The Bitter Roots

The Bitter Roots

Norman Macleod

Introduction by Joanna Pocock
Afterword by Gabriella Graceffo

RECOVERED BOOKS
BOILER HOUSE PRESS
UNIVERSITY OF MONTANA PRESS

Contents

Introduction
by Joanna Pocock

In 1940, writing through the night, cigarette clamped in his mouth, Norman Macleod conjured *The Bitter Roots* in a mere eight months while living in a log cabin up the Rattlesnake. As he wrote, there was a fear across the US that Americans would be pulled into World War II. *The Bitter Roots* begins in 1917, as the US was poised to join another great war in Europe. The first big event in the book, however, is a local tragedy – a boyish prank gone wrong. It seeps into the text like a deadly portent of the future. The "Canuck" kid, Honey Pie, is thrown into the raging Clark Fork, the river that famously runs through Missoula. "Honey Pie never really came to the surface," Macleod tells us matter-of-factly. Casual cruelty runs throughout the narrative. The main characters – all of them teenage boys – pile bravado onto callousness to protect themselves from the adult world with its corruption, its wars and its workers revolting against a system pitted against them. Fistfights are commonplace between the boys of Missoula and the scrappier kids from the union town of Butte, 90 miles southeast of Missoula.

Macleod uses the copper mining city and its importance in the International Workers of the World movement as a foil for what he sees as the slightly more genteel lumber town of Missoula.

Writing from a democratically omniscient perspective, Macleod inhabits the innermost thoughts of his characters – yet the central focus is on Pauly Craig: the unmuscular, unmanly, twelve-year-old, whose mother marries a well-respected Missoula doctor. When Pauly's mother and stepfather have a son together (as did Macleod's mother and stepfather), Pauly feels excluded and alone. He is unpopular with girls and not tough enough to be part of the gang of boys who jump trains, exchange blows, score touchdowns, have sex and generally flex the muscles they think will pump them towards manhood. This thread of the novel – the world as seen through Pauly's eyes – is classic *bildungsroman*.

Women in Macleod's novel function as objects of desire: they are flirtatious and mildly disdained or simply unknowable. In real life, however, Macleod's mother – to whom the book is dedicated – held a variety of academic and professional posts across the US and abroad. Macleod also clearly admired Montana congresswoman Jeannette Rankin, whose famous anti-war message – "I want to stand by my country, but I cannot vote for war" – begins the novel. His indifference to female characters seems to stem from the fact that Macleod is interested in the people who, at that time, were affected most by war and manual labor – those whose bodies were sent down the mines and whose lives were being used in battles to shore up a fragile democracy. Other minorities don't fare so well. Slurs for Native Americans, African Americans, Jewish and Irish people as well as those who are gay are ugly reminders of a society whose foundation was built in part upon stolen land, slavery, and prejudice. Homosexuality is seen as a challenge to the brand of manhood Pauly has been taught is the only correct one. Macleod's novel demonstrates that although some aspects of our society – war, inequality and the growing pains of childhood – are constants, other aspects have and continue to be within our ability to transform.

By the time Macleod had written *The Bitter Roots*, he had one novel and three books of poetry under his belt. His writing owes much of its style to imagism and modernism. Unsurprisingly, William Carlos Williams considered Macleod a major literary force and dedicated poems to him. Macleod inserts into the novel's narrative newspaper headlines, extracts from articles and newsreel voiceovers. You might get clippings about the Missoula Rodeo, followed by *"America to blind Germany with planes,"* then *"Pavlova, in a photoplay, with carnations, for the ladies at matinees … and the forest fires raging in one of the driest drouths in twenty-five years..."* After this, we might be led straight into Pauly and his gang shoplifting at the five and dime on Higgins Avenue. The collage effect creates a sense of facts being dislocated from reality, perhaps reflecting the chaos of war. What I felt acutely while reading *The Bitter Roots* was Macleod's need to express disorientation, bewilderment, agitation, a need to communicate to his readers that the world is not playing by the rules we thought it would, that things are out of whack.

Among this polyphony is Macleod's own powerful voice. His descriptions of Missoula are those of a poet: "Many wild lads had grown up to die in these valleys," he writes. "Their bones were fertile of madness in the memory of days gone past." Any sentimentality Macleod held for the West is undermined by the hardness of the lives he describes: "the girls who had been swept by the wind into marriage" and their children who could be "heard talking in the saloons" while others "died of drink on the Flathead." Macleod's affection for the land with its "evergreen smell" of "wind and the chinooks in season" – an affection that gripped me when I lived there and which has yet to let go – rises up like mist through every gap in the narrative:

The languid and forest-fired summers when grouse thundered in the underbrush, the brooks burdened with the liquid talk of trout. Not to forget the burnt bravery of autumn when the moons seemed as large as all expectation! Cottonwoods yellow among the deep gutturals of the wind in the tamaracks. ... the smell of cold frost that would announce—

Winter had come again!

By the end of *The Bitter Roots*, after the town has been battered by a faraway war, with some locals killed, others returning wounded, shocked and shattered, it feels as though it isn't just the boys who have grown up: the whole town, perhaps the whole world, has been forced to confront the naked folly of the First World War and its aftermath.

Fittingly, the novel ends with a dream. Pauly has to imagine the world he wants to live in because it simply doesn't exist. Like the novelist who created him, Pauly must also create something out of nothing. What stayed with me long after closing *The Bitter Roots* is the sense that perhaps the only thing a child can rely on is what is inside them: that small nugget of spirit we are born with which becomes eroded over time as we watch the world dissolve into wars and flames.

The Bitter Roots

by Norman Macleod

A Note from the Publishers

This book was originally published in 1941. It is a historical text, and for this reason we have not made any changes to its use of language. By reprinting the text, we do not endorse putative values that today's readers may find objectionable, especially with respect to Indigenous cultures. We encourage readers to ponder the text's complex relationship to the culture and time it depicts, including its use of irony and multiple perspectives to highlight clashes in values during tempestuous times.

For my mother

The [Montana] State flower is the bitterroot. Flathead Indians who used its root for food gave it the name later applied to the valley, river, and mountains of the region where it was found most abundantly. It is small, with a rosette of twelve to eighteen leaves; its low-set pink blossoms turn white after a few days in the sun.

— *Montana: State Guide Book.*

Section 1
1917–1918

Van Buren Street bridge, Missoula

Chapter 1
Introduction to War

The resolution declaring that a state of war existed between the United States and Germany, already passed by the Senate, passed the House shortly after three o'clock in the morning by a vote of 373 to 30. Miss Rankin of Missoula, Montana, the only woman member of Congress, sat through the first roll call with bowed head, failing to answer her name, twice called by the clerk—

"I want to stand by my country, but I cannot vote for war."

For a moment, then, she remained standing, supporting herself against a desk, and as cries of "vote, vote" came from several parts of the house, she sank back in her seat without voting audibly.

She was recorded in the negative.

The house on Connell Avenue was a soft brown bird in early silence. Not yet was the meadowlark of the sun come over the mountains. To the southwest the Bitterroots were febrile in darkness, but Squaw Teat Peak to the northwest and McLeod Peak to the north over the Rattlesnake country quickened in the sky. Then Jumbo

17

and Mount Sentinel to the east—the cold and separate rock that housed Hellgate Canyon, through which the Clark Fork of the Columbia flowed west to the salmon-lidded eyes of the Pacific. Southeast, the Sapphire Mountains....

Many wild lads had grown up to die in these valleys. Their bones were fertile of madness in the memory of days gone past. And many were the girls who had been swept by the wind into marriage; their children were heard, talking in the saloons, and fishing along the Blackfoot. Some married the Kootenai and died of drink on the Flathead.

Yet, it was a good land with the evergreen smell of the wind and the chinooks in season. The fishing followed the creeks and the hunting fought through the canyons. In separate coulees men had made their homes, sometimes raising sugar beets and orchards, bright from scarlet summers that faded into the mellow memory of autumn. The dogs took over terrain from coyotes, who had faded back into the dark murmur of the hills.

The cows were sheltered in these valleys, and the land itself was safe enough; but youth was a wild laughter through the years; and it grew up, sometimes shrill; and young men turned upon themselves like trapped beavers.

Along this course of history, the sun came over, moving westward. As it crested Mount Sentinel, Squaw Teat Peak could be seen blushing into rose. The light fell carelessly over the streets of Missoula. From Pig Alley, behind the newspaper plant, newsboys radiated to their separate destinations.

As the day became secure, a newspaper curled to hit the front porch of the house on Connell Avenue. It bounced and hooked into a corner of the door mat.

It was April 6, 1917.

When Mrs. Craig opened the front door of the house on Connell Avenue, her eyes were blinded momentarily by the sun. A robin in the young grass glanced at her, shook its head and hopped off through the brightly beaded dew, his beak as sharp as a dart. Mrs. Craig drew one hand over her forehead and stooped to pick the newspaper from the mat. Turning slowly, staring at the immense headline, she moved back into the house and closed the door behind her.

"Paul!" she said, with his name stiff in her throat. "Paul! Paul! Wake up! It's War! Thank god, you're not old enough to go."

Pauly rubbed the sleepy frogs of his eyes and untangled the bed clothes from around his feet.

"Do you realize what it means?" his mother said. "Pauly, look at the headlines. War! It's all over the front page."

Outside, the sky was one enormous golden glow. The air came through the windows fresh from its mountainous descent. Not anywhere could sound be heard but the singing of the birds. And yet his mother struggled with the newspaper as if it were a flock of telegrams bringing bad news. Pauly couldn't understand what all the noise was about. He had seen his mother tired, worried, distracted over her work. But usually she ran her hand through her hair and sank on the couch to rest. This was when she was tired. And many evenings, after coming home from school, he would see her lying in the dark, a cold compress over her eyelids.

But never in all his life had Pauly known his mother to talk so much! About what was said in the papers, at any rate.

"So what's it to us?" Pauly asked.

He walked out into the kitchen and splashed some cold water on his face. Drying his cheeks cursorily with a dish towel, he returned to the living room to pick up his clothes from beside the bed. "What difference can it make to us?" he said.

His mother took him by the hand and drew him down beside her on the couch.

"I hope it won't last, Pauly! But boys not much older than you will go away and many won't come back. And our life will change! But no matter what happens, you'll come to me? No matter what worries you, you'll tell me, Paul?"

"Sure," Pauly agreed, as he wriggled out of her grip. "Sure, ma! Don't I always ask you when things don't break right?"

He was embarrassed. His mother was always talking over his head, or making fun of him, it seemed. Either way, it was disconcerting. He went over behind the breakfast table and pulled on his clothes. He wondered what Wolf was doing? In a dogfight again, he bet! That was the trouble with a dog that was half wolf and half collie. What could you expect? Fights every night! Wolf was no sheep killer. That much was certain. There was too much good dog in him for that. But Wolf butchered bulldogs like poodles. Never had Pauly seen a pup to equal Wolf in a fight!

Pauly went out the back door and yelled. Wolf came skidding around the corner of the house like a five-alarm fire and leaped to slide on all four feet into Pauly's arms. Pauly, as he fondled the dog, felt for the tell-tale clots of dried blood behind the ears and under the throat, but there weren't any. Wolf must have stayed at home during the night. It was good having a dog like Wolf around. And not only a dog, but a friend, a fighter!

And yet, Pauly had more than that to be happy about. A houseful of rabbits he had, too. The hutch he had built himself. You unlocked the door at the center front where the building was high enough to allow a boy to stand up. And you walked into the semi-darkness. On either side there were tiers of rabbit apartments, with windows and wainscoting of chicken wire sharp and bright to the touch.

Locking Wolf outside, Pauly placed bran, fresh clover leaves, and water in each separate pen. The rabbits were of all sizes and colors like the rainbows of the morning air. The New Zealands with the soft tan of their fur and the white ones with their pink eyes, and their tender flesh and the smell of their sex. The Belgian hares with long, grey bodies. The Flemish Giants. Mongrels, too, of all descriptions, spotted, long-limbed, and various. The nostrils of the rabbits sniffing at the bran lifted a fine dust of hay fever in the hutch. Always, there were those rabbit noses moving back and forth, giving and taking the air, like some dynamo of delicacy still undiscovered to man.

Pauly, gripping a big white buck by the celery of his ears, moved from in front of one cage to another. He tossed the twisting electricity of its flesh into the pen of a large black doe. This should be fun! It was time that he had some new tenants to fill the empty apartment below. Pauly sat down on an overturned barrel and prepared to watch. He wondered what colors the bunny babies would be. You could never tell with that black one—God knew what her ancestry had been! Last spring she'd had eleven different color combinations. And with this white buck the pickings should be good! They'd come in all their grey and walrus nakedness into the borrowed black nest of the mother's hair. Eyes stuck fast in sleep and blind, to grow into the wonder and surprise of their peacock-furred coats. Tumble around all bunched up and funny as they hopped, two legs by two.

The white buck stamped in the corner with his hind leg. The impact was dangerous, electric. He rushed the doe and almost caught her. But the large black rabbit leaped to one side, scuttling a can of water as she bounced.

The buck whirled on a dime, stamping his left hind leg in anger. Pauly could smell the sharp scent of its sex as the white rabbit bunched his muscles and struck again at the black object of his desire. There was a quick flash of a small pink tendril as the buck lifted up and somersaulted backwards, the bounce of his long ears flat behind him. This time the doe had been lifted up from the rear. She had settled for one hard moment on the horn the white buck had rammed into her. She had risen with him in mutual motion and fallen back to the floor. It was almost too quick for the eye to catch, but Pauly had seen it. And now he smelled the sharp burnt odor of the buck. There would be babies!

But Pauly thought it better to leave the rabbits together for a time. No use his taking any chances. He wanted a good batch of bunnies to sell on the fall market.

Pauly went outside, locking the door behind him. As he walked eastward towards the university campus and the mountains above it, Wolf loped along at his side. It was strange about rabbits and their quick brutality. One lightning leap, a rip of naked sex, and it was over. The doe didn't seem to want it. Yet never ran too far. The buck was urgent enough always. But what could be the worth of such a second? Could a rabbit feel so quickly and remain content? It reminded him of a story he had heard about some creature that was consumed by sex. The male sought out the female and out of his death children were born. There must be much of dying in love. With men, perhaps, it was not so obvious because not so soon.

But with men, too, sex might kill!

If what his mother had told him was true.... A rapid knowledge of love, and disease would come tearing his nose off. His flesh would decay. He would die. Was that the reason that his mother feared the news in the paper? War! Was it another kind, yet similar kind, of madness? But Pauly knew one thing only for certain: He loved Betty Darling with every ounce of his mind. Whenever she rode past him with her dark eyes asking questions, he felt like running, his heart a tight hard ball in his breast. As if he had been the white buck in the rabbit hutch, leaping at the dark fur of the doe's flesh. And Pauly felt like shouting, but kept his lips closed. And he was afraid of this conflict of feeling, recognizing it as a sort of death. It made his blood cascade like waterfalls coming down the side of the mountain. And it was a quickening that threatened the unknown. There was danger abroad when the heart and the mouth and the brain were swept by this continual flow of fear and excitement

But boys grew up!

They became men, married, and had children, and they didn't die. Not always! Perhaps, there might be safety in marriage. If you waited for a preacher to say some words over you. The announcement in the papers. The blessing of parents. Because it was certain that not all men died of sex. But many boys who had not waited had come to grief. He had heard it was so.

As he walked toward the mountains, Pauly's mind moved in nervous speculation. Out this way there were few houses. His home on Connell Avenue was the last building which had been erected in the direction of the campus. The grass was tall in the valley. He stooped to pick a shooting star in its purple and yellow splendor.

Wolf was looking for jackrabbits, but Pauly knew his search would be fruitless. It was too close to town for wild life in this part of the valley, though he sometimes had seen the Indians come to camp on the flats to look for the camas roots in season.

Pauly walked through the university campus. The stadium was over against Mount Sentinel, but he wouldn't go that far today. He thought he would climb the clock tower of Main Hall, where his mother's office was located. He would look in and say hello, if she weren't teaching.

In any case, there was a window in the tower through which he could look out over the campus and watch the college boys and girls with their books under their arms. Some of the football men would be wearing their varsity sweaters.

Betty Darling was wheeling her bicycle around the bend of the campus oval. She was bored and didn't know what to do about it. Her brother, Lonely, was drunk and had passed out on the billiard table in her father's basement. There was no use her hanging around home under such circumstances.

Sometimes, the cellar was fun when Lonely's friends were there drinking. You could play the victrola. A boy might dance with her. Betty liked Lonely's companions. The kids her own age were too soft and speechless! She preferred the older boys with their hard arms and whiskey breaths around her. Sometimes, they moved her about as if they could be in earnest, but they were afraid of Lonely, who'd have no funny business with his sister.

But Lonely was drunk—sleeping it off on the billiard table. Betty pulled to a halt in front of Main Hall, the clock tower striking against the mountain above her. She looked up as the bells rang out high noon and a recess from classes.

"Hey, Pauly, come on down!" Betty called, hitching her overalls up over her belly button.

But Pauly, like a frightened rabbit, ducked out of the window and disappeared.

"Hey, Pauly!" Betty yelled.

Maybe he was coming down at that, though he might have answered, Betty thought. She looked around at the university kids heading for assembly. It would be something about the war, probably. Everywhere she had been this morning people were talking about the Germans. Not the kids her age, of course. But the war was the reason Lonely was drunk. Or so he had said. Her brother never lacked a reason for drinking. So the war was a good opportunity for Lonely.

Betty began to wonder what had happened to Pauly. It was taking him plenty of time to come down from his roost. To hell with him! He'd probably ducked. She decided to ride over to the Van Buren bridge and go swimming. She could hide her clothes under some rocks and swim around under the bushes. There weren't many kids about at this time of the day and, in any case, they wouldn't get tough with Lonely at the back of their minds.

It was good to have a hard guy for a brother!

Pauly's heart skipped five beats and sank into the pit of his stomach. For there was Betty, waving to him, and calling him by name! "Come on down!" she had said. Pauly loved that litte girl, but he was brave only in his dreams. If he went down to talk to

24

her, what could he say? He'd make a fool of himself, for sure. You couldn't talk with your eyes and heart alone.

But if he could approach her, saying: "Betty! Let me know what it means to be friends with a girl. Tell me how to talk!"

Then, he could go swimming with the gang in the Clark Fork of the Columbia. But maybe Lonely wouldn't like it?

Pauly was scared.

He ducked below the edge of the window, sped down the winding stairs of the tower, and out the back door of Main Hall. He whistled twice that Wolf might hear him. Skirting the football field, he struck out over the flats as fast as his legs would go.

Pauly loved Betty, but it was as much as his life was worth. Girls were death!

His mother had told him so.

Chapter 2
The Kid Goes West

▞▚

Dave Witman, who insulted the United States flag by tearing one to pieces in a public place, has issued a signed apology and has requested that publicity be given it in the press of the state. He further promises to make a public salutation of the flag at a government reservation and to wear a smaller one on his coat for thirty days.... Dixieland Jazz Band in the Livery Stable Blues*.... Annette Kellermann, whose figure is the standard of feminine physical perfection, was born in Australia. As an infant her body was placed in a quart measure. Swimming made her the most perfect living specimen of her sex.*

A month had worked quite a few changes in life as it was lived in Montana. Pauly had watched the parade going down Higgins Avenue. The brass band playing "Old time feuds are all forgotten, come away come away, 'cross the sea, you and me, from Freedom's Land, where we was born in, Kaiser better take a warnin'," to the tune of *Dixie*, and *Over There*, where the Yanks were coming. The National Guard was all dressed up with some place real to go.

The Fort Missoula boys augmented by contingents from North Dakota. The traveling salesmen who operated out of Missoula were marching in a troop by themselves, with orders from the local Chamber of Commerce for the dissemination of patriotic sentiments throughout that part of God's Land.

The bright, young faces of boys lined each side of the street. They were eager, uplifted, and unafraid!

When Pauly sauntered through the university campus these days, he noticed the fever of excitement that almost eclipsed the interest in baseball games, that encouraged the petting parties on Mount Sentinel, that promised to secure the dismissal of the professors in the German Department. And the excitement entered into Pauly's flesh and blood.

From *The Birth of a Nation*, Pauly remembered the stirring war scenes, shouts and flags, the lovely gestures of despair on girls' faces, the guns going off in sublime salvos, the fire and thunder of conflict. War must be glorious! Perhaps, in a patriotic effort to reduce grain consumption, perhaps for other reasons, Missoula saloon men were planning to raise the price of single orders of beer to ten cents.

The wonderful thing about war was that everybody pulled together, Pauly thought. So much love and violence went apace, with the brightest anticipation in lips and eyes, that even the fights in movie shows took on a sharper, more particular meaning. If it wasn't for the I.W.W.! Already, there was talk of trouble brewing in the mines of Butte and the lumber camps up the Blackfoot.

The paper said that scores of men, led by a band and bearing flags and bells and horns, would ride by automobile from Missoula up the Bitterroot Valley next Sunday to warn the Garden City's neighbors that the hoe was the weapon most likely to disconcert the German submarine and that every acre of idle land was a victory for Kaiser Wilhelm.

Pauly had heard that Lonely got into a fight with some Wobblies.[1] Yes, these were feverish days! Some of Pauly's excitement communicated itself to Wolf, who came home bleeding more frequently as the summer began in earnest.

Pauly locked Wolf in the cellar of the house on Connell Avenue, so that he couldn't follow him to Van Buren bridge, where the boys and girls went swimming. He took a pair of blue trunks, tucked them under his shirt, and proceeded in the general direction of Hellgate Canyon. Upon reaching the middle of the bridge, he descended to the island. To the northward was the Clark Fork of the Columbia and to the southward the irrigation ditch where the water was comparatively shallow. It was in there that most of the South Side gang were splashing around—Augie Storm, who was the Pastor's son, Honey Pie Buchard, and others whose names were not known to Pauly. Stiff Sullivan of the North Side gang was there, too, a big shot from across the tracks whose father had died in a railroad wreck somewhere in the Idaho mountains. Lonely, who wasn't swimming, sat on a rock watching the fun. His sister was off to one side splashing around under the bushes.

Pauly ducked beneath the bridge and changed into his trunks. He hid his clothes under a pile of boulders and came out into the open sunlight, feeling singularly naked and uncertain about his feet. The sandy soil creased between his toes and the pebbles cut. Spreading his arms to either side in order to preserve his balance, he made his way to the irrigation ditch.

He bet the water was cold! He'd have liked it better having the place all to himself. Pauly never felt at ease with too many boys around making a racket, diving, and raising hell. All Pauly wanted was some nice, quiet enjoyment, a safe and silent swim with no noise and no waves breaking into his eyes and nose. But you couldn't have everything in this world! He'd take the swim

---

1   Slang for members of the International Workers of the World.

for what it was worth, keep his mouth shut and his ears peeled back. That way, nobody would notice him, likely enough. And he could take his swim, duck back under the bridge, dry his body with the tails of his shirt, and go home.

"Look who's here!" Augie Storm said to Lonely. "Kid who runs around with his pants buttoned! You know the punk. Lives up on Connell Avenue with his mother."

"Looks kind of unwashed behind the ears," Lonely observed. "Maybe, he's never been in the water!"

"Hey, sonny!" Augie yelled. "Come over here!"

There was nothing for Pauly to do but comply. After all, that was where the swimming was. But he didn't know how to treat these guys. Augie was a muscular kid, for certain, who could hardly walk straight, his muscles were so over-developed. Nice eyes, though. Kindly.

"What's the trunks for, sonny?" Augie asked, winking at Lonely.

"Thought I'd take a swim," Pauly replied.

"He wants to swim!" Augie marveled, his mouth wide open. "What do you think, Lonely? Should we let him get his feet wet in our private pond?"

"Come 'ere!" Lonely commanded. "I hear you been chasin' my sister. Take his pants off, Augie. I want to see what year he was born."

"OK, take the pants off!" said Augie.

Pauly was scared stiff. What the hell was the matter with these guys? All he wanted was to be left alone to go swimming. He never bothered anybody. Why the Jesus couldn't they let him alone?

"I don't want any trouble," Pauly apologized. "Just takin' a swim."

"He don't want no trouble!" Sullivan laughed, blowing his nose with his fingers. "Why don't you show him what's to be done, Lonely?"

Lonely gripped Pauly's head as if it were a basketball. "Take off the pants, Augie!" he said.

Augie unbuttoned the trunks and slid them over Pauly's kicking feet.

"Think he's old enough?" Lonely asked.

Betty Darling snickered, dived into the ditch; and, as she came up into the sunlight once more, twisted her head so that the hair swung back over her forehead. All in one swift and complete motion.

Pauly didn't say anything, but he felt like crying. What was the matter with these guys who wouldn't let him alone? He was cold and naked, ashamed. No use looking over Betty's way to see her laughing. Augie tossed the trunks into a cottonwood tree. Pauly would never get them from there! And all he had wanted was a swim and to be left alone. He'd never go out into the afternoon sunlight again unless Wolf was along!

"Why don't the punk fight?" Lonely wondered. "Don't look to me like he's got any evidence!" he sniggered. "What year you born, sonny?" he asked. "I don't see no evidence!"

Augie lifted Pauly's legs and Lonely held onto Pauly's head. They tossed him into the ditch with a splash and forgot the whole business. Pauly swam under water downstream and didn't come up for air until he reached the shadow under the bridge. They wouldn't bother him any more for today. They'd had their fun. No use his running back home with his tail between his legs! He might as well stay for a couple of swims. He could sneak out later through the bushes and pick up his clothes, shinny the stanchion of the bridge, and go home.

Pauly dug his toes into the soft mud bottom of the ditch, and felt around with his hands where his trunks should've been. He watched Augie, the boy who had started the trouble. The Pastor's son would pick on some other kid, in all probability, now that he'd had the taste of it with Pauly.

"Honey Pie, how many times you swum across the river?" Augie asked. He was genuinely interested, too, if his tone meant anything at all. The cheeks of the Pastor's son were rosy as Macintosh apples long in the sun. You'd never catch Augie doing anything unless his heart was in it.

"Let's throw Honey Pie in the river," Lonely suggested.

Sullivan tackled the Canuck kid, brought him down to the ground neatly as a pin. He was quarterback on the high school team. You had to appreciate a man who could tackle like that, Pauly admitted. But Honey Pie was yelling blue murder. He was a dark kid with sad lips and his cheeks looked green. Lonely and Augie carried Honey across the small island and threw him into the Clark Fork of the Columbia coming from Hellgate Canyon. Honey's arms reached up from under the swirling current, snatched at a stick, lost it, and sank out of sight.

"Maybe the kid can't swim?" Lonely wondered, half to himself.

Honey Pie never really came to the surface.

Augie dived neatly into the Clark Fork, went under, striking out in the direction Honey had gone. The rest of the kids on the island waited. There was no use any more going out in the river! They could yell to Augie, the way it was, if Honey was seen to come up for air. No use all of them striking out blindly in that stiff current.

Augie came up for guidance.

But there was no trace of Honey Pie! Augie struck out in several different directions, but it was hopeless. Nowhere to go, and already he was far from shore. The island was dwindling. Taking a deep gulp of air into his lungs, Augie swam strongly to the south. It was quite a fight against the current, but he'd make it!

Already, his cheeks were blue. He bit his lips to keep his teeth from breaking.

Lonely busted a stick in two and tossed it into the rapids. He skipped a couple of cobs, but the water was too rough for them to reach the opposite shore. They sank with a plop into silence. Augie climbed back on the island and lay for a moment prostrate on the beach in order to catch his breath.

"Looks like Honey's gone," Lonely observed.

Stiff Sullivan muttered under his breath, spit out of the side of his mouth, and blew his nose with his fingers. Augie didn't say anything. He tossed off his trunks and wrung them, stepped into his pants, lit a cigarette, climbed the bridge, mounted his bicycle, and rode home.

"Augie was kind of quiet," Lonely remarked. The banker's son decided he'd go down to the Bucket of Blood and pick up a few beers. Sis could take care of herself. She was a tough kid, too tough for a girl! Nice.

"Jesus," Sullivan said. "You bastards better scatter if you know what's good for yuh!"

Pauly was watching the paper. The next day they found Honey lodged in a tree that had fallen over the side of the lower island, the one under the Higgins Avenue bridge. The authorities of the town decided they would build a municipal swimming pool. The local mercantile association offered to give a thousand bucks to start things off. There would be a dance benefit. There were notices in the paper of contributions given to the pool fund. There was an editorial. *One of those unfortunate accidents suffered in childhood. The future will not bring...his unhappy parents.*

"The funeral of Honey Pie Buchard, the twelve-year-old son of Mr. and Mrs. R. R. Buchard, who was drowned in the Clark Fork of the Columbia River, will be held this morning at ten o'clock. Rev. August Storm, Pastor of the Biblical Church, will conduct the service in the Lucy Undertaking Rooms. Pallbearers will be six boys who were in the same Sunday-school class with the dead boy, namely: Tony Schumaker, James McCoy, Kitt Stanley, Rodney Miller, Otto Quast, and Henry Allen."

Chapter 3
General Excitement

Agents of the big packers are buying up Montana ranch eggs at thirty-five cents a dozen, W. J. Swindlehurst says. He advises housewives to put up eggs as soaring prices next winter are probable.... Every man (citizen or alien) born between the sixth day of June, 1886, and the fifth day of June, 1896, both dates inclusive, must register today. All the stores of the city will remain closed, but the saloons will remain open as usual.... "I envy the man who has a chance to risk his life for his country!" said Colonel Roosevelt.

At the time war was declared, Mrs. Craig had two suitors. The father of Pauly was long since dead, buried in some unknown cemetery of the past, perhaps in Baltimore, perhaps in Glasgow. Mrs. Craig wasn't sure. And it had been difficult bringing up a son while she was working for her degree. Later, she'd taught. Maybe Pauly hadn't suffered unduly. In the future, however, she would have to consider him. If he were to have a new father.... Indeed, if she were to find a man who should take care of him as a father could, she would have to ask Pauly about it.

Arthur MacMurray was wholesome, red-cheeked, and naive. Dr. William Craddock was tall, his spare frame as strong as a steel cable. A solid surgeon in the community was Dr. Craddock. with his wife dead and two sons flown, one wild in South America and the other in a California bank. Mrs. Craig felt that she could look up properly to Dr. Craddock, but MacMurray was only a boy—and one who might be a soldier.

"Pauly," Mrs. Craig said. "Would you mind if I married?"

Remembering Honey Pie stretched out in the superabundant flowers of his coffin, Pauly hardly heard his mother speak to him. The black wood had been rife with carnations and roses. The soft satin coverlet that cushioned the oblong bed must have been curiously insensitive beneath the boy's back. Nowhere could Honey Pie be defined except in that queer lack of emotion which concentrated his face.

Pauly had not known Honey Pie well, and yet he had watched Honey's death from start to finish! Only Augie had tried to bring Honey back. Lonely and Augie had thrown the Canuck in; but Lonely stayed on the island shore while Sullivan spat through the side of his mouth and blew his nose with his fingers. Now the town would build a swimming pool that no more kids should die in the Clark Fork of the Columbia! What interest had Honey Pie in this? Honey Pie Buchard stiff in his satin repose, the dark mask of his face more certain and resigned than ever in life it had been.

It was a sick curiosity that had taken Pauly to the funeral. He circled the coffin within the nice safety of the line of living boys who passed into the room, around death, and back outside again into the strangeness of sunlight. The queer family of the cemetery-minded had gone on ahead. Pauly watched the finish from the gates outside the park where all pain ended, and returned home, plagued by questions.

His mother was speaking. "What do you say, Pauly? We could move to a new home. I could stop teaching and be more with you. Most of the university students are going to war. Mr. MacMurray—he's always been kind to you—what about him?"

Pauly looked sour.

What kind of a father would Mr. MacMurray make? He acted no better than a baby! Always mooning around the place, hoping for mother to marry him. Every so often he would bring Pauly some candy. What the hell use was candy? Pauly preferred a man that could tell you how to fight well, throw Betty Darling around, catch fish.

Pauly knew damn well, if Mr. MacMurray married his mother, Betty would laugh in his face!

It was no fun not knowing how to talk to boys and girls your own age! After all, Pauly had yet to smoke his first cigarette. And Mr. MacMurray would make a small adviser with his childish, trusting ways. Pauly knew with a brutal instinct that MacMurray would never make his way in the world. No stooge ever got much out of life! Nice eyes, big red cheeks, farmer ways, earnest, believed in ideals....

"I saw Honey Pie's funeral," Pauly answered his mother. "He sure was dead!"

"Pauly!" his mother said. "I thought I told you to stay away from the Buchard funeral. Sending flowers was enough."

"Well, candy's no good to Honey Pie," Pauly observed. "I'd rather stay here."

Pauly was restless. He walked over to the bay window looking out to the Cabinet Mountains far in the west, where the Clark Fork of the Columbia would have carried Honey's body had it not been for the island under the Higgins Avenue bridge. If he had a quarter, he could buy some cubebs[1] and take in a show. He bet *The End of*

---

1   An ersatz cigarette made with ground cubeb berries in place of tobacco.

the World would be a honey! *A stupendous, spectacular production in six stirring, gripping parts, depicting the catastrophe following the collision of a comet with the earth. At the Empress!*

Or Charlotte Walker in *Sloth*, one of the seven deadly sins. A stirring five act—Of course, if he could look like sixteen, he could see *Where Are My Children?* And he might be able to find the answer to a lot of things that bothered him.

A modern sociological photodrama which pictures one of the most important questions of marital life. Children under sixteen not admitted. Pauly knew that Augie would make it. The Pastor's son was a husky kid for his age and could lie with that sweet Presbyterian smile on his face better than holy murder!

But what made it imperative: Pauly had seen a picture in front of the theatre that looked just like Betty Darling, only with some drapes kind of slung carelessly over the naked body.

Jesus Jumped Up Christ!

"Pauly," his mother said. "You're not listening. Would you like it better if I married Dr. Craddock? He would be good to you and take you fishing and hunting even. You remember his lovely ranch in the Bitterroot Valley, up near Lolo? And we could move into the house on Kootenai Street. There is a big barn there and it wouldn't be far from school. What do you say?"

Pauly was fiddling with a new scout knife he'd stolen from the hardware store on Higgins Avenue. It was a sweetheart with blades for everything, even a corkscrew, and can-opener. It would be slick on a camping trip! He would take that knife with him on a trip up Hellgate Canyon one of these days. If he could get a scout hatchet to go with the knife, he could borrow some of his mother's blankets and go up, spend the night, build a bonfire, open a can of beans, bury some potatoes under the coals, and bake them to a T.

Nothing like the smell of a burnt potato in a campfire out in the open under the sky!

But his mother wanted to know about Dr. Craddock.

You had to respect a man like Doctor. He was six and a half feet, wide shoulders, spare frame, large yet tender hands, and a head that was as rugged as the sawteeth of the Bitterroot Mountains. Doctor had never spoken much to Pauly, but he had taken him along with mother when they had driven to Lolo one time. There was a swell swamp on the ranch, good fishing, and duck-hunting in season. They'd taken a boat out into the slough and fished for hours. Rainbow and speckled, even salmon trout. The flesh was soft pinkish yellow and tender to the taste. The brook trout was brown under the edge of the skin and white in the center. Boy, if he had a real rod, not this switch sort of business, but a bamboo rod and a lot of fishing tackle, flies, and rubber boots, perhaps.... If Doctor would give him a fishing outfit! And why not? Doctor had more rods and tackle than he could possibly use. It would be fun riding around in the big Cadillac car of Doctor's, too.

And if Betty saw him driving around in that large automobile all by himself, would she sit up and take notice! Doctor was a figure in the community and had a grand car.

If Pauly could get his mother to invite the Darlings up to the ranch with Doctor's permission, he might be able to find his tongue and talk about fishing, rabbits, Wolf, and things he knew. He could lead up gradually to what it means to talk to a girl and hold her hand, kiss her, and understand what a young girl thinks and feels. He could find out what she likes to do.

It just occurred to him: Never in his life had he kissed a girl! Not even faintly. He wouldn't admit it to Augie or to any of the other kids he knew. It would be as much as his life was worth!

"I like Doctor," Pauly admitted.

Crystal Craig lifted Pauly up in her arms, as far as she was able, and kissed him. It was strange how youngsters struck at the truth so quickly. Pauly couldn't know all the reasons why Doctor was best.

Poor Mr. MacMurray! He would enlist. Of that, Crystal was certain. He had as much as told her. But she could not marry unwisely and, although Doctor was older than she was, Mrs. Craig respected him and cared for him in a way she never had loved another man.

She hoped Pauly would be happy.

Pauly needed a man!

Lonely was standing on the carpet in front of his old man. Small, grey, Mr. Darling looked coldly at his son. Lonely, a tall and dissipated-looking youngster, drunk as hellfire and shooting off his guns.

"I stop your allowance!" the old man said. "I want to see how my son looks sober."

Lonely felt sick, the whiskey sour in his nose, his tongue parched; he appeared to be more mean than he really was. There was no use arguing with the old man, however. For too damn long there had been small rotten talk about his fighting and drinking!

"You hadn't run my mother to the grave, I'd be sober," Lonely said.

That was the only thing he knew would make his old man mad. If there had been any hope of softening him down.... But sooner or later you had to make the break. You couldn't stay tied to the bank's apron strings and not get weak. This was a wild country. You weren't mean and you got nowhere. He'd drink and damn if the old man wouldn't take it and like it! He didn't care much for a uniform, Lonely didn't. But there was fighting across the water. Most of the boys in this man's town were growing out of their diapers. With the war, there wouldn't be any but kids left, babies! And even punks like Augie, Stiff Sullivan—it was small time stuff playing around with them. He liked Sis, but Sis could take care of herself.

"See what I mean?" Lonely said. "You stop my allowance and my mother turns over in the dirt."

"Get out till you're sober!" the old man said.

He sat down in the Morris chair in front of the library table.

"You heard me," Mr. Darling said. "Get out!"

Lonely looked at his father. His lips drawn dryly together, Lonely licked them with his tongue. OK, the old man would cut out his liquor, would he? He didn't see the boys crowding the Bucket of Blood and the other saloons on Front Street every night for nothing! Plenty of brawls, visits to the madam. They even took care of you after it was over! They saw that you didn't get sick. OK, let his old man have it! To hell with the registration for the draft. That was for dopes. If there was anything doing, Lonely wanted to be in at the first.

"Like you want it," Lonely said, as he turned to go. "But—I enlist!" he informed his father.

Let the old man drown in his spit.

Chapter 4
The Troops Go to Butte

|:|:|:|:|:|:|:|:|:|:|:|:|:|:|:|:|:|:|:|:|:|:|:|:|:|:|:|:|:|:|:|:|:|:|:|:|:|:|:|:|:|:|:|:|:|:|:|:|:|:|:|:|:|:|:|:|:|:|

Following investigations which have been conducted for the past two days, C. Duke and Peter Janhanian, the latter a Finn, who are believed to have been implicated in spreading anti-draft and anti-registration literature in Missoula and Bonner, have been arrested and placed in county jail.... Over two hundred are dead at Butte in State's worst mine disaster. The flames and poisonous gases cut off lives of the entrapped miners. Only sixty-one bodies have been recovered.... Pro-German Plot is seen in Labor agitation in Butte. The I.W.W. swarm into grief-stricken city. Agitators circulate bulletin calling upon all mine workers to strike.

Augie Storm and Stiff Sullivan were crouched behind a line of empty boxcars to the north of the main-line Northern Pacific track. The railway station was comparatively quiet for this time of day. A fast mail was due and a few people milled around on the platform waiting for the train to show. On the other side of the boxcars and slightly to the west lay the shops. The water tank stood like a toy on its red stilts. The stacks underneath waterworks hill and the general smoke and grime of work hovered over the land.

Augie and Stiff were garbed in overalls, sweaters, and caps that were large enough to pull over the face to cut off some of the cinders. Not that it would be much use in any case. When they got up into the canyon with the wind blowing a gale and the double locomotives pulling over the continental divide, the cinders would cut into their lungs.

"Feel like moving, now that Honey Pie kicked off," Augie confided.

"Wasn't your fault," Stiff Sullivan said.

"OK, but I still feel lousy."

They peeked under the cars and down the track to the west. The mail must be coming past De Smet, for already they could hear the whistle. It wouldn't be long now. There was only one yard bull and he was on duty nights. OK, so they'd pull out in the afternoon and get to Butte by night.

Sullivan's old man had been born in the mining city. Stiff liked to go back occasionally. Vice was rampant in Butte night life and violence was vicious at any hour. Not only blackjack, poker, twenty-one, faro, but they played the horses in Butte!

It was a wide-open town, and now with the strike coming and the excitement of war in the air, and the mayor making an ass of himself as usual, almost anything might happen. It would be fun to look up his uncle, Mike Sullivan, who was something like Stiff's old man, who had died in the Idaho mountains.

The Northern Pacific mail train pulled up in front of the station, its wheels grinding to a stop. The smell of oil and cinders, the steam whistling to each side of the engine, as guys with oil cans went running up and down, all combined to lend an atmosphere of hustling excitement to the usually lifeless station.

Stiff lighted a cigarette and waited. You know, he thought to himself, that Augie is a tender guy to be so tough! Worrying about Honey Pie all the time. So OK, it was too bad. But how could anyone know the punk couldn't swim? Augie went after the kid didn't he? He did what he could! "Buck up, Augie!" Stiff advised, tapping the Pastor's son on the chest with his fist. "You did what you could, so forget it!"

Augie buttoned his sweater about his neck. It would begin to get cold going through Hellgate Canyon. That was where the blizzards came through in winter and it was cold enough up there at any time, when the train got going fast.

"Got any butts?" Augie asked. "Get a drag before she pulls out."

"OK, soldier!" Stiff said.

They could see the train was getting primed to start. All the passengers had climbed back on board. Slowly, gathering momentum, the wheels began to turn. It took some time for those big babies to get greasing the tracks!

The locomotive was going by. Two cars behind the tender had already passed. "Come on, Augie!" Stiff yelled above the clamor. "Time to get going!" They ran quickly, skipping from one roadbed to the next, in the direction of the engine ahead. The train was still going slowly enough for them to catch up.

Stiff swung behind the tender. Augie after. The train was already out of the yards and gaining speed.

The kids climbed up the ladder to the top of the tender and crouched down out of sight. They lit cigarettes.

The best way in the world to keep yourself warm when the wind got rough!

"All right, do we have a drink or do we don't?" Lonely said, getting slightly sore in the head.

MacMurray felt rather uncomfortable in the rough khaki stuff he was wearing. What in the devil to do with the long gun and the bayonet on top of it like the tent pole of a circus? That was the question. He wasn't used to this sort of thing at all. After learning that Crystal Craig was to marry Dr. Craddock, he had joined the army. But he'd expected to go overseas right off the bat. He had thought to hit the front with General Pershing. Stop the Kaiser! Save the world for democracy and American womanhood! Now, he was in Butte. There was trouble at the mines. There were strikes. German spies were inciting the copper-miners to riot. The *I Won't Workers* were causing a lot of grief. So the army had been put on the train and sent to the seat of the trouble, fighting the war at home. Lonely, another young fellow just joined up, was sent with him on a special detail to the Northern Pacific station in Butte. There was going to be trouble tonight! The mayor was worried, for they were sending the Butte boys west to Camp Lewis.

"All right, all right!" Lonely was waxing impatient. "You're in the army now, so do we drink or do we don't?"

"I suppose you know best," Mr. MacMurray agreed.

Stopping momentarily in front of The Bar of Justice, Lonely kicked through the swinging door and went in. Mr. MacMurray followed. They both walked over to the long bar which looked out at its end on Galena Street. Lonely hoisted one foot on the brass rail and spit dexterously out of the side of his mouth. This was to impress Mr. MacMurray with the fact of his leadership.

"John O'Farrell," Lonely said to the bartender. "What'll you have, Mac?" he asked.

Mr. MacMurray was undecided. "A short beer, perhaps," he said tentatively.

The bartender set down the bottle in front of Lonely and brought two short beers. He looked sourly at the banker's son. He didn't think much of these new soldier boys, he didn't. He belonged to a union himself. Butte was a union town, and these kids would find it out soon enough.

Stiff and Augie swung off the tender as the N.P. train pulled into Butte. Their legs were cramped from the uncomfortable crouching position they had assumed on the journey. Their fingers and faces were cold and black from the soot. Seen from a short distance, they looked like Negroes.

"Better get washed up," Augie suggested.

They hit across the tracks to a hash joint, went into the kitchen, and cleaned up.

"What'll you boys have?" the second cook said. "No feed, no soap."

"OK, skip the soap but give us a rag to wipe ourselves off," Sullivan said. "We're eating anyways, and none of your lip!"

"Tough kids, eh?" the cook laughed as he threw them a towel.

Out in front, they felt better.

"Ham and eggs, spuds and java. For two," Augie ordered, as they sat at the counter, their faces rosy, and clean, shining from health and the wind biting into their skin and the scrubbing they'd given themselves. They wolfed their food as soon as it was set before them, picked their teeth, finished the mugs of coffee, and lighting some fags, felt great.

"Nice ride, eh kid?" Sullivan said, feeling his age. He was a little older than Augie and already a pretty good quarterback on the high-school team. Augie Storm was just graduated from grade school. Yet, you had to give the Pastor's son his due. He came away every Sunday, from taking up collection, with enough in his pockets for all afternoon of pool.

Good billiard-player, too! Sullivan thought.

Well, it was time to be getting over to see his uncle. He hadn't seen the guy since fall. Might be dead by this time. You never knew in Butte!

"Come on, Augie," Sullivan said. "We'll go over to the church." They paid the Greek who owned the joint and walked across the railroad tracks and up the hill to the Church of the Seventh Day Adventists. It was a square two-story building on the corner of a street that topped the rise and it had a modest steeple on the southwest roof. Peeking over the edge of the second-story window, as they approached, snarled the snout of a machine gun. Nobody in sight, though. It was quiet.

"Kind of a funny church," Augie commented, thinking back on the one his father had.

"Yeh, they take their religion serious here," Sullivan agreed. "This is the workers. The other guys moved out!"

They climbed the stairs leading into the church and entered, taking off their hats from sheer force of habit. On the side opposite the pulpit they saw Bill Dunne pounding away on a typewriter. "Damn that son-of-a-bitch!" Dunne swore, as he pounded three typewriter keys into a jam and could go no further.

"What's the matter?" Stiff inquired. "I never see you run one of them things before."

Bill Dunne looked around at the youngsters. He was a broad man, not tall, but heavy and forceful in the very looks of him, probably a good drinker, too. He carried a revolver in his belt.

"My stenographer left me, the bastard!" Dunne exploded. "Joined the colors and left me holding the sack. And after last night, at that! Three sticks of dynamite they toss over the alley behind the hotel. The mayor's on top of the hotel," he said as an afterthought. He turned back to the typewriter and with fingers like baseball bats tried to untangle the s, v, and y.

"Was he hurt, the mayor?" Sullivan wanted to know.

"Hell, no, they only wanted to scare him! The troopers don't bother us. But they was getting too friendly with us, so I hear they sent up another company from Fort Missoula. You boys know anything about that?"

Augie was nudging Stiff in the ribs.

"Who's he mean?" he asked. "The stenographer? Who's the stenographer he's talking about?"

"My uncle," Stiff bragged. "Uncle Mike. The guy I was telling you about. Toughest son-of-a-bitch in our whole family."

Damn! It was no use. The typewriter wouldn't work! Might

48

as well give it a rest, anyhow, Dunne thought. He got up from the apple-crate in front of the typewriter, slammed on his hat, and started across the floor. Looking over his shoulder, he remembered the kids who had come to see him.

"You might as well tag along if you want," he suggested kindly. "We'll meet Mike sooner or later. He's taking a train to Camp Lewis with the rest of the boys who joined up. We might as well see them off. You kids need somebody to look after you, anyways! It ain't safe, here. Those machine guns upstairs sometimes go off!"

The kids followed Dunne down the steps to the street. Descending the hill, they reached the center of town near the newspaper office. That was where the district was—right behind the newspaper plant. But Bill was hitting for the biggest saloon. That was where you met everybody. Anybody you wanted to meet in Butte, you hit this saloon. If you didn't find him there, you went around the corner to the next one and so on down the line. There were four big joints. The rest were small fry and didn't count much.

"You kids drink?" Bill asked.

He knew Stiff Sullivan took after his uncle. Best damn stenographer he'd ever had! But what about the other little shaver? He didn't look so tough as Stiff. After all, the Sullivans were Irish.

"What about you, sonny? What's your handle?"

"My name's Augie," the Pastor's son said.

They all stood up to the bar.

"Two ginger ales and a mickey finn," Dunne winked at the bartender.

Stiff and Augie looked around the place. It was really a honey! It made Front Street look like a kindergarten and that was no lie. A gang of slot machines that took quarters, half-dollars, and dollars, tables all over the place with guys playing poker, blackjack, faro, and twenty-one for keeps. In the far end of the room a section was curtained off for playing the horses. The saloon was about the size of a city block and the bar ran from one end of the room to the other. All along the rail, feet were working about nervously. Guys who would have just got out of the mines if it hadn't been for the strike were drinking heavy. And yet, there were bodies still to be dug up out of the mines, and trouble was brewing. And plenty of bastards were looking mean tonight with the business about the draft and their best pals murdered in them pits and all on account of the corporation. Bill Dunne was looking towards the door.

He saw a couple of plug-uglies come in thick around the hips. He turned to the youngsters. "You kids, come here!" Bill Dunne said. When Augie and Stiff were near enough to listen without his having to shout, Bill put an arm around each kid. "You youngsters stick out over there in the corner and don't come back until I tell you to! And keep your eyes open. You might see something good!" And Bill Dunne winked.

The two strong-arm guys separated and went their separate ways, one to each side of Dunne at the bar. Each of the guys had his hat pulled down over his face. The bartender brought a couple of bottles of whiskey. He seemed to know what all the noise was about. Pausing, he looked significantly at Dunne.

"Hey, Jack!" Bill Dunne said to him, laughing. "You know what I hear? This will kill you!" He moved his elbows out to make sure he had plenty of room to move and shoved his hat to the back of his head, but his right hand stayed pretty close to his belt. "You know what?" he repeated. "I hear the company gets a couple of tough mugs to come down to a saloon after a guy I know. The company figures maybe this guy I'm speaking of is up to no good and gets along too well with the miners, who got plenty of trouble these days! So the company sends these two mugs all armed to the teeth to get this bastard, no matter what! Tells them the cops'll cause no trouble. It's all in the clear, all gravy. So these two saps shove into the saloon and they get on either side of this guy's gotta be knocked off. They figure it's easy that way. This guy can't move. Either way, one of them will get him in the back.

"But you know what?" Bill Dunne laughed, as he wet his lips with a glass of rye and winked. "They forget about the miners on each end of the bar. These guys seen plug-uglies before, company thugs, they know what to do to them guys!

"But that's playing it sissy. Looky here, Jack!" Bill Dunne pulled out his gun. He patted it on the side affectionately and laid it on the bar. "Either way," he said, "I get one son-of-a bitch."

The bartender didn't say anything. He was tense, waiting. The guys on either side of Bill Dunne were getting restless; they drank their whiskies straight. They eased away from the bar, turned, and left the saloon. The door swung back behind them.

"Ever seen such yellow sonsabitches?" Bill Dunne asked.

"Take it easy!" the bartender said. "Guy was killed here only last night."

"You see what I seen?" Sullivan said.

"Those guys didn't want none of it!" Augie agreed.

Up and down the room the miners were getting ugly.

Chapter 5
Mother Gets Married

Practically all of the Indians on the Flathead reservation registered for conscription on Tuesday. A few Indians at St. Ignatius shipped to the hills and there were some slackers in Ronan, but almost all of the eligible reds were enrolled, however, and nowhere was there trouble.... It is the bitterroot season. Down from the Flathead where the flower is rare, the older Indians have come to harvest their spring crop of roots. One will try to learn from them in vain why they have come. Here is an old squaw, sitting beside the irrigation ditch near her dirty tepee, washing a great heap of roots. "What are you doing?" Ugh! "Making bread?" Ugh! Ugh! No savvy!

"Jesus, I never seen anything like it!" Augie exclaimed, as they were riding back to Missoula behind the electric locomotive of the Milwaukee train. "Your uncle gets on the troop train and it's already beginning to pull out when he says: 'Stop! I got to shake hands with the mayor!' And they stop the train. Your uncle muscles his way out of the car and greets the mayor who's standing on the platform. After all, I guess the mayor's happy about it, seeing as how he's not so powerful popular the way it looks to me. The guys throwing the candlesticks over the hotel, where he's standing on the roof, into the alley where they blowed up four garbage cans! And the striking miners and the troops. No, I guess the mayor liked it when Sullivan stopped the tram. Your uncle sure got class!" Augie marveled.

"Mike's all right when he's not too drunk," Stiff agreed.

"But then when he grips the mayor by the hand," Augie continued. "Says, 'listen, you black bastard. When we come back, we'll finish you off!' And then gives him an uppercut to the chin that spreads his tongue like a bleeding mattress all over his face!"

"I wouldn't want none of that!" Augie said.

"Yeh, some stenographer!" Stiff Sullivan agreed.

Jesus, the wind was blowin' so hard you spit it came right back in your face, but these Milwaukee trains were clean. No cinders. Humming along with the electricity of the wind.

Nice!

After Pauly's mother married Doctor, they all drove up the Flathead in the big black Cadillac. This was Pauly's first ride up into the Indian country. It felt grand! The top was down and you could see in every direction to the farthest corners of the sky. Doctor, with his yellow gloves and duster, looked very impressive driving beside Pauly's mother in the car. In the back seat, Pauly lolled at his ease, trying every conceivable position: flat on his back, now with head to the west, now with head to the east, and then lying on his belly with chin in his hand. You could hide in the bottom of the car, too, and nobody would know that a boy was hidden there! Finally, however, Pauly decided it was better to sit up straight, with the blankets around his knees—real Hudson Bay blankets, four beavers, too....

Pauly clutched the left side of the car as they began to mount the rocky road through the Coriacan Defile. Winding around sharp curves, the hills prickly with pines and tamarack, they suddenly reached the top of the plateau. Doctor pulled the Cadillac to one side of the road, took off his leather gloves, and lit a cigar.

Ahead of them, across the large sweep of the valley, loomed the Mission Range, the rugged peaks of which rose a sheer seven thousand feet above the valley. They were covered with snow at the top. Occasionally sharp grey promontories of rock jutted out into the sky, bare and wind-blown. Pointing with the ash of his cigar to the crag north of the southernmost peak, Doctor turned to mother.

"Got my last Big Horn there," he said. "Pretty difficult to get now. It's a long trip. Only if you get on top of them do you have a chance to approach them unseen. The Big Horn never look up! They figure the danger below."

Pauly was moved. These were the highest, most rugged mountains he had ever seen in his life. He'd heard that they were home to the Grizzly and that white men had never penetrated certain sections of this range. The Salish Indians had, of course. In the early days, these mountains had been their summer hunting ground.

Doctor drove on, the fragrance of his cigar reaching Pauly in occasional drifts of smoke. The big car bounced crazily over the road. When Pauly looked over the side of the automobile, it seemed as if the ground were miles away, the car was so tall! But it was comfortable, although a little bouncy, and the springs were strong. The only trouble was about gas. They had to stop at Arlee to fill up the tank. The car went only about five miles on a gallon.

After leaving Ravalli, Pauly saw the brown buffalo grazing on the round slope of a hill. To the left of him the bison, the tremendous hump of their shoulders braced against the wind, climbed the hill, cropping the grass as they went. They appeared particularly powerful, undisturbed. It was difficult to imagine them stampeding over a cliff face for the kill.

At St. Ignatius Doctor got out, opened the door of the car for mother. Pauly vaulted over the side, hit the road on his feet, and clapped his hands for the warmth to return to them. It was strange how his cheeks burned from the wind. It seemed as though his whole countenance were one delirious flame. In the modest restaurant, Doctor advised that they eat lightly, as there would be a fine fish dinner to be had at Polson.

The rest of the way was precarious going. The road was straight enough, but the Flathead Indians, with their horses and wagons, constituted a serious menace. Time and again Doctor had to blow his horn, but the Indians took their time about moving. It seemed as though they felt the country was theirs. Doctor would honk. Sometimes, the Indians looked back, but more often than not they kept their faces set straight ahead.

It was painful to see how slowly the Indians edged over.

Occasionally, tepees were white and smoke-colored pyramids on the plain. Wild horses, broomtails, dusted the valley with their fright at the sound of the Cadillac, a big black monster. The horses carried fear in their flight. Thunder-hooved, they broke into the wind, tails flying like pennants long in the red-bent breeze. And the Indians themselves were colorful enough, wearing buckskin and bandannas, and there were store blankets to disguise the native beauty of the women. They all had black hair like ravens, shiny and bright with menace as the obsidian of their eyes.

Pauly wondered which were the Salish, which Kootenai or Kalispel? They all looked the same to him with their fine pockmarked, hooked Jewish noses, the deep tan of their faces like bronze and as hard, indifferent. They moved slowly and obstinately, as if they carried a different world inside their hearts. An earth to sustain them that would carry its own fortune. The tempo of whose seasons was as strong and inevitable as the sun itself! And to the east, along the terrible stretch of that sky, was the serrated sweep of the Missions.

It was said these Indians were dying out.

It was a long drive to Polson. Once there, Doctor stopped the car at Salish House. A restaurant built out over the water of the Flathead Lake. Doctor led the way inside to a table with a view commanding the north. As far as the eye could see were these blue waters, the Swan Range to the northwest in the direction of Glacier Park. Doctor said it would be good if they could go to Glacier some day. But the roads were rough. It was a week's journey, but once there it was worth it. The rocky guts of the world were open to the sky in Glacier Park. It was unbelievable! It was once the hunting ground of the Blackfeet.

But for today they would have to be content with the Flathead. And the lake was beautiful, Pauly had to admit. Unbelievably blue! He had never imagined that such color was possible. He'd never seen it on land or sea or in fact or fiction. But there it was, bright with sunlight and full of fish.

The landlocked salmon from these waters was famous, but Doctor suggested trout. The Salish House was noted for its fine trout dinners. And Doctor hadn't had time to fish on this long honeymoon trip. It had been a real drive going up to Polson! They wouldn't reach Missoula, on the return trip, until late that night.

It was cold and darkness was coming on when they left Polson. Pauly helped Doctor put up the top of the car and the side curtains. The wind rose in the pine trees and made an eerie whistling sound like the dreams of a strange sleep. And the sky was distant in the silver moonlight, the Mission Range on their left soft as a feather floating parallel to the east.

Back down through the Coriacan Defile, they turned left along the Northern Pacific tracks, once they reached Missoula valley. The lights of the town ahead of them flickered strangely across the flats. It was like a lost man with a lantern calling for help. But there was no answer. No sound except the occasional howl of a coyote, rising to fade into a thin echo as frightening as a child weeping on top of a mountain, and as far away and lost.

They bounced over the rough pavement of Higgins Avenue, and veered to the right after crossing the Higgins Avenue bridge. They turned up Kootenai Street and there was the house before them.

A new home for a new life!

Pauly slept the first night at the house on Kootenai Street on the balcony of the third floor overlooking the garden. When the sunlight broke into his face, he woke violently. The heat dusted him out of bed. He stood up in his pajamas, wiping his eyes of slumber. It was good looking out on the garden, it was so full of flowers, red and yellow rose bushes. Trees. All sorts of greenery and lilac bushes. To the east and back of the house lay the orchard, a whole half block of it! Cherry trees, sweet and sour, apple trees, all kinds. In one corner Pauly could see a chicken house, but it was empty of hens and roosters. Perhaps, Doctor would get some later.

Pauly dressed hurriedly, crawled down the back stairs, and into the kitchen. Big breakfast, four eggs and bacon, coffee. He was hungry after the long trip to Polson and the good sleep of the night before.

Out through the back porch and on to the lawn he went. There was a barn that was a barn! It was a two-story affair with a weathervane on top. Pauly went through the garage and into the stables. Here was a good place for horses and cows, and over against the partition which shut off the space where the Cadillac was kept would be a swell place to build a rabbitry. He could have two tiers all along the length of the barn! It would make his rabbit hutch on Connell Avenue look like small stuff, indeed! He'd have to speak to Doctor to see if he could get some lumber and chicken wire to construct the thing.

Pauly climbed up into the hayloft, which was large enough for a basketball court. It would make a swell gymnasium with dumbbells and gadgets. Rings to swing from, weights to pull from pulleys against the wall. He could get a couple of chairs and some copies of *The Police Gazette*, like in the barbershop under the building in which Doctor had his office. It would make a really good club. Pauly could invite all the boys he knew to help him fix up the place.

Up through the rafters he climbed and poked his head through an aperture in the roof. There was a small observation tower on top of the barn. Pauly, wriggling his body through the gap in the roof, climbed into the freedom above and looked out over his domain. This was really a world to conquer and no less. The small tower on top of the barn was covered by a roof poked questioningly at the sky. Pauly placed a few boards over the short rafters above his head. He climbed up into this attic he had made and curled himself out of sight. Nobody would ever find him there, if he wanted to read *Tarzan of the Apes!*

Pauly returned to the kitchen and helped himself to a large piece of apple pie and downed it with a glass of milk. As he was wiping his mouth with the back of his hand, Crystal came into the kitchen and sat down.

"Do you like it here, Pauly?" she asked.

"Mother, could I get a dray to help me bring the rabbits over and put them in the orchard?" he said.

Mrs. Craddock said it would be all right. She went to the phone and called a number.

"You go over to the house on Connell Avenue, Pauly," she advised. "A man will be right over!"

It was a lot of fun bringing the rabbits to Kootenai Street. Even Wolf seemed to enjoy it. Temporarily, Pauly had the rabbit hutch placed in the orchard, beside the barn. It would do there until he could get Doctor to build him a new rabbitry inside the stables, the place he had picked out in his mind.

After the rabbits were comfortably settled, Pauly locked Wolf in the garage. He walked over toward the university and called for Lover Lemire, who lived in the house on Avalanche Avenue.

Lover was a small and engaging lad with a shock of unruly brown hair, dark eyes and a smile that was sadly twisted for a youngster of his years. The tan on his cheeks was as tender as the fur on a bunny's belly.

"Lover!" Pauly suggested, when Lemire came out of the house. "How about us catching a drag up to Bonner and seeing the mills? I hear they're out on strike up there and we can have the place to ourselves!"

Lover seemed to think it was a good idea. "OK, Pauly," he said. "Hey, Mom, I'm going over to the baseball diamond," he yelled. "Be back for dinner!"

As they trudged out toward the university campus, Pauly wished Wolf could have been with them. But a dog couldn't very well hop a train even if it was a drag going slow, trying to make the grade. These long transcontinental freight trains out of Missoula were heavy and slow going into Hellgate Canyon. Lover and Pauly trudged gradually over the flats, striking west of Van Buren bridge until they caught the tracks; and then they followed them to the east, approaching the mountains as they walked.

"Lover, you smoke?" Pauly asked.

"Nah, my mother won't let me. Says she'll tell the old man and he'll blister my bottom if she catch any nicotine on my breath."

"Yeh, I know how it is," Pauly sympathized, trying to look as if his old man would beat hell out of him, too, if he caught him being wicked. Anyway, he could feel for Lover! Lemire's old man worked out at the Sugar Mill Plant west of Missoula. He was a husky guy and would take no nonsense from kids.

"How about smoking a cubeb?" Pauly suggested. "They don't smell like cigarettes and they puff swell." He passed a pack to Lover.

"Sure they ain't got any nicotine in them?" Lover asked.

"Hell, no!" Pauly assured him. "They smell like Jesus, but they aren't real smokes."

By this time, they were well into Hellgate Canyon. They hid in some aspens that lined a curve of the grade, smoked their cubebs, and sat down to wait. It wouldn't be long until the freight showed. This was swell! The cubebs tasted like the very devil, but they made you feel like a man. It should be fun going to Bonner, Pauly thought. George Baggs, a friend of Doctor's, was head of the A.C.M. mill there. He'd told Doctor, according to what Pauly understood, that the Wobblies were responsible for the trouble. German agents come into this country under the disguise of being Americans, calling themselves I.W.W.'s, raising the devil with industry! George Baggs had told Doctor all about it and Doctor had told mother so Pauly had overheard.

It seemed the A.C.M. mill, the Clark mill, both at Bonner, and all the lumber camps up the Blackfoot had been closed down solid.

The freight was coming around the bend so gradually it looked like slow motion in the movies. Pauly and Lover waited until the locomotive was out of sight and the caboose not yet in view. Ditching their butts, they clambered up the road bed and swung aboard a cattle car, feeling great.

It was only eight miles to Bonner. It wouldn't take them long to get there.

It would be fun to see the refuse burners, like giant bullets, smokeless against the sky.

Chapter 6
Missoula Stampede

|||||||||||||||||||||||||||||||||||||||||||||||||||||||||||||||||||||||||||||||||

Of interest to women: A real General's son is Warren Pershing, 8, son of Major General J. J. Pershing, who is living with his aunt, Miss May Pershing. Dressed in a suit of regulation olive drab, given him by army officers in Washington, "Gen." Warren Pershing plays War and as son of a general commands a troop of Omaha boys and girls who are proud to serve under him. "If this war had only waited a couple of years, father would have taken me to Europe with him," Warren declared. "If the war lasts long I'll be over there helping him lick the Germans. We'll lick 'em, too!".... The Missoula Stampede lost a clever performer, but Uncle Sammy gained a good horseman and rifle shot, when Samuel Porter, cowboy extraordinary, enlisted yesterday.

These were stampede days for the boys and girls of Missoula. *The third annual Missoula Stampede. Be there and Cut 'er Loose! A thrilling Wild West, with grand parades of Indians, Cowboys, and Riders. A huge patriotic Demonstration with 150 Contestants for the World Championship titles. Five thousand dollar purse. Relay races, squaw races, cowboys' Roman races, Pony Express races, Indian relay races, chariot races, wild horse races, trick roping, steer roping, horse roping, and bucking burros, bucking bulls, and bucking buffalo! Powder River, let 'er bust! at the Fairgrounds every day and night! America to blind Germany with planes, tremendous Sky Fleet being built to take away the eyes of the Kaiser. When Pavlowa, in a great photoplay, with carnations for the ladies at matinees, and special music by Mr. Willard Fairy, on the Fotoplayer. Fatty Arbuckle and Charlie Chaplin and the forest fires raging in one of the driest drouths in twenty-five years. Featuring Pearl White, the modern Joan of Arc, in a mystic maze that is beyond comparison.*

Pearl of the Army *shows US. Secret Service men in action. How Pearl White uncovers treachery and brings a traitor to his doom. How boys and girls can help their country by keeping their eyes open and their tongues quiet. Matinees free to school children!*

Pauly, Augie, and Lover Lemire entered the five and dime on Higgins Avenue. They deployed, like the good Secret Service men they were, down the various aisles of No Man's Land. The place was fairly crowded, for it was the season of sales. Rushing madly from one end of the counter to the other, salesgirls strove to meet the customer demands. But the booths were crowded and the stock was difficult to keep in sight.

Pauly secured a pretty good-looking knife.

Augie took for himself four boxes of tacks as sharp and strong as spikes. But Lover was new at this game. It was his first time on the hunt and he brought back no booty. The boys met in front of the store, walked over to the Palace Ice Cream Parlor, and took stock. Augie was scornful of Lemire's failure.

"Hell, Lover, that's no way to get ahead in this man's war. Think where the Germans would be by now was the French to be so sissy! You gotta develop a little spunk!" he admonished.

Pauly was quick to agree. After all, he wanted Augie to like him. If he did, he might not take off his pants any more. He might treat him like a comrade. They could fight on the same front. Pauly admired the way Augie walked as they turned out on Higgins Avenue once more and struck south toward the Fairgrounds. Augie was so muscular that he had difficulty moving one thigh ahead of the other. Pauly had worked it out that Augie should learn to ride horses like cowboys on the range so's his thighs wouldn't get in the way of each other as they usually did. He never told Augie about it, though. Augie might not like it, Pauly felt.

"Think we could catch a ride?" Lover suggested.

"We don't want no lift," Augie said, as he scattered the tacks across the road. "Now, let's see what happens!"

The cars were going by on their urgent way to the Stampede. The kids watched curiously as each vehicle rattled past. It didn't seem that there was to be any reaction at all. The cars went by and rolled lumberingly up the avenue. But no—there was one hit! A Chevrolet was pulling up to the curb, it's left hind tire whinnying increasing agony. It whistled like a bullet in flight, and *swish*, the tire collapsed.

Augie didn't want any ride. They'd get to the Fairgrounds faster than those buggies would!

Crystal Craddock was glad she had married Doctor. It was good to have a home for Pauly; and in the barn, already her son had built the new rabbitry opposite the stables; and Wolf was more free to come and go as dogs liked; and that was good for Pauly! Though Doctor didn't pay much attention to her son. He seemed to wish to forget that she had been married before. Doctor never spoke of Pauly's father, but Crystal could see that he sometimes thought of him. Pauly made Doctor recall his own two sons, who were far away and lost to him. Gil had been trouble enough and was long gone in South America like a tornado and as soon forgotten. Arthur, his favorite, Doctor hadn't seen for years. Doctor forgot the past as much as he could. He liked the ranch at Lolo with his herd of thoroughbred Jersey cows and the slough where his private fishing was good. Duck-hunting in season over the swamp, and one deer each winter when the blizzards came down through Hellgate Canyon and drifted the world with snow.

But Crystal found it hard to get used to the night trips that Doctor took. There were so few good surgeons in the West and Doctor was one of the best. Calls came from the Bitterroot as far away as Darby, or from Plains or from up the Blackfoot, though these latter were infrequent; it was mostly his Bitterroot practice that called. And Doctor would wrap himself warmly, draw on his long leather gloves, go out to the barn and open the garage doors. The Cadillac became a locomotive of mercy in the black and threatening night, the stars as pale on the forehead of the heavens as ether as he drove through the mountainous dark.

Doctor was a fine surgeon. Many were the citizens of Missoula who owed their lives to him.

For ten years Crystal had lived alone with Pauly. After she had divorced Mr. Craig, she worked her way to a master's degree, taught, and finally she had landed a job in Missoula. It had been too much of a strain, the break with Pauly's father, the responsibility of Pauly himself, and the working, teaching, and studying all at once. When she arrived in Missoula to take up her job at the university, she wasn't in the best of health.

She'd been quite ill for a time, but Doctor fixed that!

Crystal was glad she had married Doctor, but no marriage could be consummated until a child was born, he said, and Doctor wanted it.

Mrs. Storm was worried. Augie had been away all night so often! Never gave reasons for his behavior a mother could believe. He just looked at her impishly with those red cheeks and merry eyes. He asked was he not his father's son and him the minister? The Pastor would smile and let it go at that. Pastor didn't believe in ferreting out the secrets of his kids. The Lord would provide and besides he had to go fishing! At nights, there was the sermon to think about. During the day, there was the ceremony of meat pie and his dishing it out to the family. Such good appetites the kids had and Augie, especially, was such a help on Sundays! He helped take up the collection. He smoked a little, Pastor suspected, but didn't drink. Norval, the older son, was a smarter edition than Augie. His nose was sharp, aristocratic as one could wish! Raspberry cheeks, dark eyes, a good head of hair, and a fine mind, too. Pastor couldn't wish for a better couple of kids.

And the Mrs. complaining!

Mrs. Storm worried, but there was nothing much she could do about it. She bustled around at her housewifely tasks, saw the week's wash properly attended to, cooked the meals, and cleaned the house. And she was happy as she moved around her home.

But she wished Augie wouldn't go to the movies so much. If Pastor only knew! He wouldn't like it at all, she thought. For instance, the new Griffith picture, called *Intolerance*, depicting Love's struggle throughout the ages with one hundred thousand supernumeraries. "Most magnificent drama of all time, positively marvelous from every point of view." A sinful spectacle, indeed!

But the whole world was crazed these days.

War in Europe.

She hoped that Norval wouldn't be called!

Augie, Lover, and Pauly sat high in the grandstand. A rider was busting one of the wild horses they'd just let out of the pen. He came out hitting hell for leather. The bronc burst to one side and then into the sky. He twisted like a tornado and the wreckage of his passage was a duststorm blotting out the world. Waving his sombrero through the sheer force of his erratic flight, the rider clung to the horse with the iron spurs of his boots. How he managed to stay on as long as he did, the devil alone could tell! The horse was bent like a buffalo and breathing the wind. The rider, losing his grip, swayed perilously to one side and then to the other, the daylight generous under his seat.

The horse somersaulted, rose, still kicking like hell.

One of his hooves bashed in the skull of the rider as he was picking himself off the ground.

His brains a bloody mess all over the prairie.

Augie was sick.

He'd tried to brazen it out after Honey drowned. He and Lonely had thrown the kid in. Augie would have done as much on any other of a month of Sundays. He couldn't have known the kid didn't swim. It happened! He had tried to bring Honey Pie back. But he couldn't find him. And then he had left, saying nothing. He'd wanted to be alone. But never until this moment had Augie faced himself. First of all, after Honey's funeral, he'd gone to Butte, trying to run away from it all. No one had talked. No one had known. Stiff wouldn't talk. Who would? Everybody had played it safe. Nobody knew.

But Augie knew! Augie felt that he was in part to blame for Honey's death. The small dark boy laid out in his coffin had never spoken, never snitched, said nothing back. The dead can't speak; and yet, had Pastor been right when he'd talked about the ghost of the Lord upon you?

Hell's fire, the God in Heaven might speak!

Augie didn't know for sure whether he believed in God. He never talked about it. Pastor himself didn't say much. Most of what Augie had heard about the Lord was in Sunday School. He never stayed long in any case, but sneaked out. He only remained for a while in order not to give his father a black eye. But Augie had never stopped to consider whether he believed in God? Well, now was a time to start thinking! Honey Pie was long since buried. *Thou shalt not kill!* Augie had helped another to die. Had he killed? He didn't think it was quite like that, but he wasn't sure.

It would never do to let on to Lonely that he thought these things. But Lonely was away at the war. He wouldn't come back, perhaps. He'd fought with his old man, the banker. He was going to France. But it would never do to tell Stiff Sullivan either, whose old man had been as tough as any in Butte.

Augie hadn't liked the looks of death in Honey's face.

The Pastor's son felt queer at night and his dreams were fed on guilt. And now as the three boys sat in the sunlight, to the grandstand at the Fairgrounds came death again! Augie saw the brains of the man splattered over the earth. The rider who had kicked like a chicken with its head cut off, and then lain still. Stopped. No reason given!

In a way, it was worse than with Honey. Here, the blame was direct. A horse's hoof and a brain went poof. Murder! It was clean and it stank.

But with Honey Pie it had been different!

All that Augie had done was to help duck a boy in the Clark Ford of the Columbia. Augie could not see farther than that. His responsibility went no further.

But could God see it that way?

Would Pastor blame him if he knew?

He felt Pastor might.

Neither Lover nor Pauly had stomach for the stampede after the rider was killed. An ambulance rushed to the scene, and picked up the parts. Sepulchral announcements came through the loud-speaker from the judge's stand.

Augie went home by himself.

He was sick!

Chapter 7
Stiff Takes a Trip

︙︙︙

The significance of the war was brought home to Missoulians in a vivid manner yesterday when the 18th Railroad Engineers regiment from American Lake passed through the city bound for "Somewhere in the East!".... Butte, August 1. (Special.) "OTHERS TAKE NOTICE! FIRST AND LAST WARNING! 3-7-77. (L). D. C. S. S. W. T" Little was the first man of seven I.W.W. leaders marked for execution by the unknown hand which used vigilante forms in carrying out today's lynching. The mysterious symbols which follow the old vigilante 3-7-77 warning are supposed to refer to strike leaders. The death list is said to be as follows: (L), Frank Little, lynched; D, Bill Dunne; C, Tom Campbell, president, Metal Mine workers; S, W. O. Sullivan, strikers' attorney; S, Dan Shovlin; W, John Williams; and T, John Timoch.

Stiff Sullivan was not strong on reading the newspapers, or anything else, for that matter. He got his grades in high school by being the best quarterback they ever had. He sat through classes trying to appear not too tough and waited for grades to be given out. Every afternoon, he lit out for the gridiron, his shoulders bulky with pads under his expanded jersey, and the wooden cleats on his boots that would rend the legs and hamstring many an opponent. Stiff never even read the funnies. Those things were for babies! But Sullivan could count; and his uncle had been a figure in Butte—though not the one in the papers—and he knew Bill Dunne and liked him. Stiff could understand easily the language talked in Butte. And now with hell wide open in Western Montana, the I.W.W.'s all over the place.... In any case, who could help but glance at the headlines, with the papers lying all around as they were in every pool hall and saloon; the scare type big enough to frighten an army of men....

And here it was every day in the papers! It got worse and worse. If he had stayed in Butte, there would have been things to see. If it hadn't been for Augie, he would have stayed a week, but Augie wanted to get back to Missoula. The kid was worried about Honey Pie; and the Pastor was expecting his son to come home nights.

So, OK, they had come back.

But here it was in black and white in all the papers! Stiff stood around reading them between billiard shots. With hand on cue, he leaned against the cigar counter in Kelly's Empress Cigar Rooms, and looked at the print.

Frank Little, I.W.W. leader in Butte, hanged! Miners declare they know who committed the crime. While Missoula would extend the glad hand to Miss Stedman in person: Speak to her, touch her, she talks! Genuine flesh-and-blood screen actresses are rare in Western Montana. Leaving this cryptic warning, printed in defiant red letters upon the corpse of the victim, seven masked men. But picture stars are just like other people. Mary Pickford, for instance, enjoys cooking and likes to play with pretty babies. This morning hanged to a railroad bridge just outside this city, Frank H. Little, chairman of the national executive committee of the Industrial Workers of the World. Anti-draft rioters were spreading terror in Oklahoma: *Armed to the teeth and ready to resist service in the army. "I am satisfied that anyone making the speeches Mr. Little is alleged to have made would not be allowed to come to Missoula and talk!" said Mr. George Baggs, director of the lumber mill at Bonner this morning.*

"All right, smart guy. Put back them balls! And none of this marking up shots you ain't made!" Stiff Sullivan said.

These pool sharks thought they could get away with murder! Sullivan rolled up the sleeve of his left arm and placed it confidently upon the green lawn of the billiard table. Click, bounce, bounce, click, bounce and click again. Don't let anyone tell you Stiff couldn't curl those balls around the table! Stiff had grown up with balls, and not blue balls neither! On a gridiron or basketball floor, diamond or pool table, the balls were Stiff's pet discipline. Them balls never got away with much when Sullivan was around! Nor the other guys who tried to get away with slick tricks.

"OK, I'm out. Rack 'em up, boy!" Sullivan said. "Want to go another round?" he asked the guy who was supposed to beat the suckers for the joint's benefit. But the punk wasn't having any. He'd lose his job if he didn't start making the cash register sing with sucker money.

Sullivan lit a fag. OK, so he'd see what was in the sheet. He noticed that Bill Dunne was marked down as the next victim on the vigilante list. But Bill ought to be able to take care of himself. Though you could never tell. If they came late at night, the machine gunner might be asleep at the switch!

Plaster cast of head and body, measurements taken of lynch victim, will keep bust at union headquarters. (The man who made the cast is said to be a German!) No speeches are to be tolerated at the funeral. Three thousand sympathizers follow body to grave. "Only men ashamed of what they are about work with masked faces at three o'clock in the morning. This was the job of hired gunmen of the A.C.M.," Bill Dunne is quoted as having said.

Stiff Sullivan spat out of the side of his mouth into a shiny brass spittoon and blew his nose with his fingers.

Then he opened his shirt at the neck, exposing a hairy breadth of swart masculine chest, and walked out on the street. The sunlight burned against his forehead, blinked in his eyes. He raised his left hand to shade them. Damn, it was getting hot! Dryest summer in twenty-five years, the papers said. Forest fires fanned by fearful winds. All around Missoula, up the Blackfoot, along the Bitterroot, in the Cabinet Mountains, at Wounded Buck Creek, and in the South Fork country, the forests were burning. They'd probably blame this on the Wobblies, too. He wondered what in hell all the fighting was about. So far as he could learn, from what Dunne said and his Uncle spilled in his cups, the workers wanted a decent wage, safe conditions in the mines and lumber camps. His old man had been a fireman and a union man, too. No Wobblies in those days, though; the old man had been dead for some time.

His old lady wouldn't know. Though, God knows, Mary worked hard enough. She did the laundry for the Darlings, the Baggs, and most of the rich people in town.

Retreating into the shade of the awning, Stiff leaned against the plate-glass window of Kelly's Empress Cigar Rooms and lit a cigarette. He saw Lover Lemire come wheeling down Higgins Avenue on his new Harley-Davidson bicycle.

"Hey, Lover, come 'ere!" Sullivan yelled.

Lover braked his machine and pulled over to the curb, leaning his bicycle against a fire hydrant.

"How's business?" Sullivan asked.

"What d'yuh mean?" Lover said.

"Skip it," Sullivan replied. "You gotta a new machine, I see. How about you and me takin' a ride? I'll drive!"

"Where we go?" Lover was ingratiating. After all, Stiff was one of the best high school athletes in town and was tough as they made 'em when he wanted to be. Lover didn't want any bloody noses or trouble from Stiff! It was better to be on Sullivan's good side.

74

"Know Harold?" Sullivan asked. "The kid who lives over on Beckwith? We'll drop by. Take a trip to see what Harold's doin'. He's always good for a few laughs. But you want to watch him, Lover! He's kind of funny, grabs a hold of your hand when you're not looking. We go over there, you watch out for your maidenhead!"

Lover looked blank.

Lots of times Sullivan said things that didn't make sense to Lover. But there was no use complaining! Stiff would take no lip off any guy. His fists were as big as red Virginia hams and there was a mean twist to his lip. But his eyes were all right. They were rather cold, and blue, but could laugh if the joke was good.

"OK," Lover agreed. "You get on first."

Sullivan climbed into the seat and Lover sat side-saddle on the bar. They wheeled slowly out through the dazzling deep brown sunlight over the Higgins Avenue bridge and down past the high school. Turning up University Avenue, they cut toward the mountains for several blocks, then switched to the south until they struck Beckwith. Harold's house was a large, white, gingerbread affair, almost on the edge of town. The eyes of the windows looked vacant with the eyelids of the blinds drawn. Nobody was tending the sprinkler on the lawn. Sullivan was sure of that, because the lawn was so wet in this one particular spot that the water was streaming over the sidewalk and into the gutter of the street.

Maybe Harold wasn't around! That would be a shame. Sullivan wanted to get Harold to take Lover up to the attic and dust him off. That would be laughs! But if Harold didn't show....

Harold took Betty Darling into the abandoned chicken coop. He closed and latched the door. Walking over to a table in one corner of the room, he lit the candle. The mellow, flickering flame struck up the interior with the smell of fire in Harold's brain. He had fitted up a couch from the attic with mattress and velvet spread. There were carpets on the floor retrieved from the closet where skeletons were locked. A busted rocking chair beside the door and plaster saints in the corner. A copy of *Nana* on the table beneath the candlestick. The place was odorous of genteel decay.

"It's a ceremony," Harold explained, as he burned some cheap incense from the five and dime.

"You lie on the bed and I stroke your head," he said.

Curiously, Betty relaxed lying on the velvet drape. She felt languorous, tired of boredom, and curious as to what was coming next. She closed her eyes as if in sleep, drinking the incense that was driving through her nostrils to choke her brain with sleep, like opium it was so sweet. Like the sound of drugs, oriental love, and the dark night! But it was curiosity that stirred her most. Her heartbeat quickened. She lay still.

Harold sat beside her, stroking her forehead. He touched softly the line along her neck from ear to breast, and traced the inside of her arms from shoulder to fingertip.

Slowly, he undressed her. He took off her blouse, overalls, and underclothes, shoes and stockings. Betty lay coldly on the couch. Harold paused for a perilous moment. She was white from tip to toe, from the dark bobbed hair and the closed eyelids, past the hard and gradual rise of her breasts to each stiff tip of the teat, down beyond the belly button tender as a blue rose, by the black crinkly hair that covered the ripped scarlet, and along the gentle thighs, the tapering legs and the small feet. Her skin was white as moonlight and touched with delicate blue veins. Color showed daintily on the lobes of her ears, her cheeks, and the tips of her breasts.

It was a work of art nearing a sculptress finish, that would grow yet, but was better as it was! Harold could appreciate a thing of this sort...though it was not for him. He had read too many books to be taken in by this kind of flesh. Girlhood was not his promise of better things to come. But he liked to know well what he was to reject. There was a fine point of evil in all this that excited him beyond measure. His eyes glowed feverishly like those of a scientist. His pulse quickened, but he felt curiously dead in his loins. It was only his mind that felt jolted and caught, like a giant spider in the snare of its own web.

Harold ran his hands caressingly over Betty's body, touching and treasuring every inch of it.

He fingered her teats and cupped the whole breast with his hands. And he tasted every red glow of Betty Darling's body. He knew it as if he had memorized every portion of her flesh and blood. In his sleep, through the veins of his flesh, with his eyes closed or dead, he would *be* that body that was Betty's. He took communion with her sex. He *was* Betty Darling. She was no longer outside him, but he was the thing itself.

Harold picked up a feather duster from a cupboard that held it. He dusted Betty's body as of germs. He clothed it once more as he had found it first. Opened the eyelids.

The ceremony was complete.

"Jesus Christ, what a sweet, unholy bastard Harold is!" Stiff Sullivan said. "You see what I see, Lover? Your knothole as good as mine?"

"Yeh," Lover said thinly. He felt as if he had snagged his throat. The words got blocked somewhere and came out only with lumpy difficulty. "Yeh, I seen. What does it mean?"

"You know what it means! Like I told you," Sullivan said. "You tag around with Harold and you hold onto your maidenhead. He ain't interested in girls. But he don't say what he is interested in! Don't know himself, for sure, maybe. Any case, like I told you," Stiff said, "you watch out for Harold or he'll get you to rights!"

"OK," Lover agreed, blankly. "OK, Stiff, it's like you say."

Lover was completely in the dark. All he knew was that Harold had done strange things to Betty Darling. He hadn't kissed her on the lips as a man should. He'd seemed uninterested in her in any personal sort of way. He touched her only with his hands.

Lover would get little sleep for some nights after this.

"Let's get away from here," Lover suggested. "Before they come out!"

"OK, Lover. It's your bicycle," Sullivan laughed.

Betty felt suddenly panic-stricken. She thought she heard voices outside the chicken coop. If anybody had seen what Harold had done to her! It wasn't like in the books. It wasn't like what the girls she knew said it was. It didn't sound like what she had overheard Lonely's fraternity brothers saying. It didn't seem like anything right.

It was wrong!

Betty was sure of that.

Guilt crowded around her heart and the tears burned under her eyes. She must get out of here or she'd scream. She'd faint. She felt ill and wicked and profaned.

If Harold had kissed her like a man should, it wouldn't have seemed so bad. Certainly, this wasn't what boys and girls talked about so much. She wasn't a baby. She hadn't had Lonely around the house for nothing. Lonely was gone, but they had grown up together. She knew that boys' bodies were not like girls' bodies. She'd seen naked kids in enough swimming pools and irrigation ditches to last her the rest of her life! At night, when the kids climbed over the high board fence around the Hot Springs up Lolo pass.

Betty knew boys!

And love was not like this.

What was wrong with her that made Harold act so strange?

If she had only been kissed!

Betty Darling brushed the hair away from her forehead, went through the door of the abandoned chicken coop, and rushed away from Harold's place forever, she hoped.

She wished she'd never seen Harold.

The filthy beast!

Harold watched Betty leave with a kittenish smile of satisfaction like cream on his mouth. Whistling unconcernedly, with hands in his pockets, he strolled the lord of the manor to the back porch of his parents' house.

Chapter 8
The Troops Want a Drink

++

Goodbye, Mother! This morning at eleven o'clock Missoula will bid farewell to the two hundred young men who have been chosen to represent Missoula county in the selective army of the United States.... Rather than return to another nine months of school, Otto Shaffer, a thirteen year old Missoula boy, contemplated suicide at Butte last night, according to word received from the mining city.... The Kaiser must surely be out of his mind. Or he would not be so cruel and unkind!

Augie and Pauly went down together to the Milwaukee station to see the troops pass through. For the past few months the troop trains had been the major excitement in Missoula. The boys who had enlisted were sent to American Lake. Later, they came back in a rush for points east. Those who were conscripted were sent away to camp. The regular soldiers at Fort Missoula were leaving. Others were coming in. Almost any week, the kids of Missoula could go down to the Northern Pacific station or the Milwaukee station to see the troops passing through. It was more exciting to see them going east. These were soldier boys from other states, for the most part, and it was gay to see them piling out of the train for the fifteen-minute stop. They bought fruit and candy and cigarettes from the station news-dealer.

Bright and adventurous times were these for the Missoula kids! You could see the excitement in the eyes of the soldiers. They were going to France. Paris, London, would receive them with open arms! All along the route, the girls would kiss them, waving them on to victory. Pauly and Augie were impressed by the masculine splendor and military might of these boisterous youths.

Augie broke a cigarette in two, putting the longer stub back into his breast pocket. Surreptitiously, holding the remaining butt in the hollow cup of his hand so that the fag would not be noticed, he lit a match and applied the flame to the tobacco. He drew deeply so that the smoke would be absorbed in his lungs and not so apparent when he next exhaled his manly breath on the platform of the Milwaukee station, with all these people around.

There was a nice smell from the nicotine on Augie's breath. Pauly wished that he dared smoke! He hoped, when the day finally came, that he would be able to handle it as nonchalantly as Augie did.

Silently, the train pulled up at the Milwaukee station. These big electric locomotives were fast and sure as the stroke of a dagger in a night with no moon out. The soldiers piled down from the windows and doors of the railway cars. They were a festive crew with the world their oyster.

The Sammees[1] had been singing in the train all the way from Spokane. As sweetly as John McCormick, they throated *Keep the Home Fires Burning*, *Yah-de-dah*, and *Goodbye, Broadway, Hello, France*.

---

1 Slang for soldiers, similar to G.I. (for Government Issue), which became common in World War Two.

There were plenty of dames waiting to receive the soldiers with open arms. They kissed them on their way to "Get the Kaiser, get him quick, get him with a hoe or a pick, get him with a bomb or bond, get him when you cross the pond.

"But get him quick!"

He shot off his finger to avoid the draft!

But the soldiers had run out of the drinks they'd carried with them from Spokane. They wanted to sing some more and feel good on their way to war. It would be a long time before they got American whiskey again, once they had crossed the pond!

"Hey, bud!" a tall, fair-eyed soldier called, pointing a finger at Pauly. "Hey, bud, come 'ere!" he said.

Pauly, in sudden surprise, involuntarily moved toward the Sammee. With eyes fairly popping out of his head, he marched toward the soldier who wanted to speak with him. The soldier's face was flushed. He smelled loudly of whiskey.

"Bud, here's five bucks! Run up to a bar and bring me a quart of whiskey. Keep the change, but hurry back! The train leaves in fifteen minutes," he said.

Pauly clutched the money in his right fist and started running up the stairs to the top of the Higgins Avenue bridge. Augie, startled by this sudden turn of events, took some time to get the situation clearly in mind. Then, he followed after Pauly as fast as he could.

Augie, puffing and panting, was running as hard as hell. Maybe, he'd been smoking too much lately, he thought to himself. His wind wasn't as good as it should've been! He caught up with Pauly halfway across the bridge on the way north to where the saloons were located.

"Hey, Pauly!" he yelled. "What's the rush? You got plenty of time. Save your breath so's you can get back as easy as you start out"

Pauly, slowing his pace, turned and looked at Augie. "Think there's time?" he asked.

"Sure, all the time in the world!" Augie assured him. "No use breaking your neck."

They jog-trotted along, saving their wind, until they reached the First National Bank. They walked past the I.W.W. headquarters that had been raided that very morning by the Federal authorities.

"Where should we get the whiskey?" Pauly questioned.

"Not down Front Street," Augie answered. "They don't pay much attention to kids down there! Too afraid they'll get in a jam with the cops. They got enough to worry about without breaking more laws than they have to. We better keep on toward the fish fountain. I can get whiskey at the Silver Dollar."

That sounded OK to Pauly. Up to now he hadn't thought about the possibility of his not being able to get the stuff. And then what would he have done? Augie was a great help! You could always depend upon Augie to be resourceful in these things. Like the way he stole the money from the collection plate every Sunday in church. Pauly would freeze with fear if he did as many tough things as Augie did. But now that the Pastor's son had provided the solution to the problem in hand, everything was all right.

"Looky here!" Augie exclaimed, as they reached the Isis theatre. He pointed to a big billboard in front of the box office. *Danger! The picture that startled America in Six Massive Parts. See opium dens in operation! The poison needle workers, the women opium smokers, the other side of life. Do you know that one half of the world never knows how the other half lives? Think it over! It is food for thought.*

"Say, we better get goin' if we're gettin' back with that soldier's whiskey," Pauly observed. He was fearful they wouldn't be able to cross the bridge in time to meet the train before it pulled out of the station.

"OK," Augie said, soothingly. "We got plenty of time."

They walked across the street to the Silver Dollar, Augie leading the way. As the swinging doors opened for the Pastor's son, Pauly handed over the money to Augie, and the Pastor's son went in. Pauly waited outside the saloon. He wished he had the guts to smoke a cubeb, but the stuff stank so much Augie was sure to find out what was going on. Pauly would be the laughing stock of the town if Augie found out he was smoking cubebs instead of real cigarettes. Pauly fished a stick of gum out of his watch pocket, undressed it, and curled it around his tongue. It should keep him occupied for the moment. That was Pauly's main trouble these days. What to do with his body when other people were looking at him. Of course, nobody was around at present, but Augie would be coming out of the bar before long.

It seemed like it was taking a helluva time, however. Pauly peered under the swinging doors to see if he could get a squint at Augie's legs. But there was no sign of the Pastor's son at all in that saloon! Panic-stricken, Pauly swung into the taproom. He walked up to the brass rail and spoke to the bartender.

"You see a boy come in here a moment ago, Mister?" he said.

"He's in back," the bartender answered.

Pauly went through the door marked "Bucks" and discovered Augie rolling a Bull Durham cigarette.

"You got the liquor?" Pauly asked, with an urgent fear on his face. "We don't get going we'll miss the train."

"We already missed it! Look at the clock on the barroom wall," Augie said. "Anyways, they wouldn't sell me the whiskey on account of my old man's the Reverend," he explained.

Pauly's heart was stuck in his throat. The train had come and gone with that soldier who had wanted the whiskey, and the five dollars was still unspent! That Sammee would carry dark thoughts of revenge with him all the way into the east. What would he think of a boy who had not returned with the money entrusted to him? Pauly didn't know, but somehow he felt crooked. Stealing from the five and dime was one thing! That was a dare. You took your chances with the rest of them. But this five bucks was like takin' candy from a baby. It didn't get you nowheres!

"But what do we do with the money?" Pauly said weakly.

"We split it! You got the five bucks in the first place so's it's only fair you should get some," Augie explained. The Pastor's son rolled his cigarette with one deft hand and stuck the fag in his mouth.

"Outside," Augie commanded, "we get the five bucks changed and you get your commission."

Augie sauntered out into the taproom and asked the bartender to change the bill. This coin was a windfall to Augie. It was much easier money than what he slipped out of the collection plate at church. Them soldiers shouldn't be drinking, anyways! The Sammees oughta keep in shape in order to lick the Kaiser. Losing that five bucks should teach that soldier something and make him fight all the harder to win the war.

Nobody could say that Augie Storm wasn't as patriotic as any kid in the land.

But it sure came in nice!

It would help him forget about Honey Pie's death. Augie'd take in that movie about the poison needle workers and buy a couple of dime detective magazines.

"Here's your split," Augie said kindly, as he handed Pauly two dollars and pocketed the rest himself.

In the deep conscience of his loneliness, Mr. Darling felt bitter and cold. The paper, unread, lay on his lap as he sat in the Morris chair in front of the empty fireplace. He thought of his earlier years, during the long winters, when he had read sitting before the blazing logs with the noise and merriment of the children around him. The comfort of his wife in those calm hours! In those days, he had been rising in the bank, and the children sought him out as he chewed upon his cigar after dinner was over. But that his wife should have died, leaving him this loneliness, that even the children couldn't invade—that had been hard!

In any case, Lonely had failed him.

But who was to know how blame should be placed? In the homes of men and in the hearts of children, or in the great world at war, who was to know such a thing? It was bitter, this war, more than the papers guessed. *Goodbye, Mother!* Indeed. He picked up the paper lying before him and read: *The Missoula Women's Patriotic Association yesterday shipped four boxes of mufflers and earpads to the boys across the Atlantic. Charles Larivire, however, spells his name in three ways, dislikes work and is a Republican. Therefore, a jury of physicians decided yesterday to send him to the insane asylum at Warm Springs.*

Not once had Lonely written to him.

The banker knew from a card Betty had received that his son was in France. Lonely had changed through the years more than his father had bargained for. If he had but spent more time with his son, fishing with him, and hunting for deer and the Big Horn! If he had done this, perhaps his son would not have gone so far to the bad!

It was difficult to think of the possibility of Lonely dead on the bloody fields of France!

His own flesh and blood, in what danger, had chosen between his father and drink and had taken war with all of its violence, inebriation, and death! Yet, it was better perhaps than that Lonely should have stayed to sour in the degenerate habits he had picked up. Mr. Darling wondered what use his banking was, now that he had lost his son? He loved his daughter, it was true, but she was a tomboy and hardly ever around. He would have to speak to her more sharply about coming home earlier at night. And now that she was in high school, she would be tearing around with a tougher crowd. Perhaps he should be more attentive to Betty's growing needs. Now, that Lonely was gone.... Perhaps, he would never see Lonely again?

Mr. Darling's eyes passed broodingly over the newsprint: *Autumn whose fluttering leaves, the cottonwood yellow along the mountain waters, and the sharp scent of winter coming in. Rivals Venus in the matchless beauty of her hair. While it was generally admitted that the army barracks at American Lake were the finest homes for boys ever made.*

They had arrested 166 leaders of the Industrial Workers of the World!

Mr. Darling cast the newspaper into the empty fireplace.

His face was bitter as the memory of his dead wife.

Chapter 9
Wolf is Banished

In view of the boisterous and disgraceful conduct that marked the last departure of drafted men from Missoula, Mayor Wilkinson and the city council are discussing plans for the closing of all saloons and liquor houses on October 8, the day set for entrainment of seventy-nine more of the county's quota for American Lake.... Brown had gone to the show instead of staying with his fellow classmen and after the show he was caught by the sophomores and with the assistance of the freshmen was painted with green paint and his hair shorn from his head. Thick molasses was then applied and he was taken out on the Frenchtown road and left to find his way home.... Local patrolman arrests slacker and receives fifty dollars bounty.

These were heroic afternoons for Stiff Sullivan. Most of last year's team had enlisted or been conscripted, like Norval, Augie Storm's older brother, and there was little competition for Stiff on the football field.

Stiff was a triple threat. He could open-field run, dropkick, punt, and pass. He was tough on the tackle, too. He stiff-armed these babies with pleasurable ease. The Hamilton team had been a snap, Great Falls was easier than it had been for years. Now Butte was coming up.

He walked around school, the hero of all the little girls who fawned upon his least word and gesture. Not that he had time for these well-behaved lassies. He was a man, Stiff Sullivan was, and he drank when he felt like it, smoked, but kept in pretty good shape on the whole on account of the games.

Sullivan had enjoyed clipping Augie's head. Pauly had no fight in him, but it had been a struggle getting the Pastor's son. That kid could use his fists! But school had settled down after the frosh had been hazed, and things were pretty quiet most of the time.

With a lineup crippled through injuries sustained in the game with Great Falls, the Missoula High School eleven lines up against their ancient rivals, the Butte High School team, this afternoon. What did these sports writers know? It made Stiff sick.

Home talent!

The Butte kids 'ud get sent back on stretchers!

"This bunch can lick the Germans right away," Phillips said, after observing the soldiers in the nude. Missoula to send a Chinaman to the front. They go wild, simply wild, over me! Resenting being called a scab, Ziki Savichevich drew a revolver and shot Verner Nelson, an I.W.W. organizer, twice through the right breast, inflicting wounds which caused death an hour later. And what were the days ahead?

Dr. Craddock had just returned from performing an emergency appendectomy at the hospital up in Hamilton. It had been a long trip coming back through the Bitterroot Valley. As he passed by Florence, the snow had begun to fall and the wind hit up, a blizzard, early for the season and this but October. He stopped the car beside a barn to protect himself from the whip of the snow and put up the side-curtains. He began driving again, going as fast as he could for fear that the snow would drift the grade below Lolo. He'd never get through to Missoula if it got too bad!

It was difficult driving. He used his left hand, reaching around the windshield, to wipe off the snow.

As he passed his ranch at Lolo, he thought of his brother who had died in the large empty grey house. The caretaker lived with his family in the smaller house between the silo and the creamery. Doctor never let anyone live in the big house after his brother had died. His brother had been Doctor's reason for coming to Montana in the first place. Back in Missouri, the tuberculosis got his brother by the throat. Doctor, by bringing his brother to Montana, had thought to loosen the bulldog grip of death.

But it had been too late for that when they reached Missoula.

Death had had the head start.

Doctor's brother lived in the big house for a few months and then died, all by himself, the orchard quiet outside his window. It had been several days before Doctor discovered him, lying forlornly on the cot in the parlor heavy with dust, quiet and pale as he had been for several afternoons past.

But Dr. Craddock loved the ranch and kept it in memory of his dead brother. He raised thoroughbred Jersey cows that won prizes at the livestock shows. He had a couple of good mares and a stallion worth a fortune. And he'd stocked the slough with fish.

He enjoyed the orchard, too. He pressed cider from the Macintosh apples, and rapidly it soured and became hard. He drank it, sometimes, before going out into the dampness and the cold, hunting ducks.

As Doctor passed over the grade which led into the Missoula Valley, he thought of his marriage to Crystal Craig. It was good not to be lonely! And Pauly wasn't so bad, for a stepson, though Wolf was becoming a problem. Coming back every morning bloody from fights of the night before! Wolf, so far, had dedicated himself to the killing of dogs. But who was to say that he might not graduate to an interest in men and women or even to an interest in babies? That dog was dangerous! If Wolf should bite someone influential, Doctor would have trouble on his hands, for sure.

The dog would have to go.

He might have him taken to the ranch at Lolo. There, the dog would be safe enough and not so likely to get into mischief. Pauly would not feel so bad, if the dog were not killed.

He'd have to speak to Pauly.

When Pauly came home after the game with Butte, his pockets were stuffed with four hundred thousand dollars in stage money. It was not real money, but it was real enough for Pauly, and very convincing to the eye. It looked like the genuine article, right enough, and filled him with a tremendous sense of power and wealth. The two dollars Pauly had received from the split of the soldier's money had brought returns. Pauly didn't know what to do with the Sammee's money at first. He didn't feel right about spending it in the usual way.

For cubebs!

Banana splits and movies, like Augie Storm did.

Pauly's conscience hurt him. He couldn't help thinking about how that soldier must feel, riding to war with no whiskey to make him feel happy. Pauly didn't know what liquor tasted like, but he knew that the Sammees drank it when they wanted to sing. *Over There.*

Or *Goodbye Broadway, Hello France!*

The best Pauly could do was to turn the money to good account. Accordingly, when Augie showed up at the football game with a lot of stage money and offered to sell Pauly four hundred thousand dollars worth for the two bucks he'd kept from the Sammee who wanted the drink, Pauly jumped at the chance.

Returning to the house on Kootenai Street, Pauly struck for the cellar entrance in order to escape observation of the maid.

Finding a cigar box sufficiently empty and suitable to his purpose, he stuffed three hundred thousand dollars into it, crawled through a cellar window under the front porch, and buried the money with all secrecy, according to a plan detailed in *Kidd's Treasure Trove*. Nobody would ever find that money the way Pauly had buried it! He'd keep it there until after the war was won. Then, he would dig it up and give it to some soldier boy come back from the front.

But Pauly's conscience was not yet clear.

He sneaked up to his room on the second floor, using the back stairs from the kitchen, and past the maid's room, and continued down the hall quietly in case his mother was about. Reaching comparative safety, he selected an envelope full of fish flies and emptied it of its burden.

Placing one hundred thousand dollars inside, he addressed it:

"For the Soldiers,

"Care of the Salvation Army,

"American Lake."

That was where the Sammees came from when they passed through Missoula on their way to the war. Pauly didn't know where the soldier who wanted the whiskey had gone, but at least he could send a hundred grand to the Sammees still at camp, and he could save the other three hundred thousand for a Yank that had come back from killing the Kaiser. He would mail that money tonight!

Outside the window, snow was blowing fast. The game with Butte had been a battle on ice. If it hadn't been for Stiff! Sullivan fought his way clear to victory in any kind of weather. Pauly was proud to know a great football player like Stiff Sullivan, who'd made the Butte lads bite the dust through several inches of snow! How the blizzard hit the window pane with the resounding impact of winter to come! Outside, the drifts were piling up in back of the house. It would be cold in the morning going to school.

Pauly went downstairs to the living room, where a fire was crackling in the grate. Large logs of cedar that smelled beautifully.

The dinner bell rang and Pauly followed mother and Doctor into the dining room. He ate wild duck and browned carrots, roasted to a turn, Boston Brown Bread, and baked beans. He finished with a small demi-tasse of coffee. Doctor didn't mind if Pauly drank coffee once a day in the evening. But he wouldn't hear of Pauly's smoking.

Doctor lit a cigar, pushed his plate from in front of him, looked calculatingly at Pauly, and spoke.

"I've been thinking about Wolf," he began. "He's a dangerous dog! I've talked with mother about it. And several of the neighbors have threatened to poison him. You wouldn't like that?" he asked.

Pauly, with fright in his fingertips, sat still, but his hand on the tablecloth shook. "No, Doctor, I wouldn't like Wolf to be killed!" he said.

"That's the right spirit! I knew you'd see it my way," Doctor agreed. "He's a dangerous dog. I've decided the best thing to do is to take him up to the Lolo ranch. You can build him a dog house there. And Wolf won't mind, because other dogs are around."

"But when will I see him?" Pauly asked.

"We go up almost every weekend," Doctor pointed out.

"Yes, Doctor," Pauly agreed.

Pauly pushed his chair away from the table, keeping his eyes down on the floor, slipped out of the room and up the front stairs. He slammed his bedroom door shut on the public curiosity of the hall. And fell upon the bed.

Pauly wept!

With the pillow clutched to his breast.

Wolf had never killed anybody!

Pauly cried to himself.

Chapter 10
The Country Gets Rough

:||||||||||||||||||||||||||||||||||||||||||||||||||||||||||||:

An American soldier of General Pershing's force, found guilty of the rape and murder of a French woman, has been executed by a firing squad.... Emil Koski, a Finnish miner, who shot and killed Mrs. Anna Jackson, a neighbor and countrywoman, while firing upon a Liberty committee which had called for a second inquiry into his seditious utterances at Red Lodge last night, is a raving maniac.... "My husband was drafted. I didn't have a job or a cent. I went to the streets and Pippi got hold of me!"

Penny liked it! Or at least it was easier than any other way of life she had known. But it was getting to be too much of a good thing with the Madam on her trail all the time; and the war, the boys kicking over the traces, one Yank after another, and even the kids were coming around. All of them were drinking so much that they hardly knew when she went through the motions of taking care of the bugs. All that window dressing half the time for nothing! Nice red medicines to make it look real. It had a sting like the

Jesus, too! Syringes on the dresser and pink curtains around the bed. But Penny was getting sick of the hysteria, the talk about German spies, the workers who wouldn't work, the Wobblies, and now the Reds over in Russia who had cut themselves a slice of the world, for sure.

And were some of her customers angry!

She got it from both sides. The Maximalists were OK. The Bolsheviki were lice. Later, she found out it was one and the same thing. But what difference did that make in her business? In any case, she had to listen. She got it coming and going. She thought of the Salvation Army Captain who had once been a Prize Ring King. He'd reformed after a life of true adventure! Was that a laugh! With his ears as big as cyclones and tougher than cauliflowers.

She'd like to have her beauty sleep on some sweet day when the men weren't coming around the mountain. But the men would be boys! And the boys would be men! It was the basis of her trade, and Penny had her trade down pat. She could go into the routine in her sleep. In fact, she was sure that she did. It was enough to drive a lady to drink. But you had to wait until you were a Madam to be able to afford that. Hot chance of getting there soon! The trade was brisk, but the Madam took most of the profit. And now with the police hot and heavy on their trail. *Third member of the trio accused of corrupting and exploiting Eleanor Doggs, a motherless fourteen-year-old child, will face charges against her in court this afternoon.*

Penny was sick of it. There were all kinds of struggle in her profession, but a lady must live!

If there was one thing in the world that was certain, it was violence. There was one man in Missoula who told how he was in Petrograd during the first revolution. He didn't see much, he said.

"I just kept indoors, where I sat down and waited for the shooting to stop!"

The shadow of the moon watched the blood spilled on the street. *"Petrograd, Nov. 9. Government forces holding the Winter Palace were compelled to capitulate early this morning under the fire of the cruiser* Aurora, *and the cannon of the St. Peter and St. Paul fortress across the Neva river. At two o'clock this morning the woman's battalion, which had been defending the Winter Palace, surrendered.*

"The women's and soldiers' delegates are in complete control of the city."

Time moved fast!

After the Anaconda game, which was the final tilt of the season, Augie Storm, Stiff Sullivan, Billy Toole, Tubby Ross, Bud Bailey, and Jake Sterling doffed their duds and tore into their daily togs. It had been a hard game on a field only partially cleared of snow. The afternoon had been cold and the Anaconda kids had been tough to take. Advantages of the home field, and the dropkicking of Sullivan, however, had won the day. The Anaconda kids had been good sports about losing. Nothing like them Butte mugs who never lost a tussle without griping about it!

The Missoula boys never had much good to say for Butte. The miners thought they were the toughest kids on the lot.

"Hey, fellers!" Stiff Sullivan said, as they left the locker room and headed for the street. "I hear them mugs in Butte has been tellin' about how that last game we played 'em was stole by dirty refereein'."

"Yeh, I heard the same," Augie agreed. "I was talkin' to a stiff come through from Butte yesterday."

Fat Tubby Ross was the first to jump for the bait. He swallowed it hook, line, and sinker. "OK," he suggested. "So how about we take a little trip to Butte and give them guys a lesson?"

Augie Storm thought it was a good idea. He still had some of the money he'd earned from the soldier who wanted the whiskey, and from helping Pauly see the thing through with his conscience by selling the stage money. If the Pastor wondered why he didn't come home that night, Augie could say he was out celebrating the Anaconda game with some of the boys. The Pastor would smell his breath, not looking suspicious at all, but affectionate like a good Christian father. Augie would see to it that the Pastor smelled nothing but Sen-Sen.[1] It was better that way, now that Norval had gone to the war. No use worrying the Pastor unduly.

Augie's mother would worry, of course, but the Pastor would take care of her.

"OK!" Augie agreed. "We pick up all the kids we see on the way down to the station. Should be just time for that seven o'clock train leaves the N.P. yards."

As they went down Higgins Avenue, Sullivan caught Lover Lemire and Pauly trying to duck out of sight in an alley.

"Hey, come 'ere, you punks!" Sullivan called.

Pauly knew there was no ignoring Stiff Sullivan.

"How'd you like the game, punks?"

Pauly and Lover were pleased that Stiff should speak so kindly to them. Usually, when either of them saw a bunch of the team coming down the street after a game and feeling rambunctious, he thought it a good idea to stay out of sight and avoid trouble. But here was Stiff Sullivan being nice. It was most unlike him, Pauly thought.

"Those Anaconda babies stink," Pauly said, trying to look as vicious as he could.

"You hear that, boys?" Augie applauded. "But maybe we better coach 'em some more," he qualified, looking at Tubby.

Ross took Pauly by the arm and pulled him onto the sidewalk. Bud Bailey crossed over to Lover and looked him straight in the eye. And then Tubby and Bailey both began talking at once.

---

1 A breath freshener, often used to cover up the smell of alcohol on one's breath.

"It's like this," they said. "The Anaconda boys are all right. They lose a game and they don't squawk. Not a peep do you hear out of them. They're friendly and nice as you please. But them Butte mugs! We been hearin' they talk out of turn! Now you wouldn't want that, would you? Tubby and Bailey asked."

Stiff winked at Augie and blew his nose. The Pastor's son was OK!

"Like you say," Pauly agreed. "Them Butte mugs need a lesson, you think?"

"Hits it right on the bone," Augie laughed. "Why, them Butte kids is so crazy with sour grapes, and cocky, their fingers droop when they're drunk."

"Yeh!" Lover said, thinking about how his old man would be sore if he wasn't home soon.

"Come on, quit gassin'," Sullivan admonished. "We got to get goin'! We're catching that seven o'clock mail for Butte to teach them mugs a lesson. Lover and Pauly are comin' along."

There was nothing else for Lover and Pauly to do. They hitched up their pants like cowboys and trailed along. It was no use to argue with Sullivan and his gang, or there'd be trouble! They go to Butte and they'd have grief for one night only. Pauly was no fighter, had never been in a brawl in his life, but he thought he might be able to duck out of the way come a scuffle because, after all, it would be dark by the time they reached Butte.

The boys had to get out quite a ways from the station on account of the cop. Joe Vuckovich, the yard bull, went on duty at six o'clock. By now, he'd be snooping around with his ugly face like a headlight, looking for stiffs. Joe never beat up the Wobblies who rode the rods, particularly on freights, because most of the brakies[2] carried red cards, and Joe was never aching to get in a fight. But with kids it was different. You could manhandle a kid

---

2   Slang for railroad brakemen.

once in a while and you never got into trouble. The kids couldn't fight back on account of Joe's Billy and the Luger he always carried in his hip pocket. The kids knew Joe Vuckovich would shoot!

If a kid got killed....

You could always blame it on the dark.

Stiff Sullivan knew Joe Vuckovich felt that way, because Stiff had an in with the guys that worked at the shops. Sullivan's old man had been a fireman and the railroad workers felt they should kind of look out for Stiff.

Stiff's old man had been four aces!

The train was pulling out. It began to go pretty fast by the time it hit the crossing over the road that went up the Rattlesnake. But there was no help for that. Already, the yard bull was losing pace as he ran alongside the cars to see that no punk got aboard.

"All right, you guys, get goin'!" Stiff yelled, as he broke from the bushes beside the road and started.

Augie shoved Pauly and Lover ahead of him, and the bunch shot out as the locomotive pulled by in deep black thunder. The yard bull was back with the Pullmans, and losing ground.

Stiff, Augie, Lover, and Pauly swung aboard the tender. The rest scattered among the blinds as the train gathered momentum. Pauly's legs had been jerked out from under him when he grappled with the iron rungs on the side of the front mail car. His shoes had struck with a resounding crash against the dark green wood of the train. And then he was safe! A bullet whistled by Stiff Sullivan as he climbed on top of the tender. But nobody was hurt. Joe Vuckovich didn't dare shoot too close to the engine. If he'd seen the kids sooner, he might have been able to wing one of them. But as it was....

All of the Missoula boys made the mail!

It seemed like a long ride to Pauly. Going over the continental divide was the worst part of the journey. But they didn't get so cold they couldn't stand it. At Drummond and Garrison, while the locomotive was taking water, they grabbed some coffee in the station restaurants. That, together with cigarettes, helped keep them from freezing. It was the first real smoke Pauly and Lover had ever had. They warmed their hands over the glow of the burning tobacco and concentrated their eyes on the golden fire of the cigarettes. It was what you called psychology, according to Augie, who'd heard his old man talk on the subject. Augie was more educated than most of the other kids, because he'd had to listen to so many sermons.

You learned things when your old man was a preacher!

The Missoula boys hit the snow hard as soon as the mail pulled past the outskirts of Butte. Trudging wearily to the station, they turned into the men's room, and cleaned up a little. Pauly's left hand was bleeding. He'd hit the ground rough, but the rest of the kids were all right—except for Lover. His teeth were chattering like angry chipmunks.

On the way up Galena Street, Sullivan explained about The Bar of Justice. "We can get drinks there and they'll warm us up," he said.

Pauly and Lover weren't having any. They stuck to coffee at the counter in back of the joint. But Tubby, Billy, Jake, Augie, and Stiff took straight rye whiskey with short beers for chasers. Augie paid the bill. The kids would have trouble getting drinks in the open in Missoula. But in Butte the babies were baptized with firewater and they grew up bottled in bond. The Missoula kids liquored up, getting ready for trouble.

"Come on, Sammees!" Sullivan commanded, after the second round of drinks was finished. "We got some night work to do. We see those guys if we walk the streets enough!"

They turned back down Montana Street, Lover and Pauly kind of stringing along in the rear. Pauly had an idea, if they met some of the Butte toughs, he and Lover could get off into an alley somewhere, hit out for the N.P. station, and catch a drag back to Missoula. If anything ever came up about it, they could say they hit a couple of guys and then got lost in the melee. After it was all over, there shouldn't be no trouble. Once they got free, that was!

Up Silver Street, Stiff Sullivan was pointing his finger. "You see what I see?" he asked the rest of the Missoula kids, rhetorically. "Looks to me like a bunch of them Butte mugs we strewed all over the field last month."

Anissimow, the Butte left tackle, Wolin, quarterback, Serafimovitch, full, Pat Casey, left end, and Mike O'Hara, who played right guard, were ambling slowly down the street. Most of them were miners' sons, though Casey's father was down at City Hall. Out for an evening, they were walking around town, looking hard. No use being the local football team unless you strolled around to take in the sights come dark! Anyways, it was only at night the town opened up. Them was the hours to see what went on. The district running high, wide, and handsome; and the gambling going full blast; and plenty of sociable drinks to be had. There was trouble, too, if you was looking for it.

Not that the Butte kids, the guys on the team, ever really had much competition on the streets at night.

Unless a boozefighter got in the way....

The town was theirs!

"Hey, suckers!" Stiff Sullivan yelled, as the Butte kids got close. "I hear you guys been talking out of the side of your mouths."

"Yeh, and so what?" Serafimovitch said.

"So we figured we'd drop by and see what you has to say," Jake Sterling explained.

"That's the way it is," Anissimow laughed. "You boys wanta play! You ain't got no referee with you, I see. How come you ain't got a referee along?"

Stiff Sullivan didn't say anything. He stepped up to Casey, whose father was down at City Hall, and let go a right jab. Casey's mouth was spitting blood so fast he looked like a fire hydrant, but he hit back. Sullivan warded off the blow and struck a left uppercut to the jaw. Casey's feet folded beneath him; and before grandma could say Jack Robinson the Butte kids and the Missoula boys were mixing it all over the lot.

Lover and Pauly ducked under cover of darkness into an alley and started running as fast as they could. No Butte mug could follow because there weren't enough Butte kids to go around as it was. And Sullivan, Augie, Jake, and the rest were giving no ground.

"Lover, you safe?" Pauly gasped, as he dashed around a corner and back into Montana Street. Lover pulled up behind him, heaving as if he'd never catch his breath again.

"That was a close shave," Lover decided.

"Yeh, them Butte kids play rough," Pauly agreed.

They walked more slowly as they neared the Northern Pacific tracks.

Wolin, back on Silver Street, was doubled up on the ice. Some bastard had kicked him below the belt!

Chapter 11
The Christmas Touch

:::

Few wounded in war who do not recover. Missoula mothers need not worry, for surgery and medical science have scored greatest triumph in history of the world.... Pupil in the Central School writes, "In this horrible no man's land the Kaiser hasn't got a stand, here the Sammees, blithe and gay are going to make the Kaiser pay!" Could bitterroot be used for food? High cost of living revives interest in State flower as staple.

Christmas was coming, and it looked to Bill Dunne, as he walked down Silver Street, as if it was going to be a really good season for some of the workers at last. Conditions in Butte were tough. All over the country, the Wobblies were having stiff going, but there'd been plenty of strikes. The workers were becoming more militant. But the "Liberty" committees that were taking into their own hands the suppression of strikes were getting out of bounds. They'd killed a couple of guys in several Montana towns. Even the Federal authorities were getting worried about talk of a congressional committee to investigate the situation. The government was taking over the railroads; and Jeanette Rankin had said her piece.

The newspapers were running wild: *Bare world plot to overthrow social order as work of Bolsheviki, I.W.W., and Irish agitators!* The way you had to figure everything, Bill Dunne reflected, was: How does it affect the progress of the war? If it was against immediate Allied victory, the papers were against it.

But that wasn't all.

The Anaconda Copper Mining Company had its finger in every kettle. But they'd better look out they didn't get boiled!

US. millionaires double number in last two years! Didn't they have any caution? If you were against the workers, how could you expect to get away with news stories like that? After all, the workers could read.

Let them think about that!

But things were getting tough with Dunne in Butte. Walking around the streets, he took a chance to get shot.

He'd been hearing a story about Stiff Sullivan, who'd barged into town a few weeks back with a gang of Missoula kids. They'd tangled with Wolin, Casey, and some of the other Butte kids, Bill Dunne had heard.

There'd been hell to pay on that fight. He didn't know how Sullivan had come out, but some of the Butte kids had themselves in a sling. Kids got tougher every day.

Good thing, too.

There'd be plenty of chance for them to show their stuff if a Lenin ever got started in the United States! As for the present, Russia was a good beginning, maybe....

At least, so he hoped!

Bill Dunne turned into the Stud Saloon and ordered himself a drink.

The Missoula High School basketball team got off to a good start, with Stiff Sullivan sinking a basket from the middle of the floor in the game against Dillon. Betty Darling sat in the balcony and cheered the home team.

Pauly Craig stumbled out of his Ancient History Class. He was thinking about getting home to a good venison steak supper. Doctor had been back in the Lolo National Forest, where he'd shot a strapping big buck, large enough to provide the family with meat for the rest of the winter. As Betty Darling tripped down the hall, Pauly rushed out of the building and into the street. He didn't know what he'd have done if Betty had stopped him.

He'd been hearing stories from Augie, who said that Lover Lemire and Stiff had seen some queer things, such as Betty naked and Harold, the strange boy from Beckwith Street, playing with her. Pauly didn't believe it, for a moment! But he'd have to ask Lover about it some day. Pauly kept Betty close to his heart, that he might dream of her, the beautiful, untarnished symbol of his hope. For some day, in a wondrous year, Pauly would be able to speak to Betty without embarrassment, mention his desire, marry her, and grow up in the world to be a surgeon like Doctor, perhaps.

With Betty beside him through the years!

But it was a good thing that he'd gotten out of the door in time. She hadn't seen him. There was no use his taking the chance of making a bad impression on her with so much in the future at stake!

Pauly hurried across Higgins Avenue.

As he was passing the candy shop on the corner, Stiff Sullivan and Augie came out on the street.

"Well, looky who's here!" Augie exclaimed, with one hand clutching Pauly's arm in a firm grip. "You see what I see?" he asked Sullivan. "The sissy who took a powder in Butte! Where's your little playmate, Lover Lemire?"

"A guy knocked me out in the alley. When I wake up you fellows are gone," Pauly explained.

"Yeh? And what's Lover's story?" Stiff Sullivan laughed, as he spit out of the corner of his mouth and wiped his lips with his fist.

"Honest!" Pauly swore. "I was never very good with my dukes. I made a pass at a guy and he knocks me colder than a mackerel. When I wake up, you guys have left. Cross my heart and hope to die!"

Augie was disgusted. He twisted Pauly around and gave him a swift kick in the seat of the pants. "You and your grandmother! You and your grandfather, too. The little yellow bastard! Leaves us in Butte to take over them guys ourself!"

Stiff Sullivan was bored. These prissy kids like Pauly and Lover Lemire didn't interest him much.

"Let's go see the girls," he suggested.

A quick stab of fear and excitement ran along the quicksilver of Augie's veins. He forgot all about the Sissy Craig kid.

"Right now, you mean?" he asked.

"Don't worry, Mrs. Storm!" Crystal Craddock consoled the Pastor's wife. "I'm sure that Norval will be all right," she said, talking over the phone in the hallway of the house on Kootenai Street. "It takes them some time to get over to France when they're conscripted so late. Maybe it will be all over by the time he gets there. Let us hope so. In the meanwhile, I've knitted a few mufflers and things he might be able to use. Would you like me to send them direct to him?"

Poor Mrs. Storm! She seemed worried half out of her mind.

Crystal thanked her lucky stars that Pauly had been too young. She hung up the receiver and walked upstairs to her room. She sat down in front of the fireplace with the logs crackling blue and red flames and casting a yellow, flickering shadow on the pale turquoise of the carpet under and around the bed. Crystal had wanted a twin-bed bridal suite, but Doctor was insulted. Crystal had given in.

Now, she was happy. If only Doctor would like Pauly more. He was such a strange little man, Pauly was, and he was worrying about Wolf more than he let on. She knew from what Doctor had said that the dog was not getting on too well at the ranch. Probably, the caretaker neglected him. The last time she'd seen Wolf, the dog looked shaggy and unkempt, and starved. There was a wild look about the eyes.

Perhaps it would be better not to take Pauly up to the ranch so often. She could use as an excuse the fact that the snows were so high that a blizzard was too much for Doctor to chance. Before the winter was out, maybe Pauly'd forget.

Pauly had a new dog, now. A black and white bulldog called Toughy, but Toughy was as bad at fighting as Wolf almost, and you could see the bloody wounds on his white and black coat more easily because the hair was short.

Crystal worried a great deal about her son. He didn't come to her as often as he had in the days before she'd married Doctor. She hadn't the slightest idea, most of the time, what Pauly was thinking about. She thought of his confusion the time she had pointed out to him a hunchback walking the streets of the town.

"I never look at anybody who's deformed," Pauly had said. "Afraid I might make him feel sick!"

A sharp stab of tenderness and pride had reached into Crystal's heart. So infrequently did you see into the mind and body of someone you loved! A husband, a father, a mother, or even a son. It was with strangers that you spent your life. Only occasionally did some casual word or gesture reveal the deep and true humanity of the people you loved. It was something that was too often forgotten in these dark days of lust and horror, with the echoes of war all about, and Sammees going over the top.

In Europe there had been too many wars!

Poor Mr. MacMurray!

Pauly slunk into the kitchen like a beaten pup that has been out in the rain too long. Toughy had come to meet him out on the lawn, but Toughy couldn't cheer him. Charlie Chaplin always laughed at reverses, no matter how bad they were. But Pauly couldn't laugh. Recently, he'd seen Jack Pickford in *Tom Sawyer*. What a bunch of sweet-acting little kids. Nothing like the boys in Missoula! Everything, according to this movie, might be a little heart-rending at times, but every cloud had a silver lining.

Grown men didn't remember how tough it was to be young.

Like having your bathing trunks tossed into the branches of a cottonwood tree. Exhibited, stark naked, ashamed and mortified, in front of the only little girl you had ever loved in your life! Knocked around, tripped, made fun of, called a sissy because you hadn't learned to move fast, talk tough, clip a guy, and knock him out for a month.

Kids were cruel! There was no kindness in kids.

Chapter 12
The Trouble With Girls

︙︙

I.W.W. no worse than La Follette. Dean Larsson discusses freedom of speech at Public Forum. Another point of view was expressed by an unknown questioner who asked: "How far do you think you would get in an argument with Max Eastman or Emma Goldman?" Charles M. Schwab, president of the Bethlehem Steel Corporation, declared in an address at a dinner here tonight that the time was near at hand "when the men of the workingclass—the men without property—would have control of the destinies of the world."

The new year had come and gone.

Betty Darling had the shakes for many months after her cruel experience with Harold. It took time to rebuild the confidence she'd had in herself. If Betty were to rope any Romeos, first of all she would have to get the incense of evil out of her mind. The letter she had received from Lonely comforted her. Her brother was learning all there was to know about France. He'd be going up to the front line trenches soon. And if the Boche[1] hadn't heard about Montana so far.... Powder River, Let 'Er Buck!

Betty went to the high-school drags that were thrown in the local gymnasium, where the balconies were draped with purple and gold brocade. The baskets were swung up against the roof.

By such simple magic, a basketball court was turned into a seventeenth-century salon. Most of the time, Betty refused to dance. She wanted to make up her mind about life and you couldn't do that very well in the arms of some boy!

School every morning. At night, there was the stiff figure of her father, the lines of worry creasing his forehead. The bank was not well these days, for people were land-poor.

When Betty went upstairs to go to bed in a lonely house, she worried; and at night she dreamed about Harold. The man who had described and questioned her body, and left it unanswered. The boy who had made a jest of her. While blizzards swept over the mountains, Betty slept in a house that was not her home. She lived in the house of her father, where smoke of expensive Havana tobacco lay heavy on the air at suppertime. The maid came and went along the dark hallways. There were too many rooms in the Darling house, now that the mother was dead, and Lonely had gone to fight the war on another continent.

Who was there now to warm the heart of a young girl in a world that was too big for her?

Betty had thought herself a tomboy. She had admired Lonely when he wasn't too drunk, but Harold had changed that! Now, Betty didn't know what to think.

When it came to the dance held at the gymnasium in January, the snow had frozen and the ground was hard. Betty appeared in a white dress that revealed her growing loveliness, with her hair

---

1   Slang for German soldiers, derived from the French *alboche* (short for *Allemand caboche* or *German cabbage-head*).

curled and a white ribbon tied neatly over her left ear. There was no use in being a tomboy, now that she was fast on the way to being grown-up. Her breasts grew larger as the winter advanced. She'd forget Harold if it was the last thing she ever did, Betty thought.

Betty was all right!

Augie was sure of that, as he came barging down the basketball floor. He'd give her a swing, Augie would, for Betty was tender. She was young as the sprout. The greener the flower, the whiter the root! Augie was definitely impressed with Betty, and the Pastor couldn't possibly object to her father. Not that Augie was the marrying kind, and him so young, but if it ever came out! Should Sullivan say, for instance, "I hear you're goin' fancy!"

The banker's bank would shut that out.

For Betty was tender!

"May I have this dance?" Augie said in his best Sunday school English.

Betty floated into his arms like a dream, her flesh was so soft and her dress was so white, and she moved like a cloud. You'd never have guessed, from the overalls she used to wear and her raucous speech, that Betty could be so lovely. But Lonely was long gone in France and Betty had changed. She should be interesting out on a date, from what Stiff Sullivan said. Augie was sure that Harold had missed a few points. Harold would! How in hell a lady like Betty had gone for that fag was more than the Pastor's son could understand.

But he'd soon find out!

Between dances, Augie sneaked out to the lockers to get a snort. Drinking was a new angle he'd learned from his last trip to Butte, when he'd tangled with Serafimovitch and that crowd. Pocketful of Sen-Sen, and you munched it hard, and didn't come home until late. Pastor never guessed what went on. Sen-Sen worked.

Betty knew that Augie was drinking. She didn't mind it if he didn't get goofed up too much. Like when she remembered Lonely's fraternity brothers and the way they had pushed her around in the billiard room in the cellar of her father's house to the fox trots they'd played on the victrola. So she knew what whiskey felt like from the breath of it on her cheek. It was better than the five-and-dime incense of Harold and his chicken coop! Augie was a boy that Lonely would've liked. It took boys like that for Betty to grow fond of! But for several months she had wondered if there was something wrong with her that Harold should have acted so bad.

She'd find out tonight!

Augie had stoked the furnace of the Pastor's house well. He could stay out as long as he pleased. He'd borrowed the Pastor's car. He'd take Betty for a ride, after the dance was over. If he got goofed up enough.

Augie would sow his wild oats while he was young, while Norval was strewing his grain on the fertile fields of France.

When Sullivan had suggested going to see Penny, Augie was scared half out of his pants. They'd gone down to the rooms of Madam Nellie's Hotel. They'd walked up the stairs to the second floor lobby. The Madam with skirts flowing like Thaïs floated up the hall.

"Yes, what will you boys have?" she asks real polite.

Augie, no kidding, is weak at the knees!

No good to let Sullivan know, so Augie swaggers up to the Madam and says, "The best in the house!"

Madam smiles faintly, but is too much of a lady to let out she catches on. She ushers Sullivan and Augie into the sitting room, and they both sit down on the edges of their chairs, formally, only Augie a little more so. He keeps his lips buttoned!

"What comes now?" says Augie.

"Keep your pants on!" Sullivan sneers. "All in good time."

So Augie droops back into his chair, but tries to get a cynical look in his face.

Well, of course, Penny comes in and she is a sight for sore eyes. Long and slinky, black hair and dark eyes. She has a kimono over her body. She's not too careful about covering up the breasts, either. Penny looks at Augie, who is new to the place.

"A friend of yours?" she asks, turning to Stiff.

"We knock around some," Sullivan admits.

The other nest takes Sullivan, and Penny goes off with Augie into her bedroom. And that was where the trouble began!

Augie fumbled with fear. His bones went soft as gumbo mud in the rain. His whole body wilted, and he thought of the sturdy rocks of mountain crags, steadfast and clean, the smell of pine cones, and the prickle of kinnikinnick,[2] whittled by the wind. The wild parsnips of summer white on the plain. Augie was new at the game, and remembered everything that his mother never told him. The Pastor, his father, believed in God, but had never gotten around to giving his son any practical advice. The only coaching Augie had ever received had been from his older brother.

But Norval was far away.

Augie did the best he could! He fought a losing fight facing the stiff current. He came up, like Honey Pie, clutching for straws. Drowned. In the soft red lushness and the simpering sneers of Penny that would make him a man! Augie had carried it off in seeing the Madam and on the trip upstairs. For the rest, it was a quick passage through strange waters, and then a battery of instruments that frightened him half out of his wits. "What d'yuh think I mean?" Penny had said. "Think I want to shake hands?" and she had laughed pleasantly in a professional sort of way. Damn! But there was a helluva lot of white fat on her behind!

---

2   The common bearberry plant.

Going back down the hallway, Augie recovered enough to become curious. "You ever go out?" he asked. "Do you go out to eat, you go out to get the air, you go out to smoke or buy a newspaper, or go to a movie or have a sundae?"

"No," Penny replied. "I stay here!"

She laughed to the other garden: "He ain't planted much around here!" Penny snickered and Stiff Sullivan looked wise. OK, the Pastor's son was all right. You'd never see a better guy with a cue or a collection plate come Christian Sundays when the Pastor was talking about the war!

"Augie'll learn," Stiff Sullivan said to the girls.

But the Madam didn't show and Augie felt like on some of those mountains at night. You're up twelve thousand feet in the snows in a barrack of rocks to hide you from the storm. You light the fire and it casts some rainbows in the sky. Eyes glow in the underbrush around you. And you measure the space between the eyes and you match coins to see whether it's a coyote, a cougar, a lynx, or a plain damn figment of the imagination. And you always win! No referee. And it's fine fun! Then, you start gassing, or remembering, about all the girls you took out that you've never seen since. You open a can of beans, fry some bacon, burn some spuds, and the fire begins to die out.

It's cold.

The dawn comes up grey over the mountains.

And you're lonely. Afraid! And you go out of the whorehouse feeling like that, and wishing the Madam was around so you could crack wise.

"Come back again when you're more at attention," Penny laughed, as she turned around her fat behind and walked down the hallway.

Augie hoped to Christ he didn't get himself in a sling. He wished Norval were around to give him some good advice!

Augie finished the bottle of whiskey in the locker room. He felt fine! Wiping his mouth with his handkerchief, he turned and walked back to the dance floor where Betty was waiting for him. They danced around the place a few times as the orchestra was playing *Home, Sweet Home*. After the dance was over, Betty wrapped herself warmly in the coat her father had given her for Christmas. Outside the gymnasium, Augie opened the door of the car for Betty to climb in. It was a sedan. Rare in these parts. And fairly warm in winter! Augie lit a cigarette and stepped on the starter.

He wondered if Betty was warm? She looked bright enough in the fair beauty of her skin. She was sweet and human in a way that Penny never had been. Augie saw that the banker's daughter was tucked in securely with the robe around her feet and thighs. Only her soft face showed clearly in the light coming from the dashboard.

Augie shifted gears.

Skidding crazily around the corner down Higgins Avenue, he gunned the car on the straightaway, pressing the throttle hard. The wind rode past like buffalo in stampede. The mountains shining in the stiff, white light of the moon, were remote as remembered desire. His car, a black beetle, shot forward in the steel-encased jacket that kept the world outside. Augie's silent exhilaration was running the clock!

With the alcohol deep in his veins and Betty beside him.

Not that Augie was interested in girls to the extent of marriage! But all of his life he'd known and admired Lonely. He'd never have dared to talk to his sister if he had wanted to in those early days. Now, Lonely was gone and Betty was no longer the stripling kid in overalls. She was full-blown and soft like a question. One he would know the answer to:

And why was Harold?

The car was parked in the blind alley of a coulee beyond Fort Missoula, where the mountains began. In the back seat of the sedan,

Betty was serving as a cushion. She felt the strong masculine odor of whiskey and cigarette breath on her cheek. The lisp of liquor on Augie's lips tasted good. At least, the Pastor's son had kissed her the way she should be kissed! She went soft under the hard muscle of Augie's body. It was clean because it was like Lonely. It was like Missoula, and Lonely's fraternity brothers, and like all of the life she had been through, and yet it was strange and undiscovered. Betty was on guard, for all her softness!

She marveled at Augie's movement and boyhood strength. His rosy cheeks were hot under the thin white threads of her fingers. But when his hands drew up along her naked thighs and felt like fever on her belly—

Betty Darling cried. She jackknifed like the snap of long and steel-sharp scissors. Nothing like Harold would come again in her life! Not until words meant something real to her heart, not until lips could speak and eyes could sense the loneliness of her thought. Silence shut in the valley of her body.

On the road back to Missoula, Augie sulked.

Returning to the outhouse of God, Augie was sore.

He hoped to Christ Sullivan had himself in a sling!

For teaching him about love.

Chapter 13
Peeping Toms

‡‡

Sedition charge faces judge of Montana court. Charles L. Crum, of Forsyth, will be asked to resign as presiding judge of the Fifteenth Judicial District, embracing Rosebud and Musselshell counties, tomorrow morning by a committee of "The Hundred".... US. transport sunk; Missoula men on board. 2,179 troops on ship when subs attack.... Five Montana men, including two from the Bitterroot valley, lost their lives in the Tuscania *disaster and have been buried on the coast of Scotland, according to an official announcement made yesterday.*

It was a principle with Doctor that a boy should earn his keep. If you started a youngster on the road to self-sufficiency early enough, he would know how to handle himself in a world of hard knocks. Doctor had to admit that his oldest son, Gil, hadn't turned out for the best. The exception proved the rule. And that was why he had decided to have a couple of the cows brought down to town from the ranch. It should do Pauly good to have to milk every morning and evening. The kid was so diffident! Some real work would help him grow up.

And yet, Pauly was not so bad now as he had been at first. The child had professed a flattering interest in surgery. Doctor had taken Pauly on trips up to Stevensville and to Hamilton. Operations! The boy had watched it all without a murmur.

And Pauly had pleased Doctor by learning all of the bones in the body. He could rattle off the names like a regular first-year medical student. As a reward, Doctor had taken Pauly down to the Lucy Undertaking Rooms to watch an autopsy. The man was long and yellow in the death laid out in the funeral parlors. The cup of his skull was sliced nicely like a cantaloupe. When the crown of his head was removed by Doctor's exact and scientific fingers, there was the brain, beautiful and intricate as a cluster of red flowers. The purple clot on the left lobe was proof of the correctness of Doctor's diagnosis. As he had suspected, the man had died of syphilis.

Doctor turned to see Pauly's pale face in the gloom.

He'd make a man of him! Start them out early. That was the ticket. If Pauly were to be a doctor when he grew up, he'd have to learn to stand blood early.

Two cows it would be!

Doctor would have them sent down in the morning.

Pauly got up out of bed early these winter mornings. He still slept on the balcony that led off the attic. The heavy Hudson Bay blankets kept his young body warm in any kind of weather, and the dirty, grey tarpaulin kept off the ram and the snow. Pauly would dash from the balcony into the comparative comfort of the attic, slip into his bathrobe and slippers, and sneak downstairs past the luxurious form of the maid who was still sleeping in her bedroom. The stairs from the attic led through the maid's room. There was no way that Pauly could avoid it. Occasionally, he'd stop to observe the deep bounty of the maid's breasts, whenever they were free of covers.

Pauly was fascinated by the maid's breasts.

But it seemed like such a terrific burden for a woman to carry around with her wherever she went. Pauly marveled that women didn't become hunchback from carrying so much around on their chests.

The smell in the maid's room even on the coldest of mornings was unpleasant. It excited and sickened Pauly, all at once. He hoped that other girls would not be like this—smelling up everything with their bodies! Sometimes, with his heart in his throat, Pauly wondered what would happen if he ever collected enough courage to place his hands on the maid's bosom.

If she suddenly awaked to find his hands upon her, what would she do? Smile sleepily? Or would she scream out? It was too much of a chance to take!

Fear tightened Pauly's throat. He slipped out of the room as quietly as he could, with his heart beating roundly.

After fixing the furnace, Pauly would tramp out through the snow, climb into the loft of the barn, toss down hay for the cows to eat, return downstairs with bucket and stool, bury his head in the side of one of the cows, and start milking.

Two soft, warm teats in his hands, the milk streaming alternately into the bucket.

The trouble with girls:

They bothered a boy's sleep. They'd never, never, never leave him alone. Like the thought of Betty Darling and all of the stories he'd been told. But Pauly never quite believed them, for Betty was the white, pure object of his dreams.

Pauly returned to the kitchen with a pail of milk and set it upon the table. The maid could take care of it. Pauly carried with him the hot close odor of manure from the barn. He'd fed the rabbits and tossed some meat to Toughy. Now, he could wash up for breakfast and hurry off to school.

Crystal's son went through his classes in a dream. Home for a quick lunch and return. During the afternoon study period, he read a copy of *Western Stories*, which he'd hidden inside his notebook. As he was leaving study room, Augie caught him by the arm.

"We're goin' around robbin' iceboxes tonight," he said. "Want to come along?"

Pauly agreed. Some way, somehow, he'd have to get on the good side of Augie and the rest of the gang. Show that he was a guy with guts! A fellow who could talk tough, smoke, and spit like a man! Maybe, tonight was the chance.

The night was dark with the moon lost in the clouds. The white snow on the ground was covered by the wind-swept shadows of winter. After a good hot dinner and milking the cows for the evening, Pauly wangled some money out of his mother. He told her he was going down town to a movie. *The Knights of the Round Table*: shows how a group of Boy Scouts clean up on a gang of roughnecks.

"All right, Pauly, but be home early," Crystal said.

Pauly kissed his mother hurriedly on the cheek, looked at Doctor faintly in alarm, put on his Mackinaw, and hurried out into the night. The snow crackled under his shoes. Hurrying over to the candy store across from the high school, he found Augie, Stiff Sullivan, and Jake Sterling already there.

Augie was smoking one of his home-made Bull Durhams.

"What kept you?" the Pastor's son asked impatiently. He was exasperated. "We was beginnin' to think you'd ducked out again!"

"Nothin' like that," Pauly apologized. "I was milkin' the cows and the cows wouldn't stand still."

"OK! No damage done," Stiff Sullivan growled. "If we're goin', we better get goin'," he said.

They began the evening's foray at Betty Darling's house. Going in back of the banker's brick building, they broke into the kitchen and raided the icebox with the greatest of ease. There was chicken left over from supper, candied sweet potatoes, and wine. They split the food four ways, but Pauly barely touched his lips to the bottle.

Doctor ever smell liquor on his breath and he'd get strapped, for sure! Not that Doctor had ever whipped him, but Pauly was taking no chances. The sound of breaking bones, as the kids tore at the fried chicken with hungry teeth, was pleasant and exciting in Pauly's ears. The gurgle of wine and the risk of getting caught.

It was great!

Pauly wondered what Betty would think if she saw him now. They wandered from house to house, skipping homes where dogs were evident, until they finally arrived at Lover Lemire's. This would be enough icebox-breaking for one evening. The kids had eaten so much they could hardly walk. But Lover's icebox must have been located in the cellar. In any case, Sullivan couldn't find it, and the cellar door was locked.

"Let's fan over to the gymnasium at college," Jake Sterling suggested. "We might be able to scare up a basketball game or something."

Right in the middle of the season like this there were usually some university guys tossing baskets and playing around. Augie thought it was a good idea and Sullivan didn't care if they did. Pauly didn't matter. They strolled across the campus, passed Main Hall, and opened the door of the college gymnasium.

"Nothing but broads," Sullivan snorted. It seemed that this was one of the evenings the girls took over the floor.

"Wait a minute! I got an idea," Augie said. He led Jake, Stiff, and Pauly around to the football field. Here, the bleachers leaned smack against the gymnasium. Softly, the boys crept up from level to level until they reached the top of the grandstand right under the windows of the shower room on the second floor. Quietly, carefully, Augie pried one of the windows loose and opened it, eager and careful to make no noise.

Augie, Stiff, Jake, and Pauly, kneeling down on the bleachers, peeked through the astonishing aperture Augie had made. Seven co-eds were naked under the showers. With tempestuous pulse compressing his heart with excitement, Pauly saw fourteen breasts, each at a different droop and angle. His eyes traveled feverishly from one to another. He observed the soft slope of the girls' thighs, the dark gardens, the napes of the neck, and the tapering of the legs to the feet. The precious pain of their bellies struck Pauly amidship. He thought quickly of the maid whose room he passed through going to bed.

Pauly hoped that Betty Darling's room was, like the shower, clean and charming to the eyes and nose.

A tall, dark girl felt inquiry sharp on her breasts. Instinctively, covering herself with her arms, she screamed like a woman provoking attack. The girls in the shower room looked up to see the salacious slant beneath the window and the line of faces behind. The girls felt masculine eyes, sharp as knives, cutting into their bodies. The girls howled like alley cats, as pandemonium imperiled their flight. Legs flying in every direction, they headed for the exit. "Get the cops! Get the cops!" one girl yelled at the top of her voice.

"Scatter, you guys!" Augie exclaimed.

The boys broke down through the bleachers, giggling hysterically with glee and excitement, and spread out over the field in flight. Pauly found his own way home through the cover of darkness.

A thin crust of snow collapsed with each step he took.

Lonely and Mr. MacMurray stood side by side, neck-deep in a front-line trench.

Over the top, and beyond in No Man's Land, they could see but one tree, bent and twisted like scrub cedar on a wind-rocked mountain top. The gnarled and embittered wood was black and rusted with murder. In the silence the occasional snag of a branch pointed accusingly at the sky. Whistle and plop of a single bullet. Silence once more! It was too damn silent! Mr. MacMurray's knees felt weak at the joints.

Lonely played bravery right on the nose; and was hoping Powder River would win. He'd never imagined war was like this. The stifling quiet and the promise of more to come! Until the barrage was laid down and death would begin. He wondered what he'd have done had he known when he spoke so harshly to his father what he knew now? The dark days dead in the past of sleep and their fitful memory where the moon came over the mountains. *Standing a moment on the Higgins Avenue bridge, looking down as the waters swirled in the Clark Fork of the Columbia. The separate and lonely lights of the town over the railroad tracks. Waterworks Hill to the north over the N.P. shops. Thinking would he get drunk again tonight? Come home in the morning when the sky began to pale and only the cops were out, looking for murder?*

Strange, he had never cared for his father.

As the deathly silence continued, Mr. MacMurray thought sadly of his Montana days. He'd been younger and more foolish than anyone would have suspected. Too young to marry Mrs. Craig. Too young to know what the war was about.

Suddenly, hell broke down around his ears!

The sky exploded.

As she turned out the light and got into bed with Pastor, Mrs. Storm thanked merciful God that her son had not been lost when the *Tuscania* was sunk by submarines.

Chapter 14
Augie Follows the Mob

"If a man who has lived under this flag and enjoyed its protection now disparages it or refuses to do his bit in defending it, for God's sake let him move under a flag he does like, or let us silence him, even if we must take him out and shoot him," said Dan A. Reed, representative of the US. Food Administration.... William Hardy, secretary of the local I.W.W., gets from nine to eighteen months in the state penitentiary at Deer Lodge. Mr. Hardy got into trouble, it will be recalled, when he neglected to pull his coat-tail over the butt end of the revolver which he was carrying in his pocket for the protection of I.W.W. property.

Augie Storm got a real scare when he heard about Jane Smith, the pretty little Hamilton girl who shot herself in the side because of the morning after the night before. Pastor was talking about it over his tea cup. Coffee was a little too strong for Pastor. But God was never too hard on those who had sinned. Mrs. Storm felt sorry for Jane, whose mother belonged to a different church than Pastor's. But Pastor's wife said nothing. She wished to preserve peace in her home at any price. There was enough to worry about, as it was, with Norval fighting in France. God should take care of her son. She prayed to the Lord every night before crawling into bed with Pastor.

Augie listened to Pastor talking. Every nerve in Augie's body was tense with concern. Like a bird dog with its tail pointed and its ears tuned in on the wind.

Jane had walked into the local hardware store. She'd come all the way from Hamilton with guilt crowding her brain.

She was a casual acquaintance of Betty Darling's. The fathers of both girls had become friends through some transaction at the bank.

Jane walked up to the counter displaying guns. *"Please, go away!" she screamed to the doctors and nurses at St. Patrick's Hospital.*

"Let me see a revolver," Jane asked the hardware clerk.

"Six-shooter or automatic, Miss?" the clerk said affably. She was a pretty girl and kind of young to be interested in guns, he thought. If it weren't for the fact he was married, he'd like to give this baby a lay. But you couldn't be robbing the cradles these days. You took too much of a risk! The girl looked rather set and serious, though, for a youngster her age. The clerk withdrew a .41 Colt from the counter display.

"Have you any cartridges to fit this gun?" Jane Smith asked. "I'd like to see how it's loaded."

She'd watched her father get ready for hunting trips, many a time. The long, sharp rifles that would catch an elk were familiar to her from childhood. But she'd seen few pistols at close range, although many Montanans wore them on the hip.

The clerk brought out a box of cartridges and handed them to the girl. The guns were not selling so much any more with the new law about registration. Good thing, too, the clerk thought, because that was the way they got that Wobbly who was head of a ring of German spies in Missoula. They'd caught him carrying a concealed weapon and they'd sent him away for a good long while.

If that young girl would only smile, by God, he'd try to date her, wife or no wife. The clerk bet this kid was a good lay!

Jane inserted a cartridge, pulled back the action, and shot the bullet into the chamber of the gun.

Went out on a joyride and a beer party on the night before, she admitted. I never did anything wrong before, she wept. Before the clerk could possibly know what was up, Jane turned the gun on herself and pulled the trigger.

"I was so ashamed, I tried to kill myself and I don't want to live," she wept.

Augie was really scared to hear the Pastor talking about it. The girl knew Betty Darling, it seemed. Jesus! If on the other night things had gone as he planned.... Stiff Sullivan was right when he talked about Penny and all the rest of the girls. No trouble, and safe enough if you knew how to keep yourself out of a sling! The best way was to pick your girl and go to her regular. No use to take unnecessary chances by sleeping with every girl in the house. It was too risky going respectable, according to what Stiff Sullivan said. Augie was scared!

"Poor girl," the wife of the Reverend sighed. She was glad that her children had been boys. No girls to worry about. Her husband was a good man and, praise the Lord, no scandal should ever soil his name! But sometimes it was a little hard agreeing with all the stern pronouncements the Pastor brought forth. Pastor was good to his sons, however. She'd say that about Pastor.

He was good to his children!

Augie felt thin streams of cold sweat trickling down his spine. Excusing himself from the table, he returned to school. Hell, Honey Pie is properly buried and long forgotten when something has to come along and remind him of death! Tough, and he beat Serafimovitch with his two bloody fists flying. He was a kid, but could fight. Back through the black storm of Hellgate Canyon he had come here to the town. Stiff Sullivan comforting as hell with the sympathetic words he spit out of the side of his mouth. No use getting weak or the heebie jeebies would get you! He'd forgotten completely about God. It was good to leave the Saviour out of these things. The grandstand crash at the Fairgrounds. The rider's brains, like a mud pie, smashed on the ground.

Went on a joyride and felt soon afterwards the effects of remorse, Jane Smith, a pretty little girl, violated, shot in the side, hoped to die, and probably would.

But Augie was beginning to regard Stiff Sullivan with suspicion. Norval was fighting for democracy and American womanhood in France, and yet Augie had allowed Sullivan to take him to Butte to see that Red, Bill Dunne! Augie felt he'd have to watch his step in the future. He knew what the score was and Stiff was getting soft in the head.

All through school that day, Augie worried. He was afraid he might see Betty Darling come tripping down the hall.

Shot in the side and not expected to live.

Augie wiped cold sweat from his brow. He'd have to collect enough courage to bluster through any encounter with Betty he might have! When school closed, Augie walked rapidly down Higgins Avenue and across the bridge to Kelly's Empress Cigar Rooms. He played a couple of games of pool with the punk who was supposed to take the customers. In spite of his nervousness, Augie beat the sap three in a row.

One thing good about the war, though! They no longer bothered kids in the pool parlors and saloons.

Augie decided Stiff Sullivan was talking too big and free for a guy that was nothing but a fireman's son. He got away with it only because he was tough, a star athlete, and a kid that was swift with his mitts.

At this moment, Stiff Sullivan walked into Kelly's Empress Cigar Rooms. He saw Augie wielding his cue with all the dexterity that religion and science could give him. Sullivan liked the Pastor's son. Augie was the only kid in town, outside of Billy Toole, that Sullivan felt at all free with. The Pastor's son was OK!

Augie was a good fighter, too.

It occurred to Stiff Sullivan that fighting went along with preacher blood and maybe it would be better if he saw the father more often, now that he was getting up in the world?

"Hello, Augie!" Stiff Sullivan said. "Was up to your place after school let out, but your old lady says you ain't at home. I was thinkin' what's new with your brother!"

Augie looked sour. But not too sour! Who was Stiff to start getting worried about the war or his brother? Augie had been hearing stories about how one of Sullivan's cousins, a ranch hand up the Rattlesnake, was up to his neck in trouble. Pastor had been telling him they'd passed a new law at Helena. Good thing, too. Get Bill Dunne and the rest of those Reds in Butte right in the neck!

"How's Herbert?" Augie replied, looking innocent as he bent over his cue, shot a fast one into the corner, bouncing, and it came back and hit the eight ball smack on its behind into the side pocket. "Hear he's been crackin' wise!"

Sullivan looked at Augie with surprise. Was the kid going to speak out of turn at this late day in the evening? It looked like Augie was listening to too much pool-room sentiment. It was too early to teach the kid a few things, maybe. Slap the Pastor's son down now and who would he have to cruise around with nights? It was a real predicament for Stiff to be in! It was no good, this Augie's getting things in his head. Pastor's son was supposed to have brains. That was one of the reasons Stiff had taken the kid to Butte to see his uncle and get acquainted with Bill Dunne.

It was a tough world and not everything went according to Hoyle. Now, the workers was all right! Sullivan's old man had always said, before he kicked off.

But Stiff wasn't sticking up for Herbert even though he *was* a cousin of his.

The farmer!

"What Herbert does is one thing!" Stiff Sullivan said, sitting down on the radiator and glancing up at Augie under the heavy shade of his eyebrows, his pupils narrowing to pinpoints of conjecture and distaste. "But guys that speak outa turn gets slapped, and slapped hard. You wasn't by any chance talkin' to me, was you?" Stiff asked.

"Go slow! I was only wonderin' how it affects you. On the level!" Augie said quickly.

"OK!" Sullivan answered. "So they make him kiss the flag. Maybe, it's good for him. But about treason, that's somethin' different."

Stiff looked out of the front window of Kelly's Empress Cigar Rooms. Augie, in the meanwhile, was running the balls off the pool table. Augie was good, but the micks were tougher! Not that Herbert was full-blown Irish. Maybe, that was why he was a farmer in everything that he did and said. Cracking out of turn! You never got hard when you had the whole mob against you, unless you wanted to get flattened. Not if you were wise, you didn't. In any case, Herbert was wrong. Instead of beefing about Europe, which was usually safe, he talked about things at home.

Sullivan saw the headlines of the newspaper on the radiator beside him. The paper was getting hot and so was Stiff. Shifting over to a bench along the wall, he lifted the paper off the radiator and started to read: *Wounded U.S. soldiers begin to arrive home. On the eve of the gathering at Moscow of the Russian Congress of the Soviets, which is to pass on the German peace accepted at Brest-Litovsk, President Wilson in a special message to the Russian people....*

Trouble with the times! Even his uncle's friend, Bill Dunne, worried too much about Europe. And it wasn't as if he didn't have troubles enough of his own!

Stiff put down the paper, thinking of his mother. Mary's yells had hit the rafters whenever his old man had come home drunk and spitting slogans.

Stiff's old man had been worse than Mike Sullivan for trouble!

Not the kind that Bill Dunne went in for, he had to admit, but Mary was a holy terror.

Mother of God and the saints preserve us!

Maybe, that's what was wrong with the Pastor's son. Too close to the Lord and the church around the corner. You treated God with respect and that was enough in any guy's language. *Familiarity breeds contempt!* That was what Stiff's father had always told him.

No use worrying the church too much.

Or Hell would come home to roost.

With Herbert getting himself in a jam, it was a good thing Sullivan was such a good ball player that nobody'd say sedition ran in his family. The girls still eyed him with fear and admiration. Not that Stiff at this late date was going respectable like Augie.

The trouble with gals! You take this Jane Smith from up the Bitterroot Valley. The way things were going with Augie, Sullivan wouldn't be surprised if another girl about town went off the deep end. That was the danger of going with respectable babies!

Is a genuine nine-year-old patriot. She has made a sacrifice which few girls would make. She cut off her hair that it might be sold to buy War Savings Stamps....

What Stiff Sullivan didn't know about dames!

Augie was in a brown study trying to figure out a shot he could make safely.

"Play the combination into the side pocket," Stiff suggested.

Augie swung his cue around, stopped, chalked the end with a dust of fine blue smoke, got set, serious. The five ball popped, and bounced back out of the pocket to the table again, a total loss.

"Tough!" Stiff Sullivan commiserated.

He got up from the bench upon which he had been sitting, stretched his legs, and yawned. It was time to go home and have supper with Mary. These were dark days for sure, and Mary would be worrying about what all her business would think, what with Herbert getting arrested and him a cousin of the Sullivans....

These days you'd better be patriotic if you knew what was good for you!

Alleged disloyal remarks, three men were taken to the main street of the town and forced to kneel in the snow, repeat the oath of allegiance and kiss the American flag....

And no more talk about the Irish Revolution, neither.

But one thing was certain, Herbert would stay in the clink!

Stiff Sullivan walked home through the gathering twilight.

Section 2
1918–1919

Missoula women dancing with soldiers in Riverside Park, 1918

Chapter 15
Pauly Takes a Sprint

‡‡‡

What is declared to be the first step in a campaign to rid Missoula county of all I.W.W.'s was taken yesterday with the arrest of sixteen Wobblies, two of whom are held on charges of criminal syndicalism and sabotage under provisions of the recently enacted law. While awaiting disposition of their cases, the men will be formed into a chain gang and put to work on the highways of the county.... Loyalty to the government with undying cooperation until the great war is won was the keynote of the Master Horseshoers' Association of Montana, which concluded its session at the Palace Hotel last night.

Pauly's head was in a whirl with the clamor of these days.

What he heard at home, caught after school, watched in assemblies, took from the boys! Conflict had caught his life, and no amount of wishing would set him free.

On Liberty Day, Pauly stood on a corner of Higgins Avenue and Front Street, watching the parade. Thousands of men and women marched down the street.

Pauly thought of the War Garden he had planted in the orchard beside the barn. Turnips and onions and radishes and lots of greens for the rabbits to eat. He'd grow them all, helping to win the war and keep Betty safe.

Augie marched in the parade, but Stiff Sullivan was having nothing to do with the fever about the flag. The Pastor claimed that the American boys would come back from France better men, in spite of the temptations said to exist.

Even Pauly's mother was not untouched by the hysteria that fevered the town. Every time she bought a sack of flour she took it up to the university to have it tested for ground glass.

If only the kids would give him a break, Pauly thought to himself, as he watched Augie march past. But they still talked about his ducking out of the fight in Butte, and kidded him about it. Augie was the worst. Stiff didn't say much, but Pastor's son was sneering out loud most of the time.

He wisecracked about that "sissy Craig kid was always runnin' around with his pants buttoned up like there was something sacred inside."

Pauly would have to take the bull by the horns. He'd tried to learn how to use his dukes, but it didn't seem to do much good. The boxing instructor at the university had given him up as a total loss. Pauly's arms got in the way of his own fists and his face stuck out to the enemy's attack like an apple on the end of a bough, ripe for injury. Ready to fall!

It occurred to Pauly, in a moment of inspiration, that if he could play a good game of basketball or run like hell on the track, maybe Augie and the rest of the kids would let him alone. Pauly decided to enter the track try-outs which the high-school coach was holding on the university field.

If Betty could be in the bleachers to see Pauly run like a hare!

Yes, that was the way it should be! If you couldn't use your dukes because they got tangled with each other in the fray, or because you'd grown too fast to be strong, your eyes got crossed and your vision was dim, or it was just plain that you were no damn good at it.

So you were no good!

But if you could flash a ball through the basket, pivot fast, tripping up the other guys with your speed, perhaps it wouldn't matter so much whether you could fight good or not! Football was out, if you're skinny and light, and the basketball season was over, but how about track? A guy that couldn't fight should be able to run. Common ordinary horse sense would tell you that. You're smelly with the mitts, so your feet are fast. It was axiomatic.

Straight poker or flush. You had to pick the game that was your style. Play ring-around-the-rosy with the boys for a while and they'd call him Speedy. He'd register with Coach Garrison for the try-outs, Pauly thought, this very morning. He'd buy trunks at the mercantile store and charge them to Doctor's account. Red, they would be; and some flashy purple jersey, yellow socks, and some good track shoes with spikes that would eat the dust.

At lunch time, Pauly went down town and purchased his supplies for the track try-outs. This was a honey! And he'd run first in the track meet, or second at best.

Would Betty sit up and take notice!

That's all right, fellas! Pauly would say, depreciating his own heroism as best he could. I didn't hit them Butte kids so hard as I might. I figured I'd save myself for the track! The old high-school spirit and all like that!

Augie would say: "Pauly, you're a great man! How about comin' down to Kelly's Empress Cigar Rooms for a game of pool? Or we could go over to the Bucket of Blood and watch the faro game."

Yes, that was the way it would be! By late afternoon, Pauly's heart was beating like a sledgehammer against the hollow crust of his lungs. Pauly took his track togs back with him to the house on Kootenai Street. There was no use changing his clothes in the high-school gymnasium with the rest of the kids that would wisecrack. Sissy's gonna run! they would say. He ran out in Butte so's he wants to try again! Pauly didn't want any of it. He'd get dressed in his own home. Get all fixed up and then walk over to the university field where the track try-outs were to be held.

In a white and black bathrobe, Pauly was ready to start for the field. Thinking of Betty, it occurred to him that he hadn't bathed for several days. He couldn't have Betty objecting to his odor if she should pass his way. He wasn't taking any chances of smelling like the maid. In any case, he wanted to be in good shape for the meet. Taking off his track togs, Pauly got under the hot shower, soaped and rinsed himself clean, and climbed into his track suit again. With bathrobe bound firmly about him so he wouldn't catch cold, Pauly headed for victory.

Would Betty like him now?

Clean, colorful, and debonair in his newly purchased raiment.

As Pauly Craig stepped down University Avenue, he heard the sound of marching men around him. He'd been called to the colors, the purple and gold of his high school, and he was the top sergeant. On either side of him, the men were moving with their bayonets struck with sunlight. The sharp candour of their eyes foretold the future. Miles and miles of khaki brown, determined, native, and bitten with victory fever.

Yet, it seemed a sad state of affairs to Pauly.

So many boys to run, so few to win!

Pauly increased his pace, the soldiers around him. As they passed the alley between the Sigma Chi house and Professor Riley's, a small, shawl-shouldered little woman stepped out from the shadow. Her fist was in her mouth, and tears were streaming down her cheeks, brave, bereaved, American!

"My son!" she whispered through the sobs of her sorrow.

"My son!" she said.

That was all! Just twice. The little mother had come to see her boy off to the track meet. But Pauly would win! Don't you fear, little woman! Pauly had said. He couldn't let her down in such a serious business. And Betty would see him come streaming home, the pennants of his talent flying in a veritable thunder of applause, in the hearts of the multitudes, in the atmosphere of tomorrow!

No longer could Augie say, pointing his finger.... Even Stiff, who was mostly silent on these occasions, would look approving.

As Pauly approached the grandstand, the place seemed vacant. There didn't seem to be any spectators or girls in the bleachers.

Betty didn't appear to be around.

Pauly ducked under the grandstand and cut through the gateway to the track. All of the members of last year's team were standing around waiting for the coach to give the signal to line up. Stiff Sullivan, in the tough tension of his muscles, was eager to plunge at the sound of a pistol shot, his breast bursting forward, and the spikes of his track shoes clipping the sod. Stiff Sullivan was a man who could kick, could fight, could spit.

And could run!

"Look who's comin' up!" Augie snickered. "Where'd you get them pants? Don't you know red's unpatriotic unless it's got white and blue to go with it? But purple! Where did you get them pants?"

"All they had in the store," Pauly lied, trying to hide his confusion.

"Comes the fire-sale boy," Jake Sterling mocked, as he hopped around like a grasshopper, trying to stretch his legs.

Pauly retired into the crowd that was gathered around the coach. He was not so confident of victory now. The coach placed him on the end of the starting line, on the outside, near the bleachers. Stiff and Augie hugged the inside of the track. The coach raised the pistol in his right hand. "Ready, set," he began.

The pistol went off with a bang! Like a couple of grouse, Augie and Stiff Sullivan set out in flight, skidding around the corners and raising a dust storm behind. Around the circle the boys spread out. The pounding fury of Stiff Sullivan's driving legs went up and down like pistons. Before the smoke had cleared away from the mouth of the starter's gun, it seemed, Stiff Sullivan was bending around the last curve and stripping the home stretch with his long lungs heaving. Augie came in second. The rest of the boys dribbled behind.

The coach examined his stop-watch.

He smiled with satisfaction. "All right, the rest of you fellows! Line up in your places. Once around the track and make it snappy." As the coach was lifting his right hand holding the pistol, he heard strange noises coming down the stretch. Stiff Sullivan turned around, as he straightened the sweat-shirt around his belly.

"Fer Chrissakes!" Sullivan exclaimed. "We forgot Pauly."

Augie like to split his guts laughing. For Sissy Craig was limping down the home stretch like a plug who's got the heaves, his nostrils spouting determination!

"Clear the track!" Coach Garrison admonished. "All right, all right, you guys! Ready, set," and the pistol went off like a crack of buckshot at a cloud of ducks on an early September morning.

Pauly slid out of sight through the bleachers.

He couldn't understand!

The hot shower had sweated all of the courage out of him.

Chapter 16
Betty Reaches the Brink

American football player hero in France: Did he surrender? No! Not Griswold! He drew his automatic and went after 'em. Three Germans fell from bullets and a fourth Griswold finished with the butt of his pistol.... No more rushing the beer bucket. Several Missoula saloons place taboo on old time sport. Buy it in bottles! Can no longer get lard pail filled for two bits.... Writes Walter Jacobson, of the sixth grade: "I'm going to make a garden out in the west, and of all the gardens mine will be the best. A nice little garden I will make, so the Kaiser will say, 'For Goodness Sake!'"

Betty Darling was proud of her brother, Lonely, who was using an army rifle for a crutch these days. He'd written in his last letter that war was not so bad, the hospitals were homey, and say hello to the old man if he looks like he wants it. Betty mentioned the letter from Lonely at dinner that night, but the banker pursed his lips, clamped his teeth more sharply into his cigar, and said nothing.

Betty read the letter over again before going to bed that night.

She tucked her toes into a corner of the blanket and drew the sheet up close around her neck, her bobbed hair brown and soft on the pillowcase. Thinking of Lonely, she wondered what girls he was going with? Betty knew that in spite of Lonely's drinking, her father cared quite a bit about his son. But he'd been disappointed by Lonely's going bad. At the moment, at least, her brother was safe. He'd been in the hospital, was now on leave, and soon would be going back to the trenches.

Betty observed the moon, which was framed by her bedroom window, coming over the crest of Mount Sentinel. Her eyes, in narrow slits, were approaching slumber. She thought of the night, a couple of months back, when Augie had tried to take her for all she had. He'd never stopped to gauge the look in her eyes. He'd approached her blindly, fastening his lips on her flesh. As if speech through the fingertips were enough!

Who did Augie think he was? He took too much for granted.

Or maybe he hadn't? The old-fashioned kind of love went out with the covered wagon. Perhaps, even in those days, it hadn't been as perfect as the old people said. Take Calamity Jane, for instance, crushing the heads of two drunks like seeded dandelions. She shot from the hip, did Calamity Jane, and cursed like a trooper. There was no time for romance in the life of Calamity Jane! The girls in Montana grew up tough, rode paint cayuses in the wind, wore breeches like a man, cursed, chewed tobacco, and played pool.

Betty laughed sleepily at the remembrance of the May Fete on the college campus. All these young co-eds flitting around in their underwear, trying to look like nymphs. Betty searched her skin each night before going to bed for the dark red scab of a poison tick that would bring her death as sudden as any in France.... As sure, at least! Discovering a hitherto unguessed soft, red mole on the lip of her belly, she would scratch until the blood came to the surface of her skin.

It was nothing but a landmark, however. The ranch of the Red Mole. X marks the spot. Betty tossed and turned, buried her head in the pillow.

She recalled how she had had hysterics when she'd seen Pauly Craig coming down the avenue, wearing his new green suit. The pants were so tight they looked like they'd split at any moment. She imagined Pauly, naked and embarrassed once more in the sharp tang of Montana air, as she had seen him once below Van Buren bridge, the day that Honey Pie had been drowned.

Betty laughed.

She had nothing but contempt for a kid so speechless and afraid of girls. And that ridiculously funny pride in his face like that of a boy who thinks he's dressed to the nines.

Betty wished Lonely were around to rip Pauly's shiny, green pants with his bayonet, to puncture his pride like a rubber balloon! Like Augie, the Pastor's son, had said: a kid who went around town with his pants buttoned up and afraid. But that was no reason Augie should feel she was easy and free to the hands! That Pastor's kid took entirely too much for granted. She wondered if he'd been out with that Hamilton girl who'd killed herself.

Those bright little boys like the Pastor's son! They were tough, and they went around with their tongues hanging out, panting for girls. But Lonely was far away from it all, hobbling around Paris with an Army rifle for a crutch. Powder River, Let 'Er Buck! If Augie ever tried to take Betty Darling again, she'd let him have it between the eyes. Betty was growing up and her breasts were as hard as her speech. She pulled in her belly, tautly, like a mare that was getting ready to buck.

Betty was on the verge of darkness!

Her eyes closed.

And her funny little girl brain turning things around in her head, trying to find out the answers, with her father sour and Lonely away in France.

It had been good having a brother around, even though he was usually drunk.

The girl with the champagne eyes....

The next morning Betty was off bright and early to school. There was a dull hour of Latin, lunch later, and a tedious afternoon. In study hall, Pauly sat quietly in his long green pants over by the radiator in a corner of the room. Augie got sent to the principal's office for raising a ruckus with Stiff and Sterling, who were conspiring with the springtime in their blood. Stiff Sullivan was wearing a sweater with a large golden *M* on its front. After school let out, Betty walked down Higgins Avenue and across the bridge, stopping in the Palace Ice Cream Parlor for a Banana Split. Across the street she saw the Bijou, whose billboards advertised: *The romantic love adventures of Egypt's Vampire Queen. Theda Bara in* Cleopatra*, the siren of the Nile. As Caesar so aptly said: "The Devil surely was her sire for through her blood ran liquid fire."*

Betty wondered whether she should stop in to see her father at the bank, asking him for money to see the show. She decided against it. He didn't like to be disturbed during business hours.

As Betty strolled past the empty lot where ice-skating went on in the winter, she saw a bunch of the high-school boys standing beneath a billboard. *The picture that blocked traffic on Broadway,* The Beast of Berlin! And there was a portrait of the Kaiser snarling through his mustache and leering at some Belgian babies who crouched at the knees of their mother in abject and excruciating fear. Betty stopped stock still on the pavement to see what was going on.

Augie had decided there was no two ways about it! He looked at Stiff Sullivan out of one corner of his eye. After all, Stiff's cousin had been sent to the clink for sedition and Stiff was acting funny these days! You never knew what to expect. Like on that trip to Butte. *Have you taken out your Loyalty Papers? Every American should have in his possession one of the new Certificates of Loyalty, bearing a red cross in the center, the name of the patriot across it, and a dollar sign, appropriately backed up, in the left hand corner of the page.* Like when Stiff had said Bill Dunne was a right guy!

Augie was gonna watch this guy Sullivan.

If he got Stiff out of the way, Augie'd be the biggest guy on the lot. But the trouble was, it was hard to get Stiff Sullivan out on a limb. He watched his step and kept his trap shut.

"How about the son-of-a-bitch?" Pastor's son asked. "We gonna stand for the Beast of Berlin holdin' up his dirty face for the friggin' slackers to be proud of?"

Stiff Sullivan spit. "It's an ad," he pointed out, calmly.

"OK, so it's an ad!" Augie snarled. "Do they have to put his face up alongside the name of the picture?" He looked around at the blank faces of the rest of the kids. "How about it, Bud? Do we help the boys went across the drink?"

Stiff was bored! He didn't see how it would do any good to bust up the billboard. The kids in Missoula were going hog wild, and there would be hell to pay before the end of the summer. He wished he'd grown up in Butte, with kids like Serafimovitch and Wolin.

OK, the Kaiser was a son-of-a-bitch! Anybody'd grant that! But why bust up the billboard? There was no excitement in that. Kid stuff! Stiff was disgusted.

The Pastor's son was getting screwier every day, it seemed to Stiff. It was a laugh!

OK, let 'er fly! Augie signaled.

Billy, Bud, Tubby, and Jake let go with cobs at the leering lineaments of the Beast of Berlin. The signboard creaked in its wooden joints. One board behind the Kaiser's nose collapsed, and the loosened paper flew in the breeze. Augie walked over to the billboard and spit in the Kaiser's paper eye. "Take that, yuh bastard!" Pastor's son said.

Augie wiped his hands on his pants. "We'll fix the Kaiser proper if he comes this way again," he said, turning to Bailey.

He looked at him wisely. "You see Stiff Sullivan? Was heavin' no stones I seen!" he said.

Betty Darling wondered if Augie had taken Jane Smith on a trip? She walked home slowly.

Pastor's son was a long way out of church, it looked like!

Chapter 17
Mr. MacMurray Crosses Divide

†††

U.S. Marines crush Hun line; Americans fight like tigers. In early morning raid drive enemy out of positions. Heights at Chateau Thierry captured. Battle for Marne supremacy still waging with coming of dark....
The officers at Camp Lewis tonight were trying to identify twenty-one men who jumped from an N.P. train of drafted men as it was leaving Tacoma early this morning.... "The boys that will take a chance/ the ones that have been tried/ are from the state of history/ where Custer fought and died./ When the war is over and the world is free/ and the Huns have pulled their freight/ you can bet they will remember the boys/ from Old Montana State!—written by a soldier from Powder River.

How the soldiers of Pershing's expeditionary force went into the battle with smiles on their faces was told by Private Harry Zody to a packed court room at city hall yesterday afternoon. "It's great. No kidding! He kept the fact he was wounded a secret because he wanted to stay and see the fun. He was buried by one shell; unearthed by another; now he is Shell Proof Mac! The Battle of the Marne. It was a humdinger! Do you know what a humdinger is?"

Norval Storm and Mr. MacMurray awaited the zero hour.

The cannonading had plugged their ears with confusion. Shrapnel cut into the eerie darkness where shells exploded like firecrackers on a Fourth of July in Montana. Airplanes were the black, zooming comets that stung the earth to palsy. The checkered diamond rattlesnakes of machine guns spitting death in the gunners' hands. They spat the dark red juice of murder.

Mr. MacMurray opened his mouth.

No sound came out at all, though he was yelling to split his lungs.

The earth's concussion enveloped heaven. A spray of gravel pitched into the trench where Mr. MacMurray was standing. Private Storm picked a pebble out of his ear and turned. He saw that Mr. MacMurray was trying to speak to him, his mouth wide open, and agony in his eyes. Storm spread out his hands like an umpire at a bush league game: *You're out, Mr. MacMurray, you're out!* the gesture said. Storm lit a fag, inhaling the smoke furiously, and crouched beneath the parapet. The enemy was getting most of it at this moment. Their guns had been taken unawares. The clamor rose in excruciating crescendo. The last of the Allied shell reserves were getting thin.

Sudden silence!

Mr. MacMurray glanced nervously at Private Storm.

All up and down the trench, the soldiers' nerves went taut, the cords standing out in their necks.

In a moment the signal!

Private Storm glanced quizzically at Mr. MacMurray. In an instant of insight, caught and as soon lost again, he saw a man stiff in his terror beside the good earth that shielded him from the future. A man who had come from an Idaho farm to Missoula to become a lawyer to uphold the rights of the poor, like Borah. A man whose ideals cut him off from the world and a boy—for he was a boy—who would never kiss a woman until she was his wife.

Mr. MacMurray was a clean man in a world he'd never made.

Storm ground his cigarette into the earth with the heel of his boot. Along the trench a nervous switch was thrown.

There was a moment of arrested motion.

Thinking of mother back home—First man over like a boy sticking his toe in the creek—Come on in, fellas, the water's fine! Freckles on their legs and faces as ripe as red Macintosh apples washed by the wind.

"Come on, Mac! Do yuh want to live forever?" yelled Private Storm, as he twisted clear of the trench and went over the top like a man insane with joy. His back was hunched over the ground so close his knees would surely hit him in the chin, it seemed. The bayonet was like an antenna in the glistening grey light of dawn as the specter of war crept over the landscape.

Mr. MacMurray went out into No Man's Land.

A man in a daze.

Automatically, he imitated the crouch and angle of Storm's position, looking sidewise as if life were passing by on a train. He saw the Senegalese, black faces glistening, their long bayonets ready to pitchfork the Boche in the first trench ahead. Machine guns chattered like hysterical apes. Men up and down the Allied line of advance began crumbling like an adobe wall in the rain.

To one side of him, four Sammees folded up, mingling their arms and legs together in a mad scramble for death.

Mr. MacMurray walked steadily forward with his rifle out feeling the dangerous air. The slow motion of the advance seemed unreal, painful as sleep, when tomorrow is questioned.

MacMurray crept up behind an enemy machine gun nest, as he had been trained to do, pulled the plug of a hand grenade with his teeth, and let 'er fly! *Another German Army was vanquished when the hero of the hour let go with both fists.* He'd come a long way from the evening he'd spoken to Mrs. Craig and asked her to be his wife!

If Crystal could see him now!

Mr. MacMurray skirted a shell hole, with modest concern, and continued abreast the advance. The Senegalese, black as the earth that had brought them forth, seemed to go on forever; but the Sammees were thinning out so fast, it seemed to Mr. Mac-Murray, that there was only Private Storm to keep him company.

Private Storm plunged into the first line trench of the Boche, both feet forward, and sliced his bayonet into a German's throat. He placed his foot on the Hun's breast and drew back the blade dripping with blood. Looking up and down along the Germans' first line of resistance, he saw the Senegalese with their dead-pan countenances cleaning them out with murderous method.

The Pastor's oldest son drew a sigh of relief. Turning around, he looked back across No Man's Land, the way he had come.

Saw Mr. MacMurray relinquish his rifle, limp as a leaf, and bury his face in the dirt.

Private Storm had said to Mr. MacMurray: *Come on, Mac!* . . .

Mrs. Roberts was a determined lady who upheld culture in Missoula, though it seemed to her like a losing fight. So Pauly didn't see much of Hutch Roberts, who had different interests than Pauly had. Hutch disliked *Tarzan of the Apes*, for instance, and read Dickens so's he'd be educated to follow in the footsteps of his father and become a great newspaper man!

Naturally, Pauly's inferiority complex deepened in the face of so much aggressive intelligence.

Mrs. Roberts suggested they stop at the Palace Ice Cream Parlor for refreshments after the show. She felt somewhat sorry for Mrs. Craddock with the baby coming and Pauly around. She felt it her duty to take Pauly out to a show, once in a while, so Mrs. Craig could get some rest.

As they arranged themselves around a table in the Palace Ice Cream Parlor, the wife of the circulation manager of the local newspaper turned to Mrs. Craddock's son. "Well, Pauly, how did you like the show?" she asked.

"I'll have a banana split," Pauly answered, looking intense.

Hutch Roberts howled. Did you ever see a kid like that! Went around with his ears buttoned up. Never heard what anybody said. Maybe, Augie was right about the Craig kid. He seemed a little foolish in the head, Pauly did!

"Mother wants to know did you like the show?" Hutch Roberts explained.

Pauly blushed. "Oh, yes, Mrs. Roberts, I thought it was keen," he said, spreading confusion with his hands. He didn't know what to do with them. Under the table they felt lost and above the table they were an obvious source of embarrassment.

Pauly felt sad. Wolf gone, and now Toughy banished, and in their stead he had a Boston Bull pup that ran away as soon as you let it out of the house. And dogs were the only friends he had!

Back in the house on Kootenai Street, Mrs. Craddock gripped her abdomen in pain.

"Doctor!" she screamed.

"Doctor!"

Chapter 18
The Baby is Born

Is Romance a dead issue in this age? War opens door to disprove theory.... Fifteen federal prisoners, mostly aliens with I.W.W. leanings, were hosed by city firemen in Walla Walla until they yelled for mercy.... Forget it, Soldier!/ Sweethearts are not for you./ Your rifle is your sweetheart/ so learn to shoot it true!

The wind was hot as a branding iron that would leave its mark on the earth. Darkness rustled everywhere and little gusts licked up the dusty trails. If it didn't rain soon, the country would curl up in the dry heat of summer and blow away in the afternoon.

Paul Bunyan slept badly in the valley that served him for a bed. He was thirsty as four hundred wildcats after a night's rampage. A mountain cut into his ribs uncomfortably. As he tossed about restlessly, jostling the mountains that wedged him in, the burnt breeze fanned his face with flame. A couple of landslides buried some towns whenever Paul Bunyan moved.

Paul Bunyan awoke!

It was too damn hot for sleep.

A river had run into his shoes from sweat and his feet were steaming with mist, but the fog from his perspiration evaporated as soon as the sun came over the mountains.

Next time Paul Bunyan slept in this valley he'd move the mountains out of the way first. America's most famous lumberjack had had an uncomfortable night.

Paul Bunyan stepped over the Mission Range and lay down in Flathead Valley to take a drink. After he'd drunk his fill, the lake was a shadow of its former self and the fish lay high and dry on the banks. Lighting a cigarette from one of the forest fires, Paul Bunyan puffed energetically. Cyclones of smoke crept over the land. The tamaracks on the Cabinet Mountains crackled like tinder and firecrackers. The sparks flew from the South Fork to Belly River, from Canada to the Bitterroots, and all of the mountains writhed in smoke.

This was a forest fire the world would remember!

When Paul Bunyan joined the I.W.W. and celebrated the Fourth of July by burning the Rocky Mountains!

Remembering the track meet tryouts, where he had so miserably failed to come in first, Pauly made up his mind to do something about his predicament. Football was out, and so was track, but basketball still held out the possibility of victory.

Pauly climbed into the hayloft of the barn behind the house on Kootenai Street and swept the floor of hay. In the future, feed could be kept downstairs between the cow stables and the rabbitry. There was plenty of room there for a couple of bales of hay. Pauly washed the floor of the loft until it shone with the sweat of his labor. First of all, the window at each end of the barn would have to be taken care of. Pauly covered each one of them with wooden slats. Above each window, and not too close to the roof, he nailed a basket. He painted the lines from which the fouls were to be thrown and indicated a circle in the floor's center for the toss-up of the basketball.

Last of all, he tore off the chicken wire from an empty rabbit hutch and took it upstairs to stretch across the open door through which the hay was supposed to be angled into the loft. Now, no player could fall out of the gymnasium. No basketball could break the windows. The loft made a splendid basketball court if you didn't mind the baskets being a foot less than their usual height. The pillars that supported the roof of the barn got in the way a little, but if you got used to them it wasn't so bad.

At least, Pauly had figured it that way!

No use complaining this early in the day.

Pauly blew up an old basketball that had belonged to Arthur, Doctor's favorite son, when Arthur had played on the local basket quint. Dribbling the ball around the loft, Pauly tossed a few baskets to test out his skill. The ball was a little dead, and didn't bounce well, but Pauly was quite good at tossing it through the iron hoop. Now, all that was needed was a little atmosphere.

The Police Gazette and a few baseball manuals did the trick. Pauly tore off the covers, pasting them on the walls of the barn. He placed a few benches along the sides of the floor for the substitutes to sit. He put up a punching bag and scattered some dumbbells about. A mattress from the attic of the house, brought over to the gymnasium in the barn, served as a good wrestling mat

He was all set!

This marked the beginning of the Lucky Streak Athletic Club. Now, it only remained for members to sign up. Pauly contacted Augie, Stiff Sullivan, Bud Bailey, Billy Toole, and Lover Lemire. Taking them up to the loft of the barn, he asked them what they thought.

Augie busted out laughing, but soon thought better of it. It might be a good thing to have a club in which you could toss a few baskets once in a while. It would be a good place to bring a few janes, too. Augie noticed with satisfaction the mattress lying over in one corner of the room.

The Lucky Streak Athletic Club had its points.

"What d'yuh say?" Augie asked Stiff Sullivan.

It looked all right to Stiff and he said as much. Billy, with his nose twisted awry from his last fight and his red hair touseled like a presidential candidate's from the Middle West, was agog with ideas.

"OK," he said. "But how about bringing up a pool table and a table for twenty-one?"

Stiff Sullivan considered that the Lucky Streak Athletic Club was definitely looking up. Pauly, trying to be helpful, offered to donate the room downstairs which was supposed to be used by a chauffeur, but never was, for card games and pool.

Augie was amenable to the idea, so everything was arranged as Billy had suggested.

And that marked the baptism of the Lucky Streak Athletic Club. Stiff ordered all of the North Side kids to join up, Billy collected the dues and was treasurer of the club. Bud had some friends down at the Bucket of Blood who gave him a faro table. With the busted-down pool table and chairs and packs of worn out cards Billy had borrowed from the cellar of the Snowshed on Railroad Street, it helped out a lot.

After all, Billy's father had set up the drinks at the Snowshed many's the time before he kicked off.

And the bartender at the Snowshed was a friend of Billy's.

It helped quite a bit.

Pauly locked the loft and the door to the chauffeur's room with padlocks. He didn't want Doctor to find out. The basketball court was OK by Doctor, but Pauly didn't know what Doctor would say about the gambling, if he ever found out.

Not that Pauly was interested in the cards.

But if he was to have a gymnasium with some guys to play basketball, he'd have to string along with the boys.

In any case, it was about time that he began learning how to play pool and spit like a man....

Bud Bailey brought a couple of brass gobboons[1] which he placed in opposite corners of the card room. While shooting a game of pool, you could practice spitting between shots.

Pauly enjoyed loping around the basketball court. Wearing tennis shoes that were somewhat large for his feet, he practiced every evening in the bright flare of the electric lights. He protected the bare bulbs from misfortune by locking them in wire cages he'd bought at the hardware store down town. If he practiced enough during the summer, Pauly figured he might make the high-school basketball team in the fall. There was no harm in trying!

He remembered reading in the paper about a corporal who cursed the Huns while he was bleeding to death. The best basketball player he had ever seen in his life, the General had said!

Pauly decided he would erase the memory of his track meet failure in one round of applause come the basketball season next year. He saw himself sinking a basket in the final second of play. The ball arched in mid-air and swished through the net as the gun went off. Score: 27 to 28 in favor of the American Army. The perfect shot of the evening! Pauly would turn on his heel and bow modestly to the crowd.

Banking the ball on the roof of the barn, it bounced back down on a pillar that upheld the roof, settling firmly into the net. Snuggle and *swish!* and the ball had gone through clean as the clip of Betty's tiny, ankling feet.

Victory!

Over the heads of the crowd that had hoisted him upon their shoulders, he was far from the shores he had known. Never again could the Huns hope to beat the Lucky Streak Athletic Club quintet. Pauly the natural hero of the event and the girls screaming

---

1 Spitoons.

for all they were worth. Naturally, under such circumstances, it would be beneath Pauly's dignity to milk cows any more. Marching down Higgins Avenue to the local mercantile store, he would get himself a part-time job, working in the afternoons. Toughy, Wolf, and the Boston Bull pup had vanished from his life. It was only right that the cows should go as well. He'd keep the rabbits to eat up the War Garden he'd planted that spring, but the cows went home to the ranch.

Doctor expected a boy to make his way in the world.

OK, so Pauly had a job in the hardware department of the local mercantile store.

But the Kaiser had never seen a basket made like that! Bounced on the rafters and banked from the roof, like a spit ball it went in so clean and natural that three Huns bit the dust.

And Betty, watching from the side lines....

Betty giggled with joy.

Doctor always walked away from St. Patrick's Hospital with his head bent over as if in thought. Slapping his thighs with the gloves he carried, Doctor slipped into the front seat of the Cadillac and under the steering wheel. Shifting gears, he coasted across the Higgins Avenue bridge and right-angled into Kootenai Street. It was like that on the day that William Tell Craddock was born. And it was like that afterward.

William Tell was sleeping upstairs in the cradle.

Doctor came home more animated than ever before. Whistling blithely, his head bent downward toward the ground and slapping his thighs vigorously with his gloves, Doctor mounted the porch steps and opened the front door.

Pauly had learned to recognize Doctor's firm step in the hall. "Where's William?" Doctor would ask.

Always it was like that! Come rain or shine, come windy or quiet weather. Doctor would swing back to the house after putting his car in the barn; and he'd spring up the porch steps, open the door, enter the hallway, and with one foot on the stairs that led up to mother's bedroom where the baby's cradle was kept, Doctor would call: "And how's William?"

William Tell Craddock made considerable difference in the pattern of Doctor's life. Gil was away in South America, and Arthur was a dry dust in some California bank. "How's William today?" Doctor would ask.

Crystal was happy to see Doctor so proud. Doctor wanted this son to be a surgeon to carry on the practice after Doctor was gone.

William Tell would grow up!

Crystal Craddock and Doctor entered upon the happiest part of their lives. Without misunderstandings of any sort. The years that were between them melted at the sound of William's bubbles exploding from his baby lips. How William drank milk from his mother's breast better than other babies possibly could, how well he looked in the morning, and how beautifully he cooed at night—these were themes that Doctor never tired of stressing, as he carried the baby through the garden to look at the rosebushes and bounced the infant on the hard long strength of his arms.

It was the period of William Tell in Doctor Craddock's life.

A time that should never stop! At least Crystal hoped it wouldn't.

Chapter 19
Billy's One Man Strike

++

Temporary wife shoots up Negro. Edna uses gun to discipline Hilary, her mate for the moment. Woman tells police her intentions were better than her aim. "Man! I sure did shoot to kill" said Edna.... Reproduction of letter written by Arthur Le Sueur, executive secretary of the Non-Partisan League, to Bill Haywood, executive treasurer of the I.W.W., after the latter was under indictment by the Federal Government for conspiracy to hinder war and call strikes. Notice the salutation, "Dear Bill"!... When we rushed 'em, we'd yell: "Over the top, fellows! Get 'em!" Then we'd rush forward, firing. That's all.

Billy Toole was Stiff Sullivan's favorite shadow now that Augie was sticking to his patriotic guns. Hating the Huns was all right in its way, Sullivan felt, but it left unsolved a lot of issues that concerned workers' sons. The trouble with Augie was that he was the Pastor's son, and preachers—not counting the Catholic Fathers, of course—liked to talk so much about God that they forgot the ordinary men who dug the copper in Butte, sheared the mountains of spruce, and the workers who ran the trains, sweated in factories, and the sons of these men.

In any case, Stiff Sullivan didn't like the way Augie was going.

So he was seeing more of Billy these days than he did of the Pastor's son. Billy was a smaller edition, but he was just as tough as they came. He was a news kid who had the best corner in town. Nobody dared to dispute his position for long. Whenever he needed assistance, the red-head called in Stiff Sullivan to help him give the boys the hotfoot who were speaking out of turn. Sullivan would hold them, one at a time, while Billy picked himself a nice, stout board and beat their shoe leather until it burned. None of the news kids got out of line after a few applications of this hotfoot discipline.

Stiff was always happy to be of service in affairs of this kind.

He liked to see these punks squirm, hear them yell, and watch the agony on their pans.

It was like sticking a butterfly for scientific study or poking a frog with a pin. He liked cutting off the necks of chickens, too, to see that headless dance that was the craze of all the kids who wanted to see blood fly around.

Billy Toole was all right! Better than the Pastor's son.

Stiff was thinking maybe he'd have to slap Augie down. The Pastor's kid was getting too free with his lip. His mouth was way ahead of his dukes. He'd have to teach Augie a lesson. But as soon as the afternoon edition rolled off the presses, Billy would hit the street. He had the best corner in town, Higgins and Spruce, where the papers went like hotcakes day and night. He'd sell not only the Missoula sheet, but the papers from Butte, Helena, and Spokane as well.

"Wuxtry! Wuxtry!" Billy Toole yelled.

On the corner of Spruce and Higgins, he hawked the news to the world. The I.W.W. were being weeded out of the lumber camps and replaced by patriotic lumberjacks, Ryan said. In spite of which, a fierce hand-to-hand struggle took place at the local hoosegow

164

when Baptise let go with a haymaker that knocked the Chief for a loop. He hit him so hard the imprint of his fist was left on the cop's chin, every knuckle perfectly reproduced!

"Wuxtry! Wuxtry!" Billy made money hand over foot! He had his regular customers. Besides these, he got most of the trade passing through town on trips. Billy was planning to buy himself in a business when he'd saved enough money.

So when Mr. Roberts called the news kids in from Pig Alley, Billy led the bunch.

"Boys," the circulation manager said. "From now on the papers will cost three cents a piece to you fellows instead of two for five. Selling them at the usual price of five cents a paper, you'll still be making plenty. Sorry I have to do this, but you know how it is!"

"All right, fellows, that'll be all!" and Mr. Roberts turned back to his office.

"Wait a second, Mister!" Billy said. "You don't go raisin' no prices on me, you don't. I don't know about the rest of these mugs, but I got the best corner in town. You jack up them prices on me, Mister, and you don't get any of your rags sold within one block every way from my corner! I'm giving you the clear dope."

Mr. Roberts paused on the heel of his boot, his mouth wide open with astonishment. A horse fly buzzed around angrily before settling upon his nose. Mr. Roberts brushed it off, his face red with annoyance.

"Beat it!" Mr. Roberts said. Walking into his office, he slammed the door so hard the glass in it almost broke.

OK! Mister! You'll be sorry for this, the red-head said to himself. Billy turned and walked through the back door and into Pig Alley. "How about you punks?" Billy asked the rest of the kids. "You gonna take it lying down?"

"We can't do nothin'," Lover Lemire pointed out. Lover was new to the game of selling papers, but he wasn't taking any chances of losing his job.

Billy turned away in disgust. No use arguing with these yellow bastards. They'd no more guts than a cottontail rabbit. OK, let them go on being suckers! Billy Toole was going to beat this rap by himself. As he walked over to Stiff Sullivan's place, Billy heard the news kids hawking the news. *Latest News of the War! Come and get it! Message to American mothers. Federal agents safeguard health.*

That evening, Billy sent off postcards to the Butte, Helena, and Spokane papers. He put it up to them straight about how the local rag was trying to do him dirt and asked them if they'd help him?

Boy, did those out-of-town newspapers come through!

The Spokane paper said that here was a hundred copies free and good luck, kid! The Butte and Helena papers sent Billy handsome bundles of each edition, free, on the house. Those guys were OK. They took a kindly interest in Billy and wished him luck. The red-headed Toole kid felt great.

He'd teach that Roberts guy where to get off, by Christ!

The next afternoon everything was all set. Billy had made arrangements with Stiff Sullivan to see that no other news kid encroached upon the territory he'd marked off for the strike. Stiff was to get five bucks for the job, and it was worth the price to Billy, who'd concentrate on selling as many papers as he could.

"Latest Butte, Spokane, and Helena papers! All the news that the Missoula Record *can't afford to print! Only three cents a copy! Almost half the price of the* Record. *And twice as many pages. Twice the news for half price!"* Billy yelled, as he fanned up and down on the corner of Higgins and Spruce.

"Wuxtry! Wuxtry! All the latest news for three cents!" yelled the one-man strike, and the local customers brought their friends. Business was growing by leaps and bounds. In one short hour, Billy's corner had become famous throughout Missoula.

"One hundred I.W.W. convicted in Chicago! Read all about it!" Billy yelled. *"Reds Plan General Stride! Haywood gets twenty years!* Read all about it! Only three cents!" Billy yelled at the top of his lungs.

Stiff Sullivan was cruising around to see that no punks got out of line. As he passed in front of the Sour Jerkin, he spotted Lover Lemire lugging a bundle of papers on the other side of the street. He was definitely in the restricted territory. With a smile on his lips, Sullivan ambled across the street.

"Hey, sonny!" Stiff said, as he approached Lover and pushed him against the wall. "What's the idea of bringin' those papers here?"

"I was just trying to get over to my block like the other guys are doin'. We gotta scatter around," Lover said.

"So! You guys just scatter around?" Sullivan smiled and Lover relaxed a little. The big fella was just having his fun, it seemed. Wouldn't bother him, probably. After all, it was no hide off Sullivan's behind what happened to Billy Toole.

Stiff curled his big fist around a hank of Lover's hair and lifted him clear off the pavement. With his other hand, Sullivan slapped the bundle of papers to the sidewalk and scattered them with a well-directed kick. "Now, listen here, punk!" he said. "Billy's a friend of mine, see? He tells Roberts none of you guys invade his territory. He tells him none of his papers are sold within a block any direction of Higgins and Spruce. You hear him say that, didn't you, punk?"

"Owhhh, leggo my hair!" Lover screamed. The pain stabbed down through his skull and struck to the tips of his toes. He was bein' scalped, by Jesus, and it hurt!

"I was just passin' through," Lover yelled. "Honest, I was just passin' by."

"Well, just pass on and see you don't come back!" Sullivan drew his fist back even with his shoulder and let it go with all the released brutality at his command. No matter how strong or weak they were, Sullivan hit as hard as he could. If he was whipped by a bigger guy and, if the guy talked out of turn again, Stiff would choose him again. That's how tough Stiff Sullivan was!

No nonsense!

Stiff hit Lover so hard he fell flat on his back, bleeding and whimpering out of the side of his cut mouth.

"That'll teach you guys to stay out of Billy's backyard," Sullivan said, as he blew his nose and wiped his hand on his pants.

On the corner of Higgins and Spruce, the papers were going like wildfire, like the forests blazing in the Cabinet Mountains, like Paul Bunyan smoking a cigarette, like the Indians on a rampage!

Billy wondered how Stiff Sullivan was making out. The redhead remembered how Stiff had choosed the scabs during the strike at Ravalli mills. A Wobbly organizer had given Sullivan fifty bucks. "The idea is," this organizer had said, "we talk tough with them scabs and they'll charge us with sedition. We're organized and we're workingclass, so they'll take us for German agents if we speak gentle to them scabs!"

On the other hand, this organizer says, "A local boy like you could do a lot of good. Fifty bucks on the line, you choose a couple of scabs!"

Money like that was music in Sullivan's ears. In any case, his old man had never had much good to say for scabs.

Stiff walks up to a baldheaded guy. He puts his hand on the top of this scab's head, playfully, and polishes the bare skull like it was a billiard ball he was getting ready to heave at a row of fancy bottles behind the bar.

"I don't like baldheaded guys!" Stiff Sullivan says. And he stiff-arms the guy in the right shoulder, swinging him around so's his left jawbone is ripe and handy to the fist. He lets go a furious haymaker that lifts the guy right out of his shoes, and plants him on his head across the lot. That was what gave Billy the idea in the first place.

"How's about five bucks to help me break this punk Roberts?" Billy had asked.

Lover Lemire picked up his papers. His lips were swollen and his tongue was swimming in blood. Torn and wounded, Lover

Lemire had no stomach for fighting. Tangling with Sullivan was like getting caught in a machine. The iron ripped the guts right out of your belly!

Lover was through.

Mr. Roberts was getting hot around the collar, but there was nothing he could do. He felt cheap and foolish, waiting in his office for Billy Toole to show up.

The kid opened the door and came into the room. Cap in the boy's hand and a sneer in his eyes. Mr. Roberts recognized the look. Asking the one-man strike to have a chair, Mr. Roberts lit a nervous cigarette and coughed delicately to show the world how calm he was. "Well, son," Mr. Roberts said. "I know when I'm licked! How about handling the *Record* again at the old rates?"

"That's what I said in the first place," Billy Toole pointed out.

"OK, it's a deal!" Mr. Roberts said.

Chapter 20
Of Dogs and Guns

╫╫╫

A near riot occurred on Higgins Avenue last night when Alberts is alleged to have made the following remark as he passed Patrolman Connors: "See that with the brass buttons!" Talking to newspapermen after the verdict, Debs said: "It is all right. I have no complaint to make. It will come out all right in God's good time".... W. Dunne, as he sat with an automatic revolver by his hand, while he pounded out editorials for the Butte Daily Bulletin, *the torch that lights the way for the I.W.W. at Butte and keeps the blood seething in their veins.*

It amused Bill Dunne, this one-man strike that Billy Toole had pulled. Bill had heard about it from one of the boys who worked on the local, A.C.M.-controlled paper in Butte. For a gag, and because he approved of strikes in any case, Bill had sent a bundle of the *Butte Daily Bulletin* to Billy. Ordinarily, Dunne wouldn't have approved of a one-man strike. The basis of the I.W.W., and of all militant workingclass movements, was the conception of organization, solidarity! But you had to hand it to the kid for pulling a strike against wage-cuts all by himself—and winning it! The Jesus knew there were damn few strikes being won these days. All you could hope for was that the workers would learn by their defeats, grow stronger, and wise enough—at least—to be able to recognize when they were being taken for a ride by the capitalist press!

Nikolai Lenin dead!

Straight from London, direct from Stockholm—

The fact of the matter being, of course, that Lenin was in Moscow. So how could he be dead in London, in Stockholm, in Paris?

He wasn't!

It was as simple as that. *Don't change jobs without consulting Uncle Sam! Go across with guns or come across with funds! Dynamiters wreck Federal Building in Chicago. Officials blame I.W.W. for deed. Revenge the motive?*

These vicious clucks!

The workers would have their revenge, all right, and come into their own, but not by dynamiting a building in Chicago! What purpose could that have?

Already, the boys were distributing the leaflets that called for a strike in the Butte mines.

Mooney, Debs, the I.W.W. martyrs of the Chicago trial, and the countless boys that had been black-listed, slugged, lynched—in the history of these times! Not forgetting Frank Little right here in Butte. From this recital, who would it seem were the perpetrators of violence? The capitalist press saying: *And Butte is fast returning to the condition of mind immediately preceding the hanging of Frank Little in the summer of 1917....*

Was that incitement to riot, lynch, and kill?

Or was it incitement to kill, lynch, and riot?

Bill Dunne scratched under his left armpit with the butt end of his revolver. Damn, it was hot! He spread his feet on the top of the table and glowered at the soldiers walking up and down in front of the church, which constituted the offices and plant of the *Butte Daily Bulletin*. These doughboys had it easy! No fighting the Huns for them. A more particular, native conflict had caught their attention. No, all these little soldiers had to worry about, as they paraded up and down in front of Bill Dunne's office, was how soon they'd get off duty and when they could visit the district.

The striker shot early this morning by a soldier on picket duty, according to the report just received from the emergency hospital where the wounded striker had been taken, was not expected to live.

Yes!

You could bet your own sweet life! Bill Dunne thought.

The name of that soldier who'd shot the striker had been withheld. If the Butte miners ever found out that doughboy's name, it would be tough on him! Not even a drink would that soldier be able to buy—the bartenders had a union themselves. This town was strong for the workers and didn't take kindly to having their boys shot down.

Bill took his feet off the table and glanced at the sheet of paper in his typewriter: "...And the workers intend to see that democracy for which we are fighting abroad is realized in Silver Bow County!" he had written. He shifted his heavy frame into a less excruciating position in his chair, and pounded his name at the bottom of the sheet: *W. Dunne*.

Drawing the paper out of the machine, he signed his John Henry above the typewritten letters that spelled out the editor's name of the *Butte Daily Bulletin*. No question about it!

They'd never keep the workers down for long—they'd get Big Bill Haywood out of the jug, some way!

Bill got up out his chair and walked around the room to limber his muscles a bit.

There were a flock of these boys coming through the sticks these days, talking up the war and comforting mothers. Sergeant Hanley had been the fanciest to date. *One of thirteen survivors of the famous Canadian Princess Pat regiment, who gave a vivid portrayal of his experiences on the battlefields. His lecture included German Frightfulness, Gas, Liquid and Curtain Fire, Belgium Atrocities, etc.*

Frank Little, dragged through the streets of Butte and tied to the end of a rope and hanged from a railroad bridge—

Those were the atrocities the workers remembered!

Bill Dunne narrowed his eyes as he glanced through the front door of the church. The boys coming up the front steps were deputies if he'd ever seen them—and he'd seen plenty during the course of his short and stormy life!

Picking up the revolver from beside the typewriter, he ran his forefinger around the collar that pinched his neck.

"W. Dunne?" one of the guys asked, as he entered the room.

"What's eating you?" Bill Dunne said.

"You're under arrest!" the guy answered. "For sedition!"

Every afternoon, as soon as school let out, Pauly would hop on the bicycle Doctor had bought him and ride over to the hardware store where he worked until six o'clock every night except Sunday. *Oh, How I Hate To Get Up In The Morning!* Now, there was a song! But there should have been one about going to work in the afternoon. Pauly was fascinated by the fishing tackle, however. One of the counters was full of it. Bitterroot coachmen, black gnats, grey hackle with a fine yellow body, cow dung, deer flies, ginger quill—a light brown number that was good for afternoon fishing—golden spinner, grizzly king, royal coachmen....

But the best flies were hand-woven.

Badger hair tackle, sandy white, and others too numerous to mention. Some of the flies cost as much as thirty-five cents a piece. But the royal coachmen were the prettiest. A really remarkable number! Red and white and bright enough to attract the eye of the most sluggish fish.

Pauly lifted a few of them against the time he would go fishing the following summer.

But his feet hurt like the dickens long before six o'clock came around. He wasn't allowed to lean on the counter or to sit down. He was expected to stand at attention practically all of the time. It was the floorwalker's position and all personnel were expected to look bright and sunny, like the Sammees going over the top. It was imperative that the whole hardware store preserve a cheerful and patriotic appearance. Had not General Pershing himself said that looks were what counted most?

But it wore like hell on Pauly's feet, this standing at attention all the time, so's the hardware sales could go over the top like the Sammees did. He was afraid that he'd get fallen arches from standing around so much. So he didn't think that anyone could blame him if he sneaked a royal coachman or a black gnat once in a while.

Missoula en masse to honor those workers of organized labor who are furnishing the sinews of war and have not yet been out on strike. 'Cause I'm Gonna Pin My Medal On the Girl I Left Behind! Attaboy! The Yanks charged over the bombed and shell-shocked terrain to capture Cantigny. While Leon Trotzky, the Bolshevik minister of war....

Under such circumstances, the war in everyone's speech and body, it seemed only natural that Pauly should gravitate toward guns.

The rifles were too long and bulky for him to handle well. But the revolvers and automatics! Those you could duck back under the counter, or slip into your pocket, and the floorwalker would never guess this side of the Armistice what it was all about!

One pistol interested Pauly more than any of the others.

It was a small four-barrel affair, evidently designed to fit neatly into a lady's purse, .22 Calibre. You broke the gun, jammed a cartridge into each of the four chambers, and closed it up. The gun had a revolving action, but the barrels did not revolve. It was the hammer that went around in a circle, knocking off one shot after the other. Pauly didn't think he'd be able to do much damage with it unless he was at close range and the target was big as the side of a barn. The pistol was too small for accurate shooting.

But the gun was neat!

It was so small he could hide it in the palm of his hand.

Pauly day-dreamed: He'd walk up to Augie with the .22 pistol sunny and snug in his hand.

Hey, sneaker! Augie would say, superciliously. I hear your mother's been throwin' a pup.

And Pauly'd let him have it! Right between the eyes. With four cartridges, he could sign the name of reproof on Augie's forehead. That would teach the Pastor's son not to crack wise again.

From here on, you leave my mother out of it! Pauly would yell with righteous anger. Or maybe, being large and lenient, he'd merely frighten Augie, crush him to his bended knees, and make him eat dirt. Honest to Christ! Augie would plead. I never meant to take off your pants or kick you in the ass like I did last Friday. It was a mistake! Stiff was urgin' me on. Don't shoot me, Pauly! Augie would say, and we'll make up a basketball team from the Lucky Streaks. You can play center!

The Pastor's son was out on a limb, for sure....

At that moment, sweetly musing, Pauly saw Harold come mincing into the hardware store. Freckles Ferguson, the music teacher at the high school, followed him through the door. Pauly narrowed his eyes in distaste. He remembered that story Lover was telling around last winter. About how Betty was stripped and tampered with by this fat kid who was weaving his way down the aisle, his fanny going back and forth like a pendulum of a clock that didn't know what time it was! Pauly didn't believe the story about Harold and Betty Darling. She was too white and pure to be contaminated by such filthy hands!

Lately, Harold had been trailing around with this music teacher who was a boyhumper, according to Stiff Sullivan.

That made Harold something really unpleasant, it seemed to

Pauly. To think that such things were allowed, when the Sammees were fighting in France for American womanhood!

Stopping in front of the gun display, Harold simpered and spoke. "What's the biggest gun you got?" Harold sniggered, as he glanced meaningfully at Freckles Ferguson.

"Single-action or automatic?" Pauly asked.

"What about a six-shooter?" Harold lisped. "Have you got a gun shoots six times?"

Mr. Ferguson was annoyed. If he didn't watch his step, the school board was going to cause him some unpleasant trouble. This fat kid was too flash! Even as it was, the music teacher knew that rumors were going the rounds about his not having married, and about his interest in Harold.

Pauly brought a six shooter to Harold's attention. It was a big one, shiny and blue.

"My, isn't it the Old Man of the Mountain!" Harold snickered.

Harold was a little too raw to take out in public! Mr. Ferguson decided.

Doctor had received a long distance phone call from the caretaker of the ranch at Lolo. When Doctor returned to the house for lunch, he talked it over with Crystal. They decided it would be best to break it to Pauly gently. They'd drive up to the ranch after dinner, taking Pauly with them.

On the ride up the Bitterroot, Pauly's feet ached. He couldn't seem to get used to standing so long on his feet. The hardware store was tougher going than milking cows, mowing lawns, taking care of the furnace. Doing nothing was damn hard work, if you couldn't sit down! But it was pleasant driving up to Lolo in the cool September dusk. The light of autumn was mellow upon the hills and the smell of summer ended. The yellow cottonwoods among the deep and persevering green of the pines. The white and slender aspen in the gullies. And the rust of remaining forest fires merged with the deeper blood of the sinking sun. The single and separate tamaracks that stood like porcupine quills erect on the ridge of the skyline.

At the ranch, Doctor parked the car in the shadow of the large and empty grey house, where his brother had died.

Pauly, before the Cadillac had fairly stopped, hit the ground running and lit out for the kennel.

Wolf was stretched out flat on the ground, an abandoned meat bone eaten with yellow beside him. His tail, stiffer than a pine cone, was pitched in the dust and his fur coat was pinched and dry as pine needles.

Winter in Wolfs flesh hugged the dead soil!

And a swift emptiness filled Pauly's heart and body.

"Died of bein' alone, I'd say!" the caretaker was explaining to Doctor. "He wouldn't have nothin' to do with anyone on the farm. Hardly touched his food!"

The slight September wind quivered for a moment in the tawny darkness of Wolf's fur coat.

It was almost night and Pauly's eyes were damp.

Chapter 21
The Influx of Influenza

┇┼┼┼┇

Surrender first! is Missoula's answer to Hun Peace Proposals.... If the people of Missoula will remember that our physicians are but human, that they are worn to a frazzle with fatigue, that some of them are already ill, they will realize the necessity of conserving the strength of the physicians by exercising a little care and consideration.... Mr. Wittrup: Meet me the night of the 8th at the big house or we will set fire to your home. Don't give news to the papers! X.

Mike Sullivan wondered what in Christ he'd joined the army for? He'd heard through the grapevine system that American doughboys were fighting in Siberia. Since when had the United States been at war with Russia? *They got there in time! They were in the fight with every faculty of their minds and bodies, with every drop of their American blood!* The stiffest fighting of the American offensive west of the Meuse was under way. In the region of the Grand Pre, the Americans threw back repeated German attacks with violent losses on both sides. The Huns were throwing kids into the breaches. Their officers drove them on at pistol-point.

Mike Sullivan wished to Jesus he'd stayed at home. This baby killing was not what it had been cracked up to be! *On the other hand, the Russian maidens under the jurisdiction of certain provincial Bolshevik Soviets had become the property of the state and were registered with the governments bureau of free love.* Bill Dunne had sent this clipping from the Butte paper owned by the A.C.M. company to Mike with appropriate exclamation marks. "Hunt a hole!" said Higbee when the Hun raid began. The Yankees were forcing the Germans back on a twenty-eight mile front.

Private Storm crouched in a shell hole.

The occasional burst of gun lightning abovehead lent a strange preoccupation to the horror of objective circumstance. But Private Storm felt very little. He'd been re-born on the first day he'd faced gunfire.

All of his Montana past vanished in that moment!

His mother bustling about the house and urgent to the Pastor's call; the tough little face of his kid brother; and the soft tension of moonlight on Montana valleys, the mountains looming to windward and against the stars.

Private Storm remembered the West like a dream before childbirth, from the womb-like world of his infancy and adolescence. No such peace existed now anywhere in the world, it seemed to him. The present facts of life referred to the tanks leveling terrain that told of terror, the big berthas, and the machine-gunners gutting the night. The swift, slick whine of rifle fire. Shells exploding. And airplanes coasting over the hawk-like corridors of carnage. This was the earth that Norval knew and all he would ever remember, when death came like T.N.T. into his heart and shot throughout his body, making complete contact with his nerves, beating into his fingers and stoppering his toes with congealed blood.

Private Storm's world was tight in his belly.

He buried his body deeper into the protecting valley of the earth some shell had exploded, considering that no lightning ever strikes twice in the same spot. He would be safe in this coulee, for the moment. He would be safe!

Cupping the match-flame with his hands, he lit a cigarette and lay down flat on his back. Even in war a smoke seemed good.

When Private Storm exploded, his face was scattered in the night wind. One hand hung innocently over the edge of a helmet that had pointed to German skies on a sometime march through Saxony. His left leg and thigh were lodged on the war-torn branch of a tree in a threatened forest that hid many machine gun nests. His belly a fertilizer for some future conflict! His right lung spread on barbed wire entanglement, red and embarrassed.

Private Storm would enrich the fields of France.

For every Yank fell with his eyes pointed, like a bayonet, unflinching toward the enemy and death....

In Missoula the War against the Spanish influenza had become more immediate than the War for Democracy, in the public mind. Dr. Craddock barely had time to drop in his office now that his patients had become so insistent. Into numerous hospitals and private homes, everywhere he went, Doctor curtained his nose and mouth with a small sheet of gauze to shut out the smell and the germs of death. If he could only keep from falling ill himself! Already, Dr. Redmond was down with the flu. The doctors in Missoula had more than they could manage. Doctor rushed from sickbed to deathbed, took long trips up the Bitterroot on emergency calls, over to Frenchtown, and never was there a full night's sleep to be had.

Doctor came upstairs after dinner to see how the baby was.

"How's William tonight?" Doctor would ask.

Crystal was careful not to go out of the house. William Tell Craddock was as healthy as any parent could wish and getting

181

rounder and pinker every day he stayed on her breast. There were special powders which supplemented baby's milk. Constant baths William had and changes of underwear. William Tell Craddock's little round bottom was tender as the flesh of a fresh young lobster just culled from the ocean's floor. And baby was the guiding force that kept Doctor going these days. For the people of Missoula were dying fast. At home and abroad they were dying. The influenza a cloud of death over the land.

The trouble was, you were feinting at shadows!

You couldn't isolate the germ. You couldn't see it, and once it had come—you didn't know what to do. It was like fighting ghosts. You breathed them in and you fought them on invisible battlefields. Already, Fort Missoula was under quarantine! How to dodge it?

Keep feet and clothing dry.

Avoid crowds.

Protect your nose and mouth in the presence of sneezers. Gargle your throat three times a day with an antiseptic. If you are poor, use salt and water. Keep in the sunshine and—

Above all, don't be frightened.

The doctors fought a losing battle. Not that Dr. Craddock ever told anyone about it! He went around efficiently, although breathing somewhat heavily as his habit was. Hay-fever season was not too far gone, and Doctor had trouble with the atmosphere.

No rest for Doctor!

No full night's sleep for weeks had Doctor had.

When school was closed against the influenza, and the theaters, saloons, and pool halls were locked as well, the Lucky Streak Athletic Club came into its own. Every afternoon and evening, Jake, Bud, Augie, and Stiff Sullivan were there. Pauly's stock went up because of the influenza. The Lucky Streak barn was the only gymnasium in town the kids could use, now that the high-school gym was closed. At night, the electric lights shone dizzily through the wire brackets that kept them from being smashed by the bas-ketball. And Pauly, because of his last birthday, had a brand new tan pigskin basketball to toss around in the barn.

Leaping high above the enemy's basket, Pauly caught the ball as it bounced from the board, ducked under Augie's outstretched arms, curved around a stanchion that braced the roof against the stars, and dribbled crookedly through and down to the end of an open floor, pivoting once or twice as he ran. It was good playing! It was great dribbling! He feinted to the left and tossed the ball in a smooth and shining arc that passed over the rafters without a discouraging sound.

Narrowly missing the roof, the basketball dropped lightly against the backboard of Pauly's basket.

There was a clean, swift *swish* as the ball slipped through the net.

It was not that Pauly was a good athlete, but that he'd prac-ticed so much in the Lucky Streak loft that he knew every crook and cranny of the barn. He could bank the ball on the ceiling. He could guess to the fraction of an inch how close he could come to each rafter and miss it. Tossing the ball against the wall, he could pivot and twist around in time to catch it on the bounce. The barn was Pauly's private ground for vindication in the eyes of the mob. If only he could arrange for some games with some out-of-town basketball teams! Like the school at Florence, per-haps, or the Indians at Arlee. Ronan, perhaps, or Camas Prairie. Any of these outfits, and bigger ones, the Lucky Streaks should be able to take in their stride!

If Augie would let Pauly play....

The only thing in the way was that the flu had canceled all football games and, if the doctors didn't get the situation in hand, there'd be no basketball games this year at all!

In any case, Pauly's stock had gone up.

Knowing the barn the way he did, Pauly gave a good account of himself. But he'd have to watch out that he didn't get *too* good.

If he did, Augie and Stiff Sullivan would trip him up and push him around. Pauly was careful to get a fair share of the baskets, but no more. After all, the other fellows liked to make a few shots. The way Pauly usually tried to work it was to get Augie and Stiff on his own team, when the kids split up for a game. Then, nothing in the world could stop him!

After dinner, Billy used to come down to the club. He didn't like to stay on the streets too long. You didn't sell many papers after nine o'clock in a small town.

With the lights bright in the card room, the kids played twenty-one. Pauly learned to play rotation while they had their fun.

Whiskey, cards and a brawl result in stabbing at St. Ignatius. Federal authorities are inquiring into the bootlegging of liquor to the Salish, Kootenai, and Kalispel on the Indian reservation. In the drawing of the jury, however, a curious situation occurred. Herbert English, who had been accused of sedition.... When it was discovered that one of the names drawn for the jury was that of Fred Vass, who is also to be tried for treason at this term of court.... Stiff Sullivan's cousin was going to get it good!

Pauly bounced the two-ball around the corner and back into the opposite side pocket. The cue ball rolled to a stop behind the three.

"Nice position!" Sullivan observed, as he rang up a gob of spit in the cash register of the gobboon.

Pauly was puzzled. He looked all over the board, but nowhere could he seem to locate the three. Not being able to find it, he began aiming for the four.

"Fer Chrissake, half-pint, I thought you was playin' position!" Sullivan laughed. "You're right up against the three ball. If it was a snake, it 'ud bite vou!"

Pauly blushed, shamefacedly. He hated to be caught napping when Stiff and Augie were around the place. But he was just learning to play pool, and he wasn't very good at it yet.

The churches were closed as well as the schools. Pastor Storm hoped God would understand the necessity for it, but it made it hard lines on Augie, who had to forego the pin money he usually filched from the collection plate on Sunday.

Augie spit into the gobboon in the corner nearest the card table while Sullivan racked up the balls on the pool table.

Augie cashed his matches and started telling Stiff about it....

"So Bud and me, we get this guy off into a corner," Augie explained, as he picked up a cue and busted the pool balls in all directions. He straightened up and chalked his stick. The fourteen ball slopped into a corner pocket. "So Bud's no slouch!" Augie continued. "He takes hold of the guy by the coat lapel. The punk can hardly speak English, he's come over from Germany so short a time before the war began. He claims he's got his first papers, but that don't bother us! We got this guy scared, see?" Augie laughed unpleasantly.

"So Bud says to him sweetly: 'Fork over a couple of fins or we turn you in for sedition,' he says.

"This punk is green, no foolin'!" Augie grinned. "He turns out his pockets without a word, his chin quiverin' like an aspen leaf.

"He's so scared!" Augie laughed.

Stiff Sullivan was looking at the Pastor's son as if he suddenly had discovered some brand new kind of filth. "Where's the money? You got it with yuh?" he asked.

"Sure!" the Pastor's son bragged. "Like I told you." Augie took the money out of his pants pocket and flashed it in front of Sullivan's nose.

Outside, it was dark as death with no moonlight out. Pauly was wondering when Doctor would be driving into the garage. They'd have to be quiet as mice when the Cadillac pulled into the barn. He couldn't afford to let Doctor know what was going on in the card room! Doctor might not like it about the gambling and cards. Pauly would switch out the lights as soon as the car turned up the driveway! He was careful, always, to see that the window was blacked out with the blind. It was all right to have the lights burning in the loft, for Doctor didn't mind about basketball.

"All right, smart guy!" Stiff said, as he snatched the money out of Augie's hand. The kids all looked up from their cards—Jake, Bud, and Billy, who was dealing.

"This coin smells of a guy would rob his own grandmother of the food she puts in her mouth!" Stiff Sullivan said. Slowly, staring the Pastor's son right in the eye, Stiff tore the money into small, terrible bits. Confetti of greenbacks like three-leaf clover littered the floor.

"I wouldn't want to see the Pastor's son carryin' this kind of cash!" Stiff Sullivan observed.

"Would you, Augie?" he asked.

Chapter 22
The World Safe for Democracy

░░░

Bolshevism is extending rapidly in the German Navy. The soldiers' councils formed at several ports have been joined by striding dockworkers and shipyard men and are negotiating on an equal footing with admirals and port commanders. At Hamburg, sailors armed with machine guns, revolvers, and bayonets.... American soldiers returning home after the war will be required to pass through government delousing plants for the removal of trench vermin.... War Ended! Berlin is seized! Armistice is signed. Last guns in mighty struggle were fired this morning at four o'clock our time.

Augie's teeth chafed with chagrin. After all he'd put up with! Stiff Sullivan's taking him to Butte and making him listen to that German agent, Bill Dunne! Not to mention the business about Stiffs cousin, Herbert. Augie had begun to wonder about Stiff long before the gang stoned the Beast of Berlin. Billy had told the story about how Sullivan had cleaned up on a bunch of mill workers. That was sabotage! And now after all these things Augie'd had to put up with, Stiff goes and tears up the money Bud Bailey and he had collected from that dumb German!

The Pastor's son had taken it right on the button.

Augie could take it, but he couldn't dish it out. Not to Sullivan he couldn't.

Even if Stiff was a Red, by Jesus, that didn't make his fists any the less to be feared! The Pastor's son knew that he couldn't whip Sullivan. It would be like putting your neck to a buzzsaw to tangle with the mick. But that didn't mean that Augie wasn't going to remember what Sullivan had done to him. Until the time he could pay the mick off, Augie would nurture this hate in his heart.

Stiff Sullivan couldn't make a sap out of the Pastor's son and expect to get away with it!

Not forever, he couldn't.

With influenza rioting throughout Missoula, and with all of the churches, schools, and saloons closed up, the farmers of the Bitterroot Valley were afraid to come to town. Augie had plenty on his mind to worry about. The Pastor's son listened to Pauly playing *Hindustan* on his mother's victrola.

"Imagine that shanty Irish tearing up my hard-earned coin," Augie complained.

"Yeh! It's like you say," Pauly agreed. "Money comes hard!" Although he was quick to sympathize with Augie's complaint, Pauly wondered whether there wasn't a principle involved? Not that he'd ever let on to the Pastor's son! But Pauly had never felt right about that five dollars he'd taken from the soldier who wanted the drink. Not until he'd buried the stage money under the front porch, that is, and sent the hundred thousand dollars in fake money to the Sammees at American Lake. When the doughboys returned from the war, Pauly would dig up the stage money he'd buried under the porch. Give it to some Sammee marching down the street. Here! Pauly would say. Have yourself a good time!

Stage money wasn't real coin, Pauly realized, but it gave the possessor a tremendous sensation of wealth! It would be nice for a Sammee to feel rich when he came back home from the war looking for work.

Maybe Stiff Sullivan was right about Augie!

Pauly didn't mind lifting from the five and dime, or stealing a few flies from the hardware store where he worked. But maybe the principle was that you didn't steal from people who would feel the pinch.

Like that German guy Augie and Bud Bailey had rolled. The Hun would go without eating, probably, on account of the money he'd lost.

You didn't take money from guys that needed it!

That was the principle Pauly had worked out.

About stores and big shots—that was different! Not that Pauly was too clear about the distinction, but there was a line that could be drawn somewhere. Like Stiff Sullivan had said: you wouldn't want to carry that kind of cash around town. Like taking candy from a baby. Like leaving rabbits to die of thirst locked up in a pen. Not that Pauly said anything about it to the Pastor's son! Pauly was afraid of Augie and made a point of treating him nice.

Betty Darling was getting over a case of the flu. Dr. Craddock said she'd been lucky to pull through so well. Betty still felt weak, but she was happy that the danger was past. And the war was over, and Lonely would be coming back. *Austrian rout.... Claws of Turks trimmed close. Valenciennes put in pocket. Down with Wilhelm! Huns cried, as they stormed the Royal Palace!* Thinking of Lonely, Betty wondered what her father would say. Sis saw little enough of her father these days. The lines of worry had deepened in Mr. Darling's face. Wherever he went, the banker carried concern etched on his forehead. Business was good, but it hadn't been good to Mr. Darling. He'd managed things badly. He was land poor. And now that the war was over....

Lonely was coming back.

Betty was beginning to feel bright and cheerful again. She thought no longer of Harold, who was waving around like a wand these days in the company of Mr. Ferguson. No wonder Harold had scorned her girlish charms! Betty was beginning to believe she had plenty to be proud of. As she convalesced in bed, feeling better and better all the time, she ran her hands softly over her body. From as far down as her hands would go on her thighs under the cover, back up past the rough brown electricity of her groin, and over the tender hills and valleys of her flesh....

She pressed her palms, feeling soft and lovely!

So why should she worry about Harold? Augie had been interested enough—if he hadn't been so rough, she might have liked him better. Had the Pastor's son thought of anything but his own haste? And now Lonely was coming back to Missoula. Would he like her the way she now was? The months he'd been gone had worked exciting changes in Betty Darling. She wondered what Lonely would think. *The sailors of Kiel, on the other hand, who had seized the German Battleships,* Kaiser *and* Schleswig-Holstein, *had placed their commanders under arrest. "Where are those Germans? Let's get at 'em!" yelled an American before Chateau-Thierry. He was going under fire for the first time. He was wild to get there. "We are constantly on the alert and are afraid the Americans are going to attack," wrote a German soldier to his wife. He was captured before he could mail the letter....*

Betty wondered how the French girls had treated Lonely. She bet they were sorry that he was leaving France! He had written her that the Frog girls were all right.

But Lonely had said that he liked Sis best!

Feeling rather adventurous, but weak at the knees, Betty inched her way carefully over the edge of the bed and out from under the covers. She slipped off her nightgown and walked timorously over to the full-length mirror that covered the closet door. She examined herself intensely in the glass. Turning her head from one side to the other, she observed critically the fine points of her flesh. Altogether, she was rapidly improving! The flu hadn't done her as much harm as she had expected. She was a little pale—and much of her summer tan was gone—but her skin looked healthy. It still retained that maiden glow she'd read about in the Sunday supplement.

Betty paused beside the dresser before getting back into bed. After showering her breasts and thighs with talcum powder, she spread perfume on the tips of her fingers and dabbed it on her nipples and under her ears and armpits.

If Lonely could see her now!

Betty crawled back into bed.

Her body felt good to itself!

Mrs. Storm bustled around the house with the happiness of the Armistice in her thought. Pastor would soon be home and wanting his supper.

Augie sat on the edge of his chair in the kitchen, looking and talking hungry, and getting in her way. But Mrs. Storm couldn't find it in her heart to scold him, for the war was over and Norval would be coming home to her. Mrs. Storm prayed that her oldest son should not be sent to the Rhineland with the Army of Occupation.

Mrs. Storm was proud of her oldest son!

But it was a good thing that prohibition was coming. There would be less temptation for Norval when he came back from France. Mrs. Storm hummed happily as she basted one of the juiciest turkeys she'd ever cooked in her life. She didn't go in for popular songs as a rule, but one appealed to her now: *There are smiles that make you happy. There are smiles that....*

But the Storms hadn't heard from Norval for several weeks. The excitement of the Armistice probably accounted for this. Getting ready for the long trip back to the states. That poor Drummond boy up in Hamilton. Mrs. Storm was touched when she read the story: *Ill health was believed to have inspired the suicide of a returned soldier whose body was found hanging from a tree in the family orchard.* She thanked her lucky stars that Norval had not been wounded.

Mrs. Storm had heard that war changed boys.

But it wouldn't have changed Norval. She was sure of that! There was too much good blood in his veins for his flesh to be corrupted....

Pastor entered the house with a festive look on his face and rubbed his hands expectantly together.

"We can begin services again at the beginning of the month," he said happily. "What do we have to eat?"

Pastor was always hungry!

Mrs. Storm smiled. Augie and the Reverend Storm sat down to the table while she brought in the dinner.

As Pastor started carving the roast turkey, the doorbell rang clamorously throughout the house. Trudging to the door, Mrs. Storm opened it. A Western Union messenger boy was standing on the porch. A tough-looking little urchin in olive-brown uniform, he touched his cap perfunctorily and held out a pad. "Sign here!" he said.

Mrs. Storm closed the door and returned to the table to stand at Pastor's elbow. Augie's fork was arrested, half-way to his open mouth. It was unusual for the Storms to receive telegrams. Maybe, it was from Norval, Augie hoped. It would be good having an older brother around the house again! Augie could talk to him about Stiff Sullivan and ask advice about what to do with a seditious guy like that.

It would be good having Norval around the house. Gay, and tanned by the outdoor life he'd been living in France; resplendent with probably some military medals pinned on his chest! Augie might be able to get Norval to let him wear one when he went over to the Lucky Streak Athletic Club.

A nice war medal would knock the kids for a loop. Even Stiff Sullivan would have to sit up and take notice. Nothing like being the younger brother of a hero come home from France!

"You open it!" Mrs. Storm said nervously to Pastor. "Please read what it says."

Pastor's ruddy face grew pale as his lips moved silently over the words the telegram contained. "Read it aloud!" Mrs. Storm asked, her fingers working furiously at a seam of her dress.

Struggling to control the muscles in his throat, Pastor read in the subdued voice of pain:

"Mrs. August Storm.

Deeply regret to inform you cablegram from abroad states your son, Private Norval Storm, marine corps, killed in action October 13. The body was interred abroad previous to termination of hostilities. Please accept my heartfelt sympathy in your bereavement. Your son nobly gave his life in the defense of his country.

George Barnard,

Major General Commandant."

Wordlessly, the Pastor's wife sank into the chair beside the supper table. Her drawn face was white in the still and gathering dusk.

Chapter 23
Bud Bailey Gets Conked

With the American Army of Occupation. Four American soldiers dispersed a mob of thousands at Esch after it had wrecked twenty-eight shops in revenge for overcharging Americans. The loss is estimated at between four million and seven million francs.... Sam Resurrection, Chief of the Flatheads, who writes letters to President Wilson, chanced to get drunk. That isn't the worst of it. Sam lay down on the sidewalk wrapped himself in his bright blanket, and went to sleep.... There is no poverty in Missoula, you say. That is what a Missoulian reporter said before he accompanied Captain Guest of the Salvation Army on his daily tour of mercy.

William Tell Craddock gurgled happily in his crib. The sunshine was pouring dizzily into the window-encircled room. Outside, the snow gleamed white as the rear end of a cottontail bunny as it bounced from one moment to the next on its cushiony, soft feet. Not that William Tell saw it like that! Indeed, it was a debatable question just what William Tell *did* see. But Doctor claimed that baby's eyes were wide open to the world. It took infants some time to learn how to use their eyes, but William Tell had progressed.

Occasionally, Doctor wished he could have an inside seat on what was going on in William's brain. Doctor wasn't a young man any longer, and the more he knew of baby's mind and heart the better he liked it.

William Tell clucked his tongue!

Jerking from amazement at the sound he'd brought forth, he paused to consider what to do next.

A rumble in his stomach settled the issue very nicely for William Tell. It was a blissful sensation, his stomach churning the milk he'd taken from Crystal's breast—and the yellow warmth of the sun felt good.

For baby felt deeply about such matters!

Doctor was sure of that.

William Tell Craddock's big blue eyes popped open with surprise. A cloud had covered the sun and baby's nose was cold. William transferred his astonishment to observe the bubble that burbled on his lips.

What a wonderful world it was, thought William Tell.

Pauly had time on his hands since the schools were still shut down. He'd practiced all the plays possible to a basketball court. He was letter perfect!

On a trip up to Lolo with Doctor, Pauly spoke to some of the lads who lived around there. Kids who had played on the Florence Consolidated High School basketball team. Their togs mildewing in the gymnasium lockers, these kids wanted a basketball game, and they wanted it soon.

"We gotta club!" Pauly explained to the Lolo boys. "The Lucky Streak Athletic Club. Why don't you guys get your outfit together and come down to Missoula and shoot us a game?"

The Lolo kids thought it was a good idea. They said they'd take it up at the first get-together they had.

Pauly felt he'd started the ball rolling. Before the end of the month, he might be able to work out a whole schedule!

He knew that he'd never be able to make the Missoula High School team. For one thing, he was accustomed by now to the lower baskets in the Lucky Streak Athletic Club. If the baskets had been the regulation height, there wouldn't have been room to sneak in the ball on account of the roof!

But he could be a hero in his own barn!

It was too bad there wasn't room for spectators at the Lucky Streak Athletic Club. Had there been, Pauly could have planned on having Betty Darling come to the game. Free! Good for one admission! The Lucky Streaks vs. the Florence High School (Unofficial) Basketball Quintet. But there'd be no place to bench Betty or any other broads. You couldn't very well perch them on the rafters, because they'd get in the way when you were tossing baskets. Betty would have to hear about his prowess at second hand.

Pauly stayed up all night planning his campaign of attack. How to get Augie and Stiff to let him play center? After all, fellows, I arranged for the game! Pauly would say. Perhaps, he'd get Hutch Roberts to have his old man run a news story in the *Record: Paul Craig Hero of Game with Florence Five. Sinks ten baskets in a row from the middle of the floor, hanging the spectator by his ears in the rafters.* (They might be able to pack one fellow in to see the game without endangering the play.)

Perhaps there'd be no audience at all!

But it sounded better in the newspaper, having the spectator falling out of his chair in the aisle.

Yes, that was the way Pauly wanted it!

In the meanwhile, in the afternoons, Pauly would trudge down to the hardware store and report for work. Standing upright busily on the flat soles of his feet until six o'clock came along.

Young man is hero! Gets flat feet during the course of the war.
The fishing tackle fascinated Pauly. Already, he'd snitched quite
a collection of royal coachmen, black gnats, and deer flies, which
he'd hidden in his room on the second floor of the house on
Kootenai Street.

But that little four-barrel .22 revolver was the number that
intrigued him most. Pauly noticed that nobody seemed interested
in buying it. If he should pick it up by mistake like, and hide it
away in the pocket of his coat, nobody would ever miss it. Pauly
was sure of that! And yet when he tried to put it up to himself to
take the gun and walk home with it.... Somehow!

His heart thumped like a rabbit's when you picked the beast
up in your arms.

With Christmas approaching, Pauly considered that he
deserved to give himself a present, after he'd got flat feet working for the hardware department all afternoon for months. He
would have to take that gun! If Lonely, come back from the war
with medals pinned on his chest, should discover Pauly didn't even
know how to shoot, what chance would he ever have with Betty?

Pauly palmed a box of .22 cartridges and picked up the
four-barrel revolver, slipping it into his coat pocket. He tried to
whistle debonairly, but nothing but a whisper came out. He cleared
his throat and, since it was already quitting time, walked to the
door with his heart stuck in his throat.

All the way to the corner of Higgins Avenue and Front Street,
Pauly felt people coming after him in the small of his back.

His left shoulder sagged with the weight of the hand that would
be clapped on him in arrest. Hey, sonny! You think you can get
away with murder? Now, come along! No trouble. You and me's
gonna have a talk with the chief!

But nobody followed him!

A young girl slopped along in her rubbers across the street.
The snow was hard and brilliant upon the earth, the air sharp as

the fin of a fish. The darkness of the sky was deeper than a blue-bell, but nobody bothered Pauly.

No one at all!

Bud Bailey knew that some guys would be having themselves a good time when Santa Claus was coming around the mountain. If he come! *Wilson to have Christmas dinner at Chaumont*—while the doughboys marched up and down. That was swell for the President, though maybe the Sammees wouldn't like it so much. And it didn't help Bud Bailey to eat!

Not much it didn't. For Bailey lived in Poverty Row across the railroad tracks.

Bud swung the empty gunny sack over his shoulder and started for the N.P. yards. He took a running slide over the fast slick surface of the ice, skidding down the sidewalk. *Oh, K-K-K-Katy, Beautiful Katy....* His old man got a job once in a while, but the old man was always drunk. Whenever he got a buck, his father bought a bottle of gin. This made things tough.

Damn!

Bud Bailey would like to get cock-eyed drunk tonight on some of the cheap booze that was floating around and never wake up for a week! Pie-eyed and carefree. He wished he could get Sullivan and Billy to come along with him on a tear. It took money to get drunk!

But Stiff was getting so's he read the papers too much. Following the progress of the Revolution, Sullivan explained. That was a howl! Any time Stiff was gonna do any work—outside of squaring off to conk a guy on the head—Bailey wanted to be there to see it. Bud didn't go in for this revolutionary stuff for the workers. All of them German agents in Butte was what had caused the commotion.

Nuts!

All Bud Bailey wanted right now was a good, hard drink.

But as it was, Bud was marching down to the N.P. yards to steal some coal so's his old man wouldn't freeze to death next time he got drunk. He hoped his ma would have some decent food in the house by the time he got home that night. Maybe the Salvation Army guy would have not of been around what with Christmas coming and the war finished and all. Bud hoped to Christ they had something to eat this side of New Year's! But the old man would have to figure a new way to get his liquor, now that Prohibition was around the corner and all of the saloons would be closed. Bud bet the soldier boys wouldn't think so much of that little trick the Christers had played on Sammee while he was over there making the world safe.

When Lonely came back from the war....

What would he find?

Damn few joints you could wrestle with the boobies, and damn few drinks with the saloons scarce as snowballs in hell!

Bud Bailey swung over the fence into the N.P. yards under cover of darkness. He hoped to Jesus the bull, Joe Vuckovich, wasn't snooping around. No trains were due for a couple of hours. There ought to be time for him to work his way over to the coal lying under the dock.

Bailey inched his way cautiously through the evening. Peering in every possible direction of alarm, he moved along slowly. Joe Vuckovich didn't seem to be about.

Beneath the shadow of the coal dock, Bud knelt and opened his sack with one bent arm and fist. With his other hand he gathered the scattered lumps of coal and dropped them quietly into the bag. If he got a good haul tonight, he wouldn't have to come back for a week! What with school opening again-

As Bud rose from his cramped position, Joe Vuckovich leaped out of the darkness. Bailey fell flat on his face in the coal dust that surfaced the snow and the bull landed on top of his back. "You little black bastard!" Joe Vuckovich snarled, as he lifted himself off the prostrate form of Bud Bailey. He jerked Bud to his feet and shook him until his teeth rattled. The kid twisted and pulled, struggling desperately to slip out of the yard bull's grip.

"All right, shine!" Joe said. "You asked for it and you get it!" Vuckovich lifted his billy and swung. Once and again and again. The club fell with sickening force into the bloody mat of Bud Bailey's hair.

Joe Vuckovich felt fine!

Chapter 24
Christers Bury the Demon

╫╫╫

At a meeting in which a Finnish chorus drew thunderous applause by waving small red flags, members of the Butte I.W.W. tonight adopted resolutions calling upon the workers of Butte and the United States to hold strikes and demonstrations demanding withdrawal from Russia of the American troops and the immediate release of political and class-worker prisoners.... And so it came about that Morrison is booked for a session with Judge Bonner in the police court today on the charge—it scarcely seems possible in a dry state—of public intoxication.

Augie Storm decided that it was time for him to get drunk. He'd never been really plastered, but it was necessary that he assert his manhood, now that Norval was dead. *And there was the case of the funny little old man who came too late. Wabbling pitifully down the streets of Missoula, looking for a drink he flattened his nose against the window of what had once been a saloon. He'd come from way up in the hills to have one last fling with the Demon Rum. And he'd come too late!*

After the arrival of the telegram announcing Norval Storm's death, the Pastor's residence had taken on the atmosphere and habiliments of sorrow. Augie left the house as soon as he could each morning. He'd no stomach for watching the agony of his mother's face, and the Pastor was so inadequate in meeting this new knowledge that he would carry with him to the grave. But the Reverend Storm had made one of the best sermons he'd ever delivered on the subject of death.

Once the initial shock had been absorbed, Pastor paid tribute to the merciful Lord.

Now, there should be mercy, Pastor thought.

Augie could not stand the sight of his mother's enveloping grief. It did not seem fitting that Mrs. Storm should so carry on. Comforting the Pastor had been her role, bustling up and down the stairs had been her life, and cooking and washing dishes and mending socks.

That was the role of Pastor's wife in the house.

She had no business crying aloud her pain! But Augie was angry at the Huns for killing his brother. It would be impossible, now, to borrow one of Norval's medals to throw into Stiff Sullivan's face when he started to crack wise.

Augie would have to carry along with no help from his older brother. He'd have to be a man in his own right. He'd have to get properly drunk!

Augie knew that Pauly's cellar was stocked with wines and whiskeys Dr. Craddock had laid in store against Prohibition, which would arrive with advent of the New Year. Augie recalled that it had been Norval's custom, whenever New Year's came around, to walk the outside railing of the Higgins Avenue bridge, blind drunk with the whiskey swirling in his head.

Augie would carry on, now that Norval was no more!

"Looky here, Pauly!" Augie said, when Pauly came out of the house. "Ain't I always treated you right? So's how about lifting a couple bottles of rye from the Doctor's private stock?" he asked.

"Do I play center in the game with the Florence guys?" Pauly countered.

"Sure, sure!" Augie agreed. "Only get me the liquor!"

The whiskey was like blue lightning in Augie's veins. He'd killed two bottles while Pauly watched. It was a good thing that Dr. Craddock never counted his stock. If he ever found out about the missing liquor, there'd be hell to pay and no mistake! Pauly thought.

While Montana went dry quietly, will it stay quietly? They can't blame a man for killing a bottle if it jumps out at him! While many less fortunate soldiers will find no work awaiting them when they get back. Was this what we meant when we promised to keep the home fires burning?

The Clark Fork of the Columbia foamed beneath the Higgins Avenue bridge. The dark night disguised the fear that was fevered in Augie's blood. Whiskey choking his heart, Pastor's son felt his way perilously, like a tight-rope walker, along the railing of the bridge. If he fell, Pastor would have no sons at all! But Augie would not slip to fall that febrile way into death where the river ran. That water had taken Honey Pie's life, but it wouldn't take Augie's! For the Pastor's son was drunk as a man should be with New Year's coming around the hills.

And proud!

Augie would cross from one end to the other the railing of the Higgins Avenue bridge.

That was the way Norval would have wanted it!

Augie was sure. The Pastor's oldest son was dead.

But, in his stead, Augie walked the railing of the bridge.

Stiff Sullivan was sore as hell when he heard about Bud Bailey's getting conked on the head. Not that Bud meant a devil of a lot one way or the other. The kid was closer to Augie than he was to Stiff, in some ways at least. But it was the damn principle of the thing!

A bull beating up a kid for no reason except that the Baileys were cold and wanted some cheer to meet the New Year's after Santa Claus had forgotten to call. Bud's folks were workers. Billy and Stiff knew what that meant. To be workers' kids! The shortage of eats, and the cold, when winter arrived ahead of schedule and the old man out of a job. But there was no use getting Billy mixed up in this thing. And Augie was drinking so heavily these days, now that his brother was dead, that he'd be little help.

Augie would be no good in a fight.

All tanked up!

And Billy had his papers to sell. No use getting Billy worked into this thing.

So the only way out was to get the Butte kids to help. No matter if the Missoula guys had got in a fight with Wolin, Serafimovitch, and that crowd. The Butte kids were workers' kids.

Stiff Sullivan took the Milwaukee to Butte. It was nice and clean on the fast electric train. The locomotive whined in the blue wind. And snow covered the ground. It was cold going over the mountains, but Sullivan wrapped himself warmly. He hadn't seen Bill Dunne for months, nor had he heard what had become of his Uncle Mike. Maybe the guy was dead!

But Bill Dunne had been sent to the legislature by a record number of votes.

Arriving in Butte, Stiff Sullivan didn't know where to find the mob. In desperation, he approached a cop. "You know where Wolin, Casey, and Anissimow are hanging out?" he asked the Law.

The cop looked down at the toe of his shoe, and spat. "Expect they're over at the Blackjack Dugout," the Law answered.

Stiff Sullivan walked up Galena Street. It was a good thing the Lucky Streaks had scheduled some basketball games, he thought to himself. What with the influenza and all of the schools and pool halls closed, the high-school athletic season had gone up in smoke. *Oh, boy! Dances will be resumed in the city at a real cabaret. Rheumatic joints get work-out as ban is officially lifted.* But basketball games were the only manly sports for this time of the year, Sullivan thought.

Sauntering into the Blackjack Dugout, Stiff noticed the long and vacant mirror behind the bar. All of the fancy bottles had disappeared from in front of the glass. This was the first time Sullivan had been in a speak. The bartender was pouring the drinks from a pitcher full of whiskey. If the Law should come in, it was an easy job pitching the liquor in the sink, thus destroying the evidence to the satisfaction of everyone.

Wolin, Serafimovitch, Casey, and O'Hara were lifting them up. Anissimow had finished his in one swift gulp. "How about givin' me another belt of that rye?" Anissimow asked.

The bartender poured the drink, as Wolin turned around to see Stiff. "Well, fer Chrissake!" Wolin ejaculated, with his mouth wide open in surprise. "Don't mean to tell me you got the nerve to show up in Butte all by your lonesome?"

"Take it easy!" Stiff Sullivan replied. "I come over here to get you guys to lend me a hand."

While Bill Dunne spoke to a jammed house in the legislative chambers, the Butte Bolsheviki paraded outside the State Capitol. Demanding the organization of an American Soviet at the National Labor Congress, in Chicago, speakers pointed to the murder of Liebknecht and Rosa Luxemburg. Governor Stewart, on the other hand, in referring to the burning of the A.C.M. lumber mill at Bonner, asserted that "Our country is now essentially a country of one flag! There is no place here for the red flag of anarchy."

Stiff Sullivan was determined to get Joe Vuckovich. And get him good!

He could have handled the N.P. yard bull all by himself, probably, but he didn't want to take any chance of a possible slip-up. The flatfoot had to be taught a lesson! That it wasn't safe to beat up workers' kids! And the Butte mugs had come through handsomely. Riding back on the N.P. train, they scattered through the blinds. Stiff Sullivan was taking the tender. That was the place Joe Vuckovich would look first. When he saw only one kid getting off the tender, Joe would figure that here was another kid handy to his Billy.

And then—

The cinders were whistling into Stiff Sullivan's nose and ears. By the time the train got to Missoula, the kids would be black and grimed as the night. Wolin was all right! He was the leader of the Butte gang and his heart was in the right place. He was closer to what was going on in the mines than any of the other kids. Because, like Wolin said, he'd been down in the earth many's the time with his old man.

Sullivan was glad he'd gone to the Butte kids for help, instead of asking Augie to lend a hand. That dumb son of the Pastor's! Walking the railing of the Higgins Avenue bridge on New Year's. Taking a chance like that for no good reason at all! Beating up somebody's got out of line was all right. That was something! But to take a chance of getting killed just on a stunt. That Pastor's kid was a little silly in the head. You couldn't depend on him to come through when there was something had to be done. Like with Joe Vuckovich beating Bud Bailey's skull into a bloody pulp. Bud was stiff punch-drunk from all them blows on his brain. Lying in the Bailey house with his face all bandaged up.

All Bud knew was that the yard buff had beat him up!

Weaving his way home, blood had crusted Bailey's eyes. He'd climbed into bed, the old lady fussing around. When Stiff had dropped by to find out why Bailey hadn't showed up at the Lucky Streak Athletic Club, he discovered Mrs. Bailey wringing her hands, and not a lump of coal in the house! It was cold as the devil and the old man was passed out. Bud upstairs was in bed with rags wrapped around his head.

Most of what Bud had said didn't make sense.

But Stiff caught on to the fact that Joe Vuckovich had knocked Bud Bailey silly in the head. On account of Old Lady Bailey had sent Bud over to the N.P. yards to gather up some coal so's they wouldn't freeze to death when the next blizzard arrived.

Hot damn! The train was pulling past the shops and morning was yet to come over the mountains. Everything was set for a perfect revenge! As the locomotive eased to a stop, Stiff Sullivan swung off the tender and landed running with both feet. Over his shoulder, he glimpsed Joe Vuckovich on his tail like a bloodhound. The yard bull had missed seeing the Butte kids, who'd jumped out of the blinds and were following him as fast as they could.

Under the increased darkness of the coal dock, Stiff Sullivan pulled to a pause, and turned around. He was waiting when Joe Vuckovich charged with raised billy club. Stiff warded off the blow with his left arm and socked the flatfoot a solid jolt on the nose. Blood gushed from the surprise that split wide open the copper's lips.

Sullivan wasted no time at all. Twisting the club out of the yard bull's grip, he drew back his right and let 'er fly. The uppercut lifted Joe Vuckovich out of his tracks. As he somersaulted and fell, Wolin and Serafimovitch caught him by either arm and pinned him to the ground. Casey and O'Hara held the cop's legs, while Anissimow and Stiff Sullivan kicked.

Their shoes bit into the brutal body that was Joe Vuckovich.

"How yuh feel, copper?" Wolin laughed.

Joe Vuckovich was yelling blue murder. He howled with the bruise of each boot striking him in the gut.

"You big Bulgarian bastard!" Stiff Sullivan snarled. "Think twice before you beat up any more kids!"

The yard bull had lapsed into unconsciousness. Wolin and Serafimovitch stripped him of his clothing. They left him bruised, bleeding, and naked on the snow.

From a pay booth in the railroad station, Stiff Sullivan called the cops. "They's a punk in his birthday suit lyin' on the ground under the coal dock in the N.P. yards," he told them.

"I wouldn't want to see the guy get cold!" Stiff Sullivan said.

Chapter 25
Pauly Has a Cigar

☩☩☩

I.W.W. and Reds plot government seizure. Senate probe of activities is authorized. Inquiry will be nation-wide. Will aim to get at root of spread in America of Soviet doctrine.... New faces for mutilated soldiers is task of woman sculptor. Spirit of mercy guides her hand. Mrs. Anna Coleman Ladd will make life worth living to Yankee wounded.... The feature of the argument that closed the trial was an address to the jury by the defendant, W. Dunne, in which he said: "So long as I have a pen in my hand, and a tongue to speak with, I will write and say these things." He was referring to the editorial on which he was convicted.

Pauly had advised his mother to marry Doctor in the first place, but the marriage hadn't worked out for him the way Pauly had expected. The rabbits had been transferred from Connell Avenue to the barn behind the house on Kootenai Street; and Wolf had tagged along, unsuspecting and blithe. But Wolf hadn't lasted long! And Toughy had come and gone in much the same way. Doctor saw to it that Pauly had plenty of warm, good clothes. Stag shirts, bright and various as rainbows after a storm; Mackinaws, woolen mittens, and a sheepskin coat. Not to forget the nice green suit Doctor had allowed Pauly to buy, to impress Betty, and to wear to school. But Doctor insisted that Pauly earn his keep. Work kept boys out of mischief, Doctor thought.

First, there had been the furnace and the lawn to mow in summertime. Then, there had been the two cows to milk. In the fall, Pauly picked the fruit from the orchard in back of the house. And now there was the part-time work in the hardware store downtown. Yet, Pauly admired Doctor. There was the large Cadillac that Doctor sometimes allowed him to drive around. When he was running the car all by himself, it looked as if nobody were in the front seat, the back of it was so high! If only Betty Darling would pass down the street some day when Pauly was driving the big Cadillac!

He gave Augie a ride once in a while, whenever he had the car to himself.

Doctor was nice enough to Pauly in an impersonal sort of way.

Pauly was hoping he could get mother and Doctor to invite Mr. Darling and Betty out on a trip some day. As soon as spring came around, maybe it could be managed. A good fishing trip up the Blackfoot or a journey to Medicine Hot Springs, past Darby, south towards Idaho.

Betty swimming in the hot-water plunge with her dark, brown hair bunched under the rubber cap!

After they got out of the plunge, they'd walk over to the hotel and Pauly'd put on some records, wind up the victrola, and they'd dance. Just Betty and Pauly. The boy and girl in the soft, intimate embrace of each other's arms. They would really dance, heart to heart, to the tune of the *Clarinet Marmalade Blues!*

But the difficulty was that Pauly had never learned how to dance. If he were to take Betty out on a trip, he'd have to begin learning a few steps!

In the meantime, there was the question of basketball suits for the Lucky Streaks to consider.

Ten thousand Yanks reported still missing ninety days after the Armistice. Lonely would be returning to Missoula soon, Pauly had heard. Norval would never come back. *Private Peat two years in hell and back with a smile, it is said.* But Augie was kicking up a little hell of his own. Ever since that telegram had arrived, the Pastor's son had been knocking the punks around in Missoula. Not Stiff Sullivan, of course.

Pauly decided to drop over to Augie's.

It was important for Pauly to keep on Augie's good side as much as he could. But the Pastor's son had been mean ever since the Pastor's wife had received the letter from the captain: *I have yours of the ninth and I will give you the details of your son's death. He was in excellent health and good spirits when we went over the top in the Meuse-Argonne battle. He was the fifth of his squad and carried the belt-loading machine and one box of ammunition. It did not explode, but he was instantly killed by the concussion and did not have a mark on his body. It came quickly and painlessly, so he never knew what had happened. He was one of my best and most reliable men.*

Always ready to do his duty, the captain wrote.

Pauly decided he'd better ask Augie's advice so's the Pastor's son wouldn't change his mind about Pauly's playing center.

With the basketball game with the Florence Five coming around the corner, the Lucky Streaks would have to have uniforms!

...cheerfully, and we will always miss him in the company and feel proud of the way he died.

On the way over to the university gymnasium, Augie and Pauly stopped in front of the house on Avalanche Avenue and yelled for Lover to come out.

Three would be better than two for the job Augie and Pauly had in mind!

"We're gettin' some jerseys for the Lucky Streaks to wear," the Pastor's son explained to Lover, as the three of them walked through the night. The Montana Varsity was playing its first basketball game of the season, now that the Spanish influenza had beaten its jagged retreat and had almost vanished.

"We go in the window once the game gets goin' good," Augie continued.

Pauly would have liked watching the game, but if the boys were to look snappy when the Florence Five came down for the tilt with the Lucky Streak Athletic Club, they'd have to get suits!

Augie, Lover, and Pauly crouched in the enveloping darkness of the bleachers that leaned up against the university gymnasium. Inside the building the game seemed to be going good. The rickety old structure that housed athletics for the State University shook with the violence of play. The referee's whistle whined sharply, like the agony in a mountain lion's scream, and the windows of the gym tinkled like Christmas Eve with Santa Claus coming over the mountains...the ringing of sleighbells, the deer tossing their heads!

Augie pinched open the blade of his jackknife, sharp against the work that had to be done.

Sliding the thin slice of steel under the lock that held the upper half of the window in place, he fished for the catch and cut it free. Carefully, with his heart in his mouth, Pauly helped the Pastor's son lower the pane. This done, the three of them climbed through the opening and dropped to the floor of the locker room.

"What d'yuh say?" Augie considered. "D'yuh think these will do?"

Pauly was definitely flattered that Augie should ask his advice. But they were sure nice. Scattered over the benches, beside the lockers that stood against the wall, were fifteen lovely white jerseys, warm and unlettered, with only the sharp red numbers on the back of each. Nice big number as clean and brilliant as an autumn moon: 17.

Another number looked nice: 23.

And each of these Gonzaga jerseys boasted a different numeral so's the players could not be confused by the referee. They would suit the Lucky Streaks fine! Pauly could cut out some letters, spelling *Lucky Streaks*, and sew them like a rainbow on the front of each shirt. Orange in color they would be on the white background of the jerseys. Red numerals on the back of the shirts.

That was it!

The colors of the Lucky Streak Basketball Quintet would be orange and red on a white background.

Neat!

Hastily, Augie, Lover, and Pauly gathered the jerseys into their arms and clambered out of the open window, closing it behind them, before turning to slip down the bleachers and out over the football field to the east. They circled the campus at considerable distance, cutting under the shadow of Mount Sentinel and back over the flats to the south. They skirted Lover's home on Avalanche Avenue and struck back toward the Lucky Streak Athletic Club.

The loft of the barn was lighted up like a church!

Pauly could hear the basketball thumping against the slats that covered the windows, protecting them from harm. Evidently some of the boys were beating themselves into shape for the Florence game.

Augie, Lover, and Pauly climbed up the ladder, through the trapdoor to the loft, and tossed the Gonzaga jerseys onto a bench along the wall.

"Do we have suits for the game with Florence or do we have shirts?" Pauly laughed.

Jake, Bud, still looking a little groggy from the beating he'd taken from the yard bull, Joe Vuckovich, Tubby, Billy, and some of the boys pulled to a stop. The basketball, which was in mid-air, bounced sloppily against a rafter, hit the floor, and dribbled crazily into a corner. Pauly could see that his stock had gone up a little with the mob.

"And I'm playin' center!" Pauly continued, looking to Augie for confirmation.

"That's right!" Augie laughed. "The Doctor's son plays center." The Pastor's son looked almost human for a moment, and it warmed the cockles of Pauly's heart.

When the I.W.W. strike leaders in Butte moved against the wage cut adopted in the A.C.M. plants, a party of sixty men, said to be bewhiskered Bolshevists from the coast, passed through Missoula over the Northern Pacific, bound for an eastern port. But Joe Vuckovich was no longer in evidence at the N.P. yards, having been confined to the hospital for an indeterminate length of time.

Returning from a movie the evening after the basketball game between the Lucky Streaks and the Florence Five, Pauly was feeling fine. He'd played center during most of the play, and had made two baskets when the Florence kids were looking the other way.

Coming back from the movie, Pauly thought happily of his new role in life. Now, at long last, he was an athlete! Although he was not on the Missoula High School team, true enough, yet he had played creditably for the Lucky Streak Athletic Club in the barn behind the house on Kootenai Street. Actually making two baskets while the Florence kids were asleep! It was handy knowing just how far you could go with the ball and still miss the rafters. That was where the Florence boys had slipped up. They'd toss the ball in the usual arc, and the roof would intervene.

But Pauly knew every crook and cranny of the barn.

He was an athlete!

Unobserved by anyone, Pauly Craig sneaked into the house. Into the darkness of the parlor he crept. Lifting the lid of the humidor that contained Doctor's fine Havana cigars, he selected one of them and slipped it into the pocket of his Mackinaw.

Outside the house he went and across the lawn to the barn.

After climbing the ladder to the loft, he clipped off the end of the cigar with his fingernails and poked it into his mouth.

Lit a match!

The fragrance of expensive Havana tobacco floated encouragingly throughout the loft.

Pauly puffed manfully.

Chapter 26
Lonely Comes Back

One man dies in fatal shooting. Drunken brawl ends in fight at Saltese bootleg cabin. Second near death.... "I could fight anything but women. They kill all they can, then bare their breasts and shout 'Kamerad.' Of course, a man would not kill them. I saw two Belgian girls with their breasts cut off," he said. He is glad to get back and proud that he had a chance to fight for the United States.... Said Judge Taylor, instructing the jury, "And if, as a result of such fight, Mr. Harvey died, but the killing was not effected in a cruel or unusual manner, in said fist fight, or otherwise, then your verdict should be one of acquittal."*

Lonely had been wounded in the leg and had used his rifle for a crutch in consonance with his flare for the dramatic. Now, he was well. Later, he'd been shot clean through the lung. It had taken Lonely the rest of the war to recover. Altogether, he hadn't had a bad time. And now he was coming home!

But when Lonely swung off the Milwaukee train at Missoula, there were no brass bands waiting to receive him. Betty was nowhere in sight and Mr. Darling was probably working at the bank. When the Sammees hit New York, they'd marched up Broadway in triumph. The confetti and torn pages of Manhattan telephone books had showered the Yankees with visible evidence of the town's admiration.

Broadway knew how to treat its returned heroes!

But when Lonely got off the train at his home town in Montana, nobody shouted, nobody lifted him into the air on the shoulders of a crowd, and carried him up the stairs to the top of Higgins Avenue bridge where a delegation from city hall was waiting to greet him!

Checking his bags at the railroad station, Lonely laboriously climbed the stairs to the top of the bridge, walked east, and pulled up before Kelly's Empress Cigar Rooms. There should be some of the kids he knew hanging around and shooting a game of pool!

"Well, *Look What My Boy Got in France!*" Stiff Sullivan laughed, as Lonely came marching in. "Where's your medals?"

Augie laid down his cue on the pool table, spread his legs apart, and grinned.

"Hey, bo!" Augie said agreeably.

"H'lo," Lonely answered, a picture of despondency. Stiff Sullivan was amused. He imagined the world must seem tame to these soldier boys returning from France. Not much excitement in Montana. The only fights were with the Law, between kids, or about the unions. Not much like the fighting had gone on across the water!

"Hey, cowboy!" Sullivan began, by way of getting better acquainted with a boy who had been beating up the Huns for so long a time. "So what do you do now?" he said.

"Get a job with my old man, if he'll have me!" Lonely replied.

Augie leaned hard on his cue and busted the balls in every direction. It was a nice break!

We're ready for you, soldiers who are returning to civilian life! We're ready with the new waist-seam styles and the famous Varsity cuts. The joint committee of inquiry on the high cost of living, however, submitted a final report. It declared that the price of gasoline and lubricating oil was fixed by the Standard Oil; that a packers' trust fixed the prices of meat; that a grain-dealing association controlled the prices for grain; that a miller's combine regulated flour and feed; and that none of the above-mentioned corporations were formed to protect the ultimate consumer.

Oh, How Ya Gonna Keep 'Em Down On The Farm? Now that they've seen Paree!

It was a rather formal dinner for a homecoming, it occurred to Lonely. Sis knew better than to speak out of turn, but her eyes were gleaming with a look Lonely had never seen before in any girl's eyes.

Sis was all right!

Mr. Darling carefully stirred the sugar in his coffee cup and lifted the spoon to lay it on the saucer. He cut the end of his cigar with a penknife, and lit up. The smoke which arose in aromatic clouds above the banker's head seemed to assure Mr. Darling of the course he should take when he spoke.

"And now, what are your plans?" Mr. Darling asked, glancing along the fine length of his cigar. "You joined the army because you wouldn't cut out the drink! So now, what do you expect?"

Lonely showed plainly his thorough disgust. Lonely was sore! Here he'd been fighting for his old man and for American womanhood—And what did he get? Lonely had blistered his hands bucking a machine gun that blasted the Huns just so's his old man could sit at home on his stiff behind and worry about the bank.

"You could give me a job," Lonely pointed out to his old man.

Mr. Darling had worries. The bank wasn't going so well these days. Money was short. The bank was land poor. Some of the deals he had made were turning out badly. Occasionally, the banker wondered how much money was in his pocket. It had come to that! But he never looked. It was better to know as little as possible about such things. And Mrs. Sullivan, the wash-woman, worrying him about the laundry bill all the time! The trouble with the working-class; they didn't realize how hard a banker's life could be. When times got hard, the bankers took it on the chin. They got it first!

"So you want me to give you a job in the bank?"

"You got ears!" Lonely replied.

Mr. Darling knocked the ash from his cigar into his coffee cup.

It was not only that the bank was not doing well. Responsible men in the community had much to worry about! The thousands who were dying daily in Petrograd proved that the Reds were no people to be running a government; and the Chinese soldiers in the Red Army who were actually selling human flesh for food. Just think of that! *Will your family be left in poverty when you die? Give your dollars a fighting chance by investing them in the bank!* Not to mention the Bolsheviks in Butte. William Dunne having the crust to run for mayor of Silver Bow's county seat! It was a national disgrace.

That's what it was!

"Son," the banker said. "I wish to speak straight with you on this. When you left to join the army to fight in France, harsh words were spoken. But your mother would want it that way! If I don't exercise some moral authority, I can do you no good at all. You were drinking when you last left this house. How do I know that that has been changed? That I could count on you to come to the bank regularly? Soberly!" the banker said.

"So we gotta play games!" Lonely spat out the bitterness that jammed in his teeth. "When Uncle Sam asks us to stick a bayonet in a Hun's guts, he don't say nothin' about our not takin' a drink! So now we're back, those of us who ain't dead, and we gotta clap hands!"

Mr. Darling stared sternly at this monster who was his son.

"You left this house once," the banker observed. "You can do it again!"

At the Bucket of Blood, on Front Street, Lonely made his connections. In any case, it was a job that required no Sunday school practice; and it would mean increasing money in his pocket as time went on and business got good. The windows of the Bucket of Blood were boarded up tight against the Feds. But if you knew your way around, you learned the place was open, and you went around through the alley and entered the back door.

Inside, the place was much the same as it had been before Prohibition. But the bar was not so shiny as it once had been. The mirror behind the bartender was covered with cobwebs and spiders shinnied up and down the glass.

The whiskey they served, however, gave you the same warm feeling in the guts.

If the cops came, it would go down the sink!

The boozerunner made a deal with Lonely. They were talking over the details. "We pack the train over the border east of Babb. Then, we cut over the mountains if we want to get the stuff back to the reservation. That's where you come in, Lonely! You take care of the stuff once we get it to Polson," the guy was saying.

"OK by me!" Lonely agreed.

This would be a job after Lonely's heart! He'd run the whiskey down through the Flathead, stopping off at all the main towns, and conclude the trip in Missoula. Plenty of money and plenty to drink! He could buy Sis a couple of things she might want that the old man wouldn't get her. It would be simple. If he got into any argument, Lonely could teach them cops a trick or two he'd learned in France! He was good at the knife, too. But the best part about it would be the Indians on the reservation. You give the redskins a drink, and they'd sell their mothers and wives for the rest of the bottle. Put their souls in hock, by gawd, for a drink, the Indians would! Of course, you had to be careful.

Them Indians got drunk and they wanted to fight!

With knives.

"From east of Babb, naturally, some of us hits Great Falls, but that ain't none of your worry!" the runner was saying. "You got the reservation and Missoula."

Lonely felt great! This was a job he could handle. The man who had come back from the Argonne with a wound in his leg and bullet-hurt in the blue cushion of his lung saw in his imagination the Federals coming over the rough terrain. Lonely was a man wounded twice in the war. And he had done his share with the bayonet, too. He remembered the ghastly grin that froze on the guy's chin. Not more than fifteen, Lonely didn't think. He looked younger than Augie, and more unwashed behind the ears. Grew colder in the bloodstream as his life gushed out of his breast, and turned over silently to go to sleep.

Mama, I won't be home tonight!

Or whatever the Hun kids said.

Lonely lifted his glass, drinking the whiskey at one gulp. This boozerunner was OK. Lonely had used his head, he had! He saw himself crouching behind a rock barricade that crossed the Cori-acan Defile, watching the Feds coming in the dark.

He cut down on the trigger of the machine gun.

The red-breasted robins of death flew out, winging into the teeth of them boys who would keep the country dry when the Sammees needed some drinks. The heft of the gun was happy in Lonely's hand. The banker's son felt nailed without a cannon around.

They'd given him a rifle, and Lonely had learned!

The boozerunner was getting ready to leave. As he opened the back door, he turned to Lonely for one parting remark.

"About the tea and the snow!" the boozerunner suggested. "Think it over, kid!" he said.

Section 3
1919–1920

Editorial cartoon by J. M. Baer from
The New Northwest, Missoula, June 13, 1919

Chapter 27
Lover is a Lover

‖‖

The 91ˢᵗ Division, known popularly as the Powder River Division, suffered between six and seven thousand casualties. It was cited seven times for bravery. Its nickname of Powder River was taken from a Montana stream which the soldiers said was a mile wide and an inch deep.... Now, are the decent people of Butte to put a yellow stain on Montana's war record by having Butte known as the only city in the United States to choose a Red Bolshevist for mayor!... "If mothers would only tell their daughters/ of the snares that lie in wait/ they would not pay to their dying day/ for the knowledge that comes too late." —Ella Wheeler Wilcox.

Lover Lemire had no use for Harold after what he had seen in the chicken coop, the day Stiff Sullivan had taken him for a trip to the house on Beckwith Street. The months had come and gone through the seasons since that time. The snow bitter in his teeth, Lover had faced the blizzards blowing down from the blue funnel of Hellgate Canyon and spreading over the flats. Spring in its hot urgency with shooting stars, bluebells, and buttercups, tender as the thought of a young girl's breasts. The languid and forest-fired summers when grouse thundered in the underbrush, the brooks burdened with the liquid talk of trout. Not to forget the burnt bravery of autumn when the moons seemed as large as all expectation! Cottonwoods yellow among the deep gutturals of the wind in the tamaracks. The kinnikinnick sharp to the touch and the smell of cold frost that would announce—

Winter had come again!

Many icicles, frozen and stiff, had melted into the past.

But Lover had never forgotten the sight of Betty's body under the profane touch of Harold's fingers. He'd not known what Stiff Sullivan was talking about, but now he knew what a boyhumper was. A kid didn't go to high school for nothing!

The knowledge had come late to Lover. The days felt different in his blood. It was all right for Stiff Sullivan to be interested in fights. It was perfectly understandable that Augie should like to get drunk. But basketball and green suits and dogs and rabbits did not satisfy Lover, as they seemed to satisfy Pauly. For Lover, these games and animals, these actions and attitudes, were not nearly enough!

Lover ached for affection that could be felt and caught.

He'd never forgotten Betty. For nights and weeks after observing Harold's caresses, Lover could get little sleep. Occasionally in study hall he managed to sit beside Betty. He'd danced with her once or twice, and she spoke to him now on the street. Betty was growing up! No longer was she the innocent, but tough-minded little youngster who had gone swimming under the Van Buren bridge, where Honey Pie had been drowned.

Lover lifted his long dark fingers and felt the fuzz on his upper lip.

After Lonely Darling had been ordered out of the house again, Betty got up from the dinner table. It made her face hot and cold by turns to think that her brother should be treated so. *Why Do*

They Call Them Babies? Because they didn't have enough caution to take care of themselves! Betty had learned a thing or two at school and Harold had fallen into permanent disgrace. You heard queer tales in the out-of-the-way places the girls gathered after school.

Betty had followed Lonely out of the house, catching up with him as he walked west toward Higgins Avenue.

"What're you doin' here?" Lonely asked.

"How do they make love in Paris?" Betty answered, almost forgetting that she never blushed.

Lonely laughed out loud and clapped an arm around his sister's shoulder.

"You're all right!" Lonely said, approvingly. "Come on with me. We'll take a little walk and leave the old man to his sour pretzels."

They turned down Gerald Avenue, walking north. *But the cops had another story to tell about the diary written by the two little Anaconda ladies who ran away from home only to be picked up by the police in Missoula. The diary these little girls kept was a complete account of what transpired, even events of the most private nature, and was a remarkable and vulgar narrative, hardly believable.* Betty walked with Lonely down to the Bucket of Blood.

Lonely ushered his sister into one of the back rooms. Returning to the front of the saloon, he spoke to the bartender. "Couple of drinks for me and the lady. She's my kid sister," he explained.

The bartender leered.

"And lay off the wise looks," Lonely snarled. "I ain't robbin' no cradles. She's my sister!"

Betty snaked the whiskey into her throat, where it fought back and forth until it finally settled in the hot corners of her body, and warmed her heart. The tips of her breast stiffened as the blood raced blithely along her veins and outward from her belly. The whiskey reached even to the tips of her ears. She felt weak!

But Lonely was the best brother a girl ever had! He'd been places, her brother had! To France and England and all those countries she'd never seen. She wondered whether Lonely had met any of the Belgium girls with their breasts cut off. *Forced to dig their own graves, they were buried alive with their babies still unweaned, the favorite pastime of the Bolshevik beasts of Russia....*

The whiskey was a golden light that electrified her body.

"Please, Lonely!" she said. "So what're the French girls like?" Lonely laughed importantly, swelled up with memories. *Running through the barrage, one hundred yards in advance of the front line, attached the enemy at several points and blasted a Hun machine gun nest, killing the gunner with a hand grenade, shooting another member of the crew with his pistol, and returned through the barrage, single-handed, with eighteen Germans at the end of his bayonet. But the girl had gonorrhea and he'd have nothing to do with her—*

"It's like this!" Lonely explained. "Girls are the same anywheres! But you take care of yourself, you understand? You get into trouble and you come to me! You hear?"

Betty was glad her brother was back.

Lover Lemire called Betty Darling on the telephone and arranged for a picnic. He asked his mother to put up a lunch. Wrapping up a blanket in a short tarpaulin, he stuck the bundle under his arm. Carrying the lunch in a haversack, Lover walked over to the banker's house and knocked diffidently upon the back door.

Sis was wearing a skirt and jersey, socks and hiking shoes. Her face looked bright and happy as her eyes danced dark and sweet. Lover's heart beat swiftly beneath his sweater. His lips quivered and broke when he spoke.

"You ready to go, Betty?" he asked.

"What does it look like?" she laughed.

Walking arm in arm over the flats, they passed the university and reached the trail which led at an easy jigsaw up Mount Sentinel. There were no trees on this face of the mountain, but it wouldn't take long for them to reach the summit. Occasionally, they paused for a breathing spell and drank water from Lover's canteen. On hikes through the hills, you always got thirsty.

As they rose into the sky, Betty breathed keenly the sharp and shining air. Spring was palpable in every step she took. The blood coursed inspiritingly through her body, and the wind broke over her as she reached the mountain top. Far below, she could see the timid speck that was her father's house. It was springtime and the flowers were fresh on the young grass. Later, and soon enough, the flowers would fade into the brown sparrows of drouth.

And forest fires would roar through the mountains. Lightning would break.

But now, the simplicity of the sun was soft and encouraging on the rose-like cheeks of Betty's face. She was young, and she loved the smell of the high earth. Over the round top of the mountain they climbed. On the very summit, the top-most point toward heaven, they stopped. Here, the wind verged upon the velocity of a gale that would sweep them from their feet. Laughingly, Betty pressed Lover Lemire for support. She liked this kid who looked so much the way Honey Pie Buchard would have looked, had he lived. In some curious fashion, since she resented Augie and what the Pastor's son had tried to bring so bruisingly about, she felt that Lover and Honey were the same in her heart.

Betty looked up into Lover's eyes and smiled.

Some Day I'll Make You Glad! Betty sang, as they continued along the rim of the mountain and dropped down the steep slope that walled Hellgate Canyon to the south. Betty was beginning to get hungry.

Down through the under brush, the kinnikinnick, and the pine trees, Lover led the way. He knew of a cave in the side of the mountain that was splendid for camping. The cavern was cut cleanly into the high black surface of the rock. It had a smooth floor wide enough for Lover's blanket, and they could build a fire at the cave's mouth. Following the trickle of a spring that, farther down the mountain, would become a leaping, unleashed cataract, Lover divided the spruce and tamarack for Betty's passage. Already, he felt warmly the friendship that had shot up between them. The memory of Harold and Betty in the chicken coop was but a faint fever in his veins.

Betty was clean!

That Wonderful Mother of Mine....

Not that his emotion for Betty was quite like that! But as nice. Betty was beautiful, lovely and young as a shooting star, whose bright red lips would split to the softest touch like Bitterroot apples to reveal the sharp, white fruit of her teeth. Fragrant, and tense, as the perfume of her breath, which had stabbed at his tongue when she'd reached out to him for support on the mountain top. It was the excitement of being with Betty alone, her walk siding with his. Her sweet movement, limber and level, as it pressed from one step to another on the staircase of the skies.

"Here it is," Lover said proudly. "What do you think of this place to stop?"

Betty sat down.

Play up your good points! says Golden Apple girl. Betty pulled in her belly and smoothed the girdle of her skirt.

Hurriedly, Lover gathered wood for the fire, and struck a match. Spreading the blanket warmly over the ground, he unwrapped the parcels of food his mother had packed for him. Wieners, which he toasted to a turn, after the potatoes had been properly burned. Sandwiches of cheese and ham, cake and sweet cider.

It was a beautiful meal!

"Come here, Lover," Betty suggested languorously, as she leaned on one elbow to watch the coals of the fire sputter and glow in the gathering dusk.

Lover lowered himself and lay down beside her, the nerves of his body taut from tip to toe. Reclining along the sharp, cool length of Betty Darling, the inch that separated him from her burned in his consciousness like flame.

"How's Lonely?" Lover asked.

"Lonely? Lonely's fine!" Betty answered. She slipped from the wedge of her elbow to lie flat on her back with her bobbed hair floating around her face like a halo. Betty felt sleek as a cat. She placed her hands behind her head, spread-eagling her arms, and looked at the ceiling of the cave which arched over her body and out into the open sky like a swallow in flight.

"And you?" Betty laughed.

"Oh, me?" Lover said. "I'm all right!" And he blushed.

Betty lifted one hand from beneath her head and brushed it across Lover's lips. It burned like nettle. It was swift and free as the wind. He turned, falling into Betty's arms, and crushed her mouth to his. Her teeth bit into his lips and her breasts cut into him like ivory. Her belly was soft and receptive under the pressure of his hard muscles. It was getting dark outside the cave. With the wind coming up, the sound of the pine trees was frightening as the howl of coyotes in the black night. Slowly, the coals of the fire blinked and went out. Smoke curled softly in the starlight....

Lover's young heart melted as in some furious furnace of conflict, his whole life was twisted out of him by the soft white movement that was Betty's body, and blood broke like a cloudburst over the rock. Lover felt drenched, swept swiftly along by some silent, completely enveloping river, and drained.

Betty brushed the tears from her eyes.

It would be dark going down into Hellgate Canyon.

Chapter 28
The Vigil on Jumbo

!!!

Police shot down during May Day riots. Red flags torn from soldiers; believe all bombs intercepted. Tanks are used in Cleveland to disperse mobs; one person killed, many hurt seriously.... Budapest, by the Associated Press: May Day has been an orgy of red. Thousands of Red Troops marched to red music through red-bannered streets. "Oh, Mother! look up in the evening sky,/ let your weeping eyes behold/ against the blue, so clear and bright,/ God's Service Star of Gold!" — written by the Mother of a Western Montana Marine.

Crystal Craddock grew very fond of William Tell and, because of his bubbles and the soft feeling of the baby's lips on her breast, she felt closer to Doctor than ever before. She enjoyed going on long fishing trips with him. Usually, she remained in the car taking care of William, and watched Doctor angling with his long bamboo rod as he waded, thigh-deep in rubber boots, through the stream he'd picked out for himself. *When I go fishin' I want fish that bite, and tobacco that don't!* But Doctor always smoked cigars.

He didn't think it fitting for a professional man to be seen with a pipe. There were certain standards of behavior that a respected member of the community had to observe.

Crystal was glad she had married Doctor! Returning to the parked Cadillac, Doctor carried a basket of fish on his arm.

"I caught some squaw fish," Doctor observed. "But I threw them back in the brook. These bull trout and Dolly Varden should do the trick." And he smiled happily at William Tell and the fish.

Crystal could thank God until her dying day that she had taken to Doctor instead of to Mr. MacMurray, the poor boy who had died in France.

William Tell Craddock gooed.

As Doctor pressed his foot to the starter, turned over the engine, and steered the big Cadillac back into the Lolo road, he thought of his last conversation with George Baggs. The man was growing blind, Doctor knew. If George didn't watch out about his smoking and the worrying about the Reds, he'd lose his eyesight sure as Doctor's basket was full of fish! Doctor had remonstrated with George. Time and again, he'd said: "George, stop worrying about the Reds and the A.C.M.! If the Bonner mill was burned, it wasn't your fault! You couldn't have done any more than you did. You've kicked the I.W.W. out of your mill. So why worry? You'll lose your eyes, for sure, if you don't watch out."

George Baggs was working entirely too hard, Dr. Craddock thought.

Mrs. Craddock wiped baby's lips, while she thought of the innocent, round, pink face that was Mr. MacMurray.

Mrs. Craddock felt sad to remember—

The clear white light in Mr. MacMurray's eyes, and the earnest hope on his lips!

Pauly, entirely aware of his responsibility, passed into the wine cellar and out through the small, cobwebbed window which led under the front porch. After digging furiously, according to the directions he had written out for himself on a card, he brought forth the box with the three hundred thousand dollars of stage money in it. Pauly's heart beat fast with the excitement of all that wealth in his fist. Maybe that money wasn't real money, but all riches were an illusion, Pauly had heard. In any case, it looked like the real thing. It gave you a tremendous feeling of power coursing heavily along the red blood in your veins.

Pauly emerged from the cellar with three hundred thousand dollars in stage money clenched in his fist.

He would walk down to the Milwaukee and wait for a train to come through. Here! Pauly would say. Have a good time! And he would pass the crisp green bills into their care-worn fingers. Go on a bender! he would say....

The engineer of the Milwaukee locomotive turned off the power. Quickly and quietly, the train pulled to a stop.

Pauly noticed the lean face of a soldier through the window that stopped abreast of him. The Sammee was leaning against a pillow in the pullman seat. As Pauly walked down the aisle of the car, his heart-strings twanged like those of a guitar—his emotion choked him so! Here, if ever, was his chance to pay his debt in full to the soldier who had wanted to get drunk on the five dollars Pauly had stolen.

"Here, soldier!" Pauly said, holding out the three hundred thousand dollars in one propitiating palm. "So's when you get home you won't have to go looking for work."

The Sammee looked startled. He turned his head back from the window to see if his crutches were still secure on the seat opposite to him.

"Why, sure, sonny!" he said. "Thanks!"

The Butte High School squad had taken the lead in the interscholastic track meet. Buckshot Wolin had established a new state record in the 220-yard dash. After the Butte kids had helped Stiff Sullivan beat up on Joe Vuckovich, they returned home. Wolin, Serafimovitch, and the rest of them. They'd still fight the Missoula kids at the drop of a hat. But when Stiff had come to them fair and square, saying: "I'm putting the lug on you guys! I need some help and it's like this."—Why, there was nothing else they could do! Wolin, Casey, and Anissimow were glad to lend a leg. For yard bulls were yard bulls the whole West over, and they shouldn't get no bad ideas about beating up workers' kids, the Butte guys thought.

Not if they hoped to live, they shouldn't!

Serafimovitch got a helluva kick out of sapping Joe Vuckovich, and Wolin smiled in his sleep whenever he dreamed of it.

But much blood had been spilled since that winter night they had pushed Joe Vuckovich around, and here was the Interscholastic Track Meet. Buckshot Wolin beat Stiff Sullivan by a hair's length in the 220-yard dash. Augie did fairly well in the pole vault, but all the rest of the Missoula team came in too slowly to count. But Bailey would have been a help, but his head was still screwy on account of he got conked. He went dizzy whenever he ran fast. And the idea in a track meet was that you should run as fast as you could!

Serafimovitch took honors in the shot-put.

Stiff Sullivan was sore as hell! He was going around with a new dame he'd picked up in front of the Bucket of Blood on Front Street. She was walking down the avenue, Sarah was. Her face was all scarred up on one side like she'd been kicked by a horse. Funny damn thing! She was pretty as a picture until she turned her head—if you saw her from her good side first. Nice nose, full lips, blonde hair and, Jesus to Jesus, she could spit out cusswords like a rattlesnake. But Sarah had showed up at the track meet plastered to the eyeballs. She sat in the bleachers with her legs spread out so wide she looked like she was flagging a train.

Stiff Sullivan knocked over the seventh hurdle and fell flat on his pan.

That bitch had no business chippying[1] around like that!

By Christ, he'd slap her down once he got her upstairs in the bedroom over the Bucket of Blood! No little chippy he was going with regular was going to make an ad of herself like that!

Sarah would play clean or he'd leave her alone.

But the worst of it was, in the relays, Wolin, Serafimovitch, Anissimow and O'Hara beat the Missoula team by three lengths! *We rode down the trail and forded the river there in 1858, the old-timer told the man with the stop-watch. That was many years ago. Silhouetted by the ray of the setting sun over the Western mountains, they made a picture I'll never forget, he said.* A reporter from the *Record* who was covering the track meet perked up his ears, and moved closer to the man with the stopwatch so he could hear more clearly what was being said. *Why, there's my uncle's wife, Mrs. Alexander Big Knife! An attractive Indian girl, like you see on the bank calendars, was puffing a cigarette. With an elk-horn, T-shaped, the flower was quickly pried out of the ground and with a deft motion, the skin of the root was peeled off, leaving the root white and clean as a boiled onion.*

Try as hard as he might, Stiff Sullivan couldn't run any longer! He'd won a couple of dashes, but the coach worked him too much. The Missoula squad was way in the back, way out of sight, in fact. It looked like the Butte team would cop most of the honors. Stiff could see the tepees of the Salish Indians, who were gathering the bitterroots, south of the field on the flats.

The name of the mountain was Sinemko, the oldtimer said.

Not like in our time!

At one time, they used the sunflower for food. But the name of the river was Red Willow, then.

---

1   *Chippy* was slang for a prostitute or "loose" woman.

Stiff Sullivan was crocked with anger.

He'd get that chippy.

But good!

Pauly hoped that the soldier to whom he'd given the three hundred thousand dollars was happy. It had been a good winter, all in all! The two baskets he'd made in the game with the Florence kids. Also, the game with Frenchtown had turned out well. Augie had been in an ugly mood. Consequently, he'd allowed Pauly to play only the first half, but they'd won the game. At Ronan they were beaten. Stiff Sullivan had been away in Helena playing with the Missoula High School quint. Without Sullivan, they'd had no chance at all of winning. The Salish Indians playing on their home floor were too fast and too tough. So the Lucky Streaks had won two games and lost the other.

It was not bad for a beginning.

But next year!

Next year would be better yet, Pauly thought.

After a fine trout dinner, Pauly went upstairs to his room and put on the Lucky Streak jersey over his shirt. After the jersey came the Mackinaw. It would be cold staying out all night on the side of Mount Jumbo, watching to see that the high-school letters, which were painted on the hill, were not busted up by any of the visiting kids from Butte. Pauly looked forward to the night's vigil on Jumbo. Reaching behind Ridpath's *History of the World* on the lower shelf of his bookcase, Pauly brought forth the .22 calibre pistol he'd swiped from the hardware store down town where he worked. He filled his pockets with cartridges and broke the gun to see if he had properly loaded it the last time he had put the rod back in its hiding place in the bookcase. If those Butte kids came up the mountain looking for trouble tonight, Pauly wouldn't duck out. Not this time he wouldn't! With the pistol perilous in the palm of his hand, Pauly felt ready for anything. Even those Butte kids, did they want a fight!

Pauly bent his arm once again behind Ridpath's *History of the World* and brought forth a package of Camels. He'd be properly armed tonight. With a pistol, the Lucky Streak jersey bright on his chest beneath the Mackinaw, matches and cigarettes, the night held no terrors.

Shaking the dust of the South Side from his feet, he sped his way past the N.P. station and past the Rattlesnake. Mount Jumbo was steep to climb. There was no mistake about that! Half-way up the mountain a fire blinked bravely in the upright blackness of the night. Few stars were out.

That fire was evidence that the Missoula kids were standing watch. Not the important members of the track squad like Stiff Sullivan, of course. But Billy Toole would be there and, perhaps, Augie. After all, the Pastor's son had already competed in the single event he was expected to take.

The fire lit up the large letters of the high school that were spread out steeply on the mountain in their fresh, white paint: *M.H.S.*

It was the defiance of those letters that should tempt the Butte kids to come up the side of the mountain. They could try, that is! But no Butte kids were going to disarrange those letters on the side of Mount Jumbo! Not if the Missoula kids had anything to say about it, and they had plenty to say! None of the other kids visiting in Missoula would be interested. Helena, Bozeman, Anaconda, and Billings had special rivalries of their own to take care of, and couldn't be bothered about the Butte-Missoula fight.

Jake Sterling spread out his legs and stared into the fire. It would be good to tell a couple of stories to while away the hours until the Butte punks made a pass at the *M.H.S.* on the mountain.

"Did I ever tell you about the time the calf chewed up my vest on the ranch at Stevensville?" Jake said, turning to Augie.

"Nuts!" Augie remarked.

"Well, it was like this!" Jake went on. "In my vest pocket was a gold watch granpappy give me. You know I had a granpappy?" Jake asked.

"So you gotta granpappy," the Pastor's son laughed.

"That was when I was in diapers," Jake continued. "After I entered high school, pa come to me and he says: 'Son, we butcher Lucinda tomorrow, because her teats are broke and she don't give no milk!' Next day, I took a butcher knife and I split Lucinda open from stem to stern. And you know what?" Jake Sterling prompted.

"Green light. Make your own traffic," the Pastor's son said.

"OK, so the watch is lodged in the cow's bronchial tube so tight the respiration has wound that clock for fifteen years! Was two minutes ahead of Western Union!"

"I was very fond of Lucinda," Jake Sterling explained.

The fire had guttered. Down through the mist that was rising from the valley, Pauly heard menacing movement.

"Them Butte kids is comin'," Augie whispered.

Pauly lifted his pistol and nosed a .22 bullet into the wind.

Chapter 29
Run, Sheep, Run!

░░

Babies, God bless them, have always been loved and made much over, but now their importance in the world is finding greater realization than ever before. The future of this country and the peace of the world depend upon the babies of today, and the better babies movement deserves the commendation of everyone.—Advt. for the Missoula Mercantile Co..... Gannon testified that he heard Vanlandingham say: "There's some more of your damn war stuff. The Boy Scout movement is English propaganda".... What I would like to say you would not be permitted to print. If the fellow that found the pocketbook kept the money, should read this story, I want him to know what I think of him is not fit to print.

Pauly had a new bitch bird dog, but he didn't think much of it. She was black and white, slinky, and pretty as a picture, but if Pauly so much as frowned at her, she ducked her tail between her legs and crept off in a corner to weep. It got so that Pauly couldn't stand the sight of her. Compared to Wolf, she was a sorry spectacle. It made Pauly sick to think of it.

Now that the peace had been signed by Austria and the Huns, the newspaper was full of the stories told by doughboys returned from the front. When Pauly was looking for the funnies, he often ran across such yarns. They were better than *Action Stories* and kept a boy informed about what went on.

So smile and the world smiles with you, but cry and you cry alone! "Whew!" the soldier exclaimed, as one of the shells burst close on the Archangel front. "Those Bolshy artillerymen sure can shoot!" he said. "But why don't they send us home now that the war is over?" He claimed they were not particularly excited by the Russian barishnas *(young girls, to you) and had a Yankee contempt for males who kissed each other in the streets and spoke a jaw-breaking language.*

...Cut another notch on the butt of his rifle.

Pauly had shot at the stars that night on Mount Jumbo the Missoula kids had been expecting the Butte kids to come up the mountain to disarrange the *M.H.S.* and fight. The Butte kids must have been too tired from the excitements of the track meet to show, for they never appeared at all.

Augie, Billy, Jake, and Stiff Sullivan were playing a fast game of blackjack in the card room of the Lucky Streak Athletic Club. It was too hot to be shooting basketball. Summer had come suddenly. Spring had but waved her hand and passed on.

Augie had come out of his last drinking bout with a sneer permanently plastered on his face. The distortion reminded Pauly, somehow, of Sullivan's chippy, who'd been kicked in the jaw by a horse. *During the course of the retreat, I saw a young fellow sitting at the side of the road. His nose was torn off. It seemed to me that I could see all the way to his belly button. I tell you it was horrible! At this moment, we were swamped in the counter-attack. I heard somebody yell: Gas! Taking no chances, we put on our gas masks as quickly as possible. Then came the new information: No gas! Fix bayonets and charge! In front of me, I saw six bodies distributed over the ground and three of them were entirely unrecognizable....* Pauly wondered whether this was the way that Norval had died?

Billy was dealing.

He was by far the best player in the club. Pauly was fascinated by the red-head's expert manipulation of the cards. Standing beside the wall, beyond the green glare of the light which was hung over the table, Pauly was content to be the observer. He had no hand for gambling and he didn't see any use in making a fool of himself.

Augie broke away from the table and lit a cigarette. Leaning against the drawn window blind that shut out the night, he turned to Sullivan.

"How's Sarah doin'?" he inquired, as he blinked the smoke out of his eyes and cocked his head to one side. "That your brand on the side of her face?" he laughed.

"You stumble bum! Why don't you wipe that slaphappy grin off your mouth and get wise to when you're well off?" Sullivan answered. He knew the Pastor's son was aching to put in his two cents, seeing as how he was still sore that his brother had got bumped across the pond.

"A horse kicked her once when she was chippyin' around a barn," Stiff Sullivan explained.

Augie grunted with distaste, dropped the butt of his tag to the floor, and ground it under the heel of his boot. Sarah had a good pair of legs, Augie considered, and she wasn't careful about how wide she spread them apart, neither! The Pastor's son was a little jealous of Sullivan's chippy.

Idly, Augie lifted the edge of the window blind and peered out into the night. Beneath the dark shadows of the trees, he saw a group of men advancing rapidly over the lawn.

"Cheese it!" Augie exclaimed. "The cops!"

With the Pastor's son leading the way, Billy, Jake and Stiff Sullivan beat it out through the stables, past the rabbitry, and climbed urgently through a window that let out on the ochre-fruited orchard of apple trees, and struck through the field at a dead run.

Pauly switched off the light.

And followed as fast as he could!

The cops completely busted up the joint. How they had learned about the gambling games being run at the Lucky Streak Athletic Club, Pauly was never to know. They didn't bother with the loft, where the basketball court was located, nor did they pay any attention to the pool table, but the faro and blackjack tables were broken and the chairs and benches were splintered like matchwood.

Pauly was scared to go home!

He shot a game of pool with Billy Toole at Kelly's Empress Cigar Rooms and, after that, he walked back slowly across the Higgins Avenue bridge, taking as much time as he could. As he approached the house on Kootenai Street, the bitch bird dog did an alligator crawl on its belly across the lawn. It was a hell of a note having a dog like that around! Wolf had been the only friend Pauly had ever counted on.

And Wolf was dead!

Pauly wondered whether he should run away from home? One thing was sure: Doctor would be sore as the devil about the gambling that had gone on in the barn. Since the cops had raided the place, it was inevitable that Doctor should know about everything that had gone on!

Doctor had never liked Pauly, anyway....

And he liked him less, now that William Tell was toddling around!

"Could it be possible, Mrs. Ohlmstead, that someone cared a great deal for you and poisoned your husband in his sleep?" the state's attorney asked. But Mrs. Ohlmstead was a sweet-faced, wholesome little woman who showed the great strain she had been under and was bravely hoping for the very best. Pauly knew that if the Doctor had found out about the gambling in the barn he'd beat his stepson's

pants off as soon as he got home! Pauly felt the approach of danger in his fingertips.

Like when Betty Darling came walking down the street and it looked as if she might pass him—

Or when Augie's tight snarl ripped the ribbons out of his ears—

Pauly was scared!

In the attic, the strap in Doctor's hand beat Pauly's bare behind. The lash leaped through the air to mingle with Pauly's cries. Anger flooded his eyeballs. He felt degraded, cheapened, and cheated of all he'd so hardly won—the partial respect of the kids, for instance, and the baskets he'd tossed in the Florence game. As Pauly's tears burned down his cheeks, he felt his hatred for Dr. Craddock growing by leaps and bounds. It had been Doctor who had taken Wolf and his other dogs from him. It had been his stepfather who'd taken his mother's love away from him. It was Doctor who'd taken him to a new house and left him a stranger therein! Crystal had no time for Pauly. Doctor and William Tell came first with her, it seemed to Pauly.

"I hope that teaches you a lesson," Doctor said.

Blinking the tears out of his anger, Pauly put on his pants, tightened the belt, walked down stairs and out of the house. He flushed with embarrassment and exasperation at the thought of the maid, who had peered at him surreptitiously from beneath the covert coverlet of her eyelids. Pauly convinced himself that he detested the maid's breasts, which bounced around like punching bags wherever she walked, and worried him half to death!

Like Stiff Sullivan would say, them boobies would be good for boxing gloves!

Remembering Betty Darling, Pauly hated her, too. The girl he'd loved for so many sleepless nights. In his imagination he saw her dark brown hair and mysterious eyes, white skin and quivering, sensitive lips.

Pauly wondered if he'd get hungry, once he was far along on the road? Brave in his paroxysm of anger, he decided to leave the house on Kootenai Street and go out into the world. He wondered whether his mother would miss him? He wondered if Betty Darling would note his absence at school when fall came around again?

He set out sturdily in the direction of Grass Valley.

The moon had arisen over the mountains, tipping Squaw Teat Peak with a silver glow that encircled the whole horizon. Passing over the plain, Pauly observed the clean, new shoots of grain coming out of the ground.

By the time he had reached Grass Valley, he began to grow tired. The muscles ached in his thighs and it felt as if his feet would break, his arches were hurting him so much. What would he eat, he wondered, once he was over the mountains and had left Missoula far behind?

It was colder, now, and Pauly's footsteps faltered with fear. As he hesitated on the road which stretched before him, he raised his quivering chin to stare at the lonely stars shining out of the sky. And then he collapsed on the rough brown sward of buffalo grass that line the edge of the highway, and sobbed aloud. In his tears, he thought of the night he'd spent on the side of Mount Jumbo, waiting for the Butte kids to show. He'd been brave that night, rolling cigarettes with one hand and blowing puffs of smoke into the dark to show how carefree he was. The encouraging, steel assurance of the pistol butt in his hand when he'd shot that bullet in the black and threatening night.

Pauly had wrapped his Mackinaw tightly about him and slept at an upright angle beside the fire. Until sunrise he'd stayed on the side of Mount Jumbo, but the Butte kids had never showed for the fight.

Now, there was nowhere Pauly could travel except into darkness. The world was before him! He hoped that he was brave enough, strong enough, to meet any blow. But it was cold without his Mackinaw. Summer was no proof against the bitter winds that blew from the mountains when night was abroad. The moon was too pale to lend its light to lead him over the pathway he must go!

Pauly wondered whether he was being punished by God? For stealing the .22 pistol from the hardware store where he worked! He'd made his peace with his conscience on that five dollars the soldier had given him for drinks. But maybe God was telling him off on the other things he'd stolen?

Pauly, imaginatively, carried his escape from the past to its logical conclusion. He saw his mother hovering above his coffin. Bleak with a dead sorrow upon his face, he was stretched out in death, with his dark eyelids limp with forgetfulness. Like Honey Pie Buchard, he had been born, had lived a few years, and died. Perhaps, even Doctor's eyes might suffer from remorse! Even Betty might be sorry she had neglected him.

Without his Mackinaw, he felt he might freeze to death!

Pauly returned wearily to the house on Kootenai Street.

As he crossed the sidewalk in front of Doctor's home, the black and white bird dog came slinking around the porch. Pauly continued through the storm of his sorrow across the lawn that paved the way to the barn. Having reached the loft, he locked the trapdoor behind him, and swung up through the rafters and out into the small tower that straddled the barn's roof.

Curling himself up like a bird dog, he went to sleep in the tiny attic beneath the weathervane that pointed the cry of the wind.

Chapter 30
The Blacklist in Butte

†††

In his address at the Mooney Mass Meeting, W. Dunne declared the dynamiting of the pay office a ruse on the part of the Anaconda company to cast odium on the One Big Union convention, now in session.... The bastille, the stockade, prison farm No. 2, and St. Ann's Hotel, also known as the brig, were the places named by the witnesses as the scenes of the alleged cruelty which were said to have extended over several months in 1918.... The section from which the Ninety-First Division took its battle cry—"Powder River, Let'r buck!"—has not been scratched by religion, stated Rev. Lingenfelter.

When Mike Sullivan returned to Butte from France, it was a different strike that was going on, but the same story. *Because the Electricians' Union had struck, the street cars would not be operated until the electricians resumed their labors, J. R. Wharton, manager of the Butte Electric Railway, announced last night.* Mike Sullivan worried about where he would get drinks now that war-time prohibition had come into effect.

At Billings, on his way home, Mike had bought a couple of the Butte and Anaconda papers. He'd loaded himself up on information pertinent to the times. He learned that *Miss Wicklund, for one year head nurse in charge of the army hospital at Etaples, was visiting her sister in Missoula. The steamer* Klondike, *however, boasted a passenger capacity of four hundred and a dining service. Left Polson three p.m., crossed Flathead Lake going in a northerly direction, and arrived at Somers at five p.m.*

Mike Sullivan turned to the magazine section of the Anaconda paper and began reading an article on the history of drink. *Egypt made beer in the fourteenth century. On the other hand, Noah is said to have been the first drunk. Bone-dry nation was first sought by ancient Chinese. King Wen ordered wine to be used only in connection with sacrificial rites, but the priests got drunk as hoot owls, and turned to opium....*

Mike swung off the rear platform of the observation car at Butte, and walked uptown on Utah Avenue. It was a quiet day, even for Sunday, and most of the saloons appeared to be closed. Mike wondered whether or not he'd find Bill Dunne at the church where the Wobbly newspaper was brought out. Not having heard from Bill for some time, Mike wondered how Dunne's trial for sedition had come out. Sullivan chuckled in his beard as he crossed Galena Street. A guy on the street corner was stewed to the eyeballs! It looked like Uncle Sam had failed to clean up Butte. *"We were housed in the barn. I ran to the window and looked out. I don't think the raider was struck but, after dropping a few bombs, he departed; and we went to sleep," he said.*

On the brow of the hill in front of him, the spire looking bleak and lonely against the sky, Mike Sullivan could see the church with machine guns pointedly poking their noses over the edges of window sills. It looked like home to Mike. *"Gave all they had! And now we are giving all we have, for it matters not when we die nor where; but how is what counts," he said. "Then, as the Salvation Army*

*lassies placed a small American flag on each of the hundreds of white
crosses stuck into the brown clay, a song leader stepped out in front
of the crowd. 'Sing it, boys, sing it!' he said."*

It was good to be back!

Mike Sullivan gripped Bill's hand as if it were a life-line.

"Well, Mike! You saw the show, but did you pay the price of
admission?" Bill Dunne asked.

"Those Germans didn't have my address!" Mike Sullivan,
laughed.

*"Scarcely had he finished, when the Hun shells began falling
among the graves. He was unsuccessful in accomplishing his mission,
but killed several of the Salvation Army girls in the process. Near me,
an orderly fell, frightfully wounded. We fixed him up as best we could
and placed him on a stretcher. Shouted in broken English: 'Go after
'em, boys! I'll be back soon and we'll beat the Kaiser in his own back
yard!' A few minutes later he was dead."*

"By the time we got over, the French had shot some of their
own officers," Mike Sullivan explained.

"So you learned your lesson. Now what?" Bill Dunne asked.

Mike sat down on an apple crate in front of a typewriter that
used to be his.

"You know you're blacklisted?" Bill Dunne said. Mike pulled
a cigarette out of his pocket, lit it, and stared moodily at the floor.
If you fought for unions you got it in the neck. The workers give it
to the corporations and the companies returned it with interest.
But the boys out in front were the fellows that got it the worst.
That was the reason the company had stopped bringing over the
Irish to work in the mines. Billed from Galway straight to the
shift boss with whom they were supposed to work. But the A.C.M.
had stopped that soon enough! If an American died in the mine,
it cost the company plenty. But it took only seventy-five dollars
to buy a foreigner his grave. That was the trouble with the Irish.

The micks became citizens as soon as they hit!

Mike Sullivan looked up at Dunne, who was pointing toward a couple of thugs that were climbing the stairs to the church. One of them was carrying a suitcase.

Bill Dunne turned to Mike Sullivan. "Them punks are up to no good, to my way of thinking!" he said.

Sullivan picked up the revolver Bill always had lying alongside the typewriter. The gat felt familiar in his big fist. It was like old times. You killed a guy in Butte, it was self-defense, and you could be damn sure it was the right guy you was killing and not like over in France. Plenty of them Germans deserved what they got, but what had the workers to do with it?

It was good to be back!

The mug who was carrying the suitcase walked into the room, dropped his luggage on the floor, and turned around to see if the other guy was strategically located to make their getaway safe.

"Well, speak your piece!" Bill Dunne said to the fellow with the suitcase. "You gotta piece to speak, ain't you?" he asked.

This guy was a tall hombre and it took him considerable time to lean down and open his luggage.

Mike Sullivan's eyes popped wide with surprise, the bag was so stuffed with greenbacks.

"This is for Dunne," the guy with the suitcase said. "If he clears out of town!"

Bill Dunne walked over to the suitcase crammed with greenbacks and kicked it down the stairs. The bag skidded from step to step, hit the sidewalk, and spread the green grass of the money all over the pavement.

"All right, you guys! Peddle your papers," Bill Dunne said.

Mike Sullivan and Bill Dunne walked down Galena Street and entered the Blackjack Dugout to get a drink.

"What'll you have?" Bill asked.

"Short beer," Mike answered.

"Your wife know you're married?" the bartender wise-cracked. "No beer here since Prohibition came in."

"Whatever you got," Mike Sullivan agreed, affably.

The bartender lifted the pitcher of whiskey and poured out a couple of stiff jolts.

"Water for chaser or straight?" he said.

The times were certainly changing fast! Sullivan thought. *Booze: Confidentially, you boys who have a little private stock of wet goods had better slip around to our office and take out some burglary insurance. Nuff said!*

Bill Dunne was amused. So Mike had gone over to see the fun! If he'd had any sense, he'd have stayed at home. The real war was going on in Butte. That stuff in the Argonne had been a sideshow. *Big Bill Haywood, militant I.W.W. leader, wrote of Butte as he remembered it: There was no verdure of any kind; it had all been killed by the fumes and smoke of the burning ore. The noxious gases came from the sulphur that was allowed to burn out the ore before it was sent to the smelter. It was so poisonous that it not only killed trees, shrubs, grass, and flowers, but cats and dogs could not live in the city of Butte. Housewives complained that the fumes settling on the clothes rotted the fibre.... The city of the dead, mostly young miners, was almost as large as the living population....*

"I'll take mine straight!" Mike Sullivan said.

Bill ordered another round.

He didn't know what the hell to do with Mike, now that he was back. Bill was used to pounding his own typewriter by this time. No need for a stenographer these days, but Bill Dunne knew that Mike was blacklisted at the mines. Something would have to be done for him. But what? *The mayor accused the Wobblies of taking pay and instructions from German agents. Another strike followed, and on August 21st, two men were killed and nineteen wounded when company gunmen fired into a picket line in front of the Anaconda plant. Martial law remained in force for some time. Breaking into the sick-room of Frank Little, bed-ridden I.W.W. organizer, they forced him to the street. Tying him to the rear bumper of an automobile, they dragged him through the streets of the city. 3-7-77 indicated the dimensions of the burial pit. In spite of this, however, they left him hanging in mid-air from a railroad trestle.*

Mike should have stayed around where his fighting would have done some good! Bill Dunne drank his whiskey and wiped his mouth with the back of his hand.

"You know what would've happened if I'd taken that money and tried to clear town?" Bill Dunne said.

"Yeh, I know!" Mike answered. "They'd have stopped you on your way out, claimin' you dynamited the pay office of the A.C.M.! All the same, them was a helluva lot of green babies."

After the One Big Union convention, Bill Dunne walked home, with Mike beside him.

What the hell to do with the guy? Mike had wanted to see the fun. And when he came back, what happened? He was blacklisted at the mines!

"I tell you what!" Bill Dunne suggested, taking Mike by the arm. "How about standing guard at the church nights, so's my wife can get some sleep?"

The streetlamps blinked bleakly through the grimed and smokey air of Butte. Bill Dunne tossed in his sleep. Behind the machine gun that poked its snout over the edge of the window sill, Mike Sullivan crouched like a periscope.

Them babies come closer, he'd cut down on the trigger!

Chapter 31
Lonely Takes to Tea

Sheriff O'Rourke and his deputies today seized what federal officials claim to be the first mountain still, eight miles southwest of Butte.... Christendom's bristling guns, and the cry for peace which religious teachers filled the world before the great war in 1914, is a striking paradox, and an unfailing sign that the end of the world is at hand.... According to witnesses, he got flip with the young woman. Only one remark did he make. The next moment she struck him in the face with a soda bottle.

It wasn't that Pauly was scared when the cockcrow of morning bent the weathervane to its golden will. Under the attic of the tower that straddled the ridge of the barn's roof, he felt warm and comfortable. His tears had dried like freckles upon his face. Rubbing the sleep out of his eyes, he stretched as best he could in such a restricted space. He wondered if the maid would be up and around the house? The more he thought about it the more likely it appeared that she would be in bed. The sun rose early in Montana summer skies. Even at four o'clock in the morning the east was grey! Pauly wondered if he'd been sissy to sleep in the barn behind the house?

In the sunshine of a new day, Pauly was reconsidering the decision he had made. If because of Doctor, and the whipping he had received, he left the house on Kootenai Street as he had planned, he'd never get to see the Chautauqua when it came to town again. He wouldn't see the hootchy-kootchy dancers at the side-show when the circus came around. He wouldn't see the Stampedes. Nor Charlie Chaplin at the *Bijou*.

But what really decided Pauly to swallow his pride: the Lucky Streak Athletic Club would go up the chimney if he left his home behind!

And the rabbits would die....

And he'd never see Betty again.

And anyway, Pauly didn't look forward to the prospect of sleeping all alone on the hard, cold earth. In spite of Doctor, it was nice to sleep in a regular bed when the night came down!

Never again would Pauly desert his affection for Betty or talk to her mean out of spite! It was enough for him that she walked the streets of Missoula and went to the same school.

And slept in the same town all night!

According to the theory upon which the sheriff was working, Lonely's liquor was being shipped to a small town east of Missoula, where it was unloaded, placed in a truck which had been rented for the occasion, and started on the last lap of its journey. For the reservation trade, they were bringing the liquor down now by way of Eureka. By boat from Kalispel to Polson was easy enough. From that point on, it was Lonely's lookout to see that business was good.

But it tickled hell out of Lonely, Betty's asking him about the girls in France! He chuckled about it as he watered some of the whiskey for his cheaper reservation trade.

He loaded the stuff into the new Buick. You had to have a fast car to elude the Feds. There weren't a helluva lot of them nosey guys in the woods, but it was better to take no chances! Even the local sheriffs were getting so's they packed shotguns.

But them French dames! *My dearest, darling Wanda: I am lonesome for the girl I left behind me. Now, my dear, in regard to my taking up with some of the girls over here. There's nothing to it. I never have been with another girl since I left you—I have been true and always will be. I don't think much of the French girls, anyway. Any young man is a darn fool who would take up with them. The good old U.S.A. has the best class of girls and I can see no reason for loving a French girl. If I was to stay here twenty years, I would never be seen with one. Dear, I love you so—I am your true and loving kid!*

Corporal F.B.T.

Lonely's car shot like a bolt of lightning through the blue darkness of the Flathead Valley. Luminous in its majestic loneliness, the Mission Range loomed to the left of his passage. Snowcapped, the imperious crags rose to the sky, unconquered, ragged and wild. Lonely's first stop was at Ronan. He skirted the edge of town and pulled up behind a ramshackle cabin. Jumping over the side of the car, Lonely made his way to the cabin's front door, knocked softly, and listened, ready to run at any disquieting sound. But all was as usual. A breed came out of the cabin and walked to the car with Lonely to help unpack some stock.

Lonely left the watered liquor at the cabin on the outskirts of Ronan. The breed carried it back into the house, and closed the door.

Imagine the gall of that guy, she told the court. Writes he'd never be seen with a French dame. And, then, comes back a wife!

Lonely chuckled with quiet amusement at the recollection of this news item. He should've clipped that one out and mailed it to Sis. As he drove rapidly through the blue night on his way to Ravalli, he turned the French girls over in his mind. The main thing he had against the Frogs—they couldn't get the wrinkles out of their legs. No matter what stockings they wore! He decided the French dames were sloppy and let it go at that. But as for telling Sis what he knew about France!

Sis would have to read the newspapers.

Lonely was keeping what he knew to himself.

It was a good thing that he had a fast car. The roads were rough, but he was burning them up with his passage. The Buick was riding swift and easy. East of Ravalli, Lonely switched into a narrow, winding roadway, and struck out toward a booze cabin in the hills. The Indians knew about the place, but none of the cops were wise. It was safe enough out there, unless some sheriff had run into the joint by accident while out on a fishing trip. Nevertheless, Lonely examined each side of the road as he drove slowly over the plain. He was taking no chances of being cut off by an ambush. If a posse appeared ahead of him, he'd pull around fast and light back down the way he had come. His bumpers were heavy enough to bust any hasty barricade, and he had plenty of guns in the car!

In the war, Lonely had become quite handy with the artillery.

It was a dark night. To the west, however, Lonely could see a faint line of fire along the foothills of the Cabinet Range. This August had been the worst time for forest fires since the summer of 1910. Lonely could smell the dry earth in his nostrils. A cloud of dust deepened the night behind him as he drove the Buick into the foothills.

Lifting a stick of tea out of his breast-pocket, Lonely lit it and narrowed his eyes with pleasure as he inhaled. These days, the forest-fire fighters used gas masks brought back from France, now that the war was over.

It was OK by Lonely!

Marijuana made you float on flame and Lonely liked it better than any smoke he'd ever known. He stopped the car just outside the entrance to a small canyon that led into the mountains.

Lonely wasn't going to be caught in no place he couldn't turn around in a hurry!

The shadow of a man rose up behind a bush and walked carefully over to where Lonely was waiting.

As silently as he had come, the shadow faded into the darkness, but he carried a box of bottles away with him.

Lonely drew the marijuana smoke deeply into his veins, climbed into the car, and turned about.

Arlee came next.

And, then, Missoula!

Lonely drove back down the winding road as rapidly as he could. The N.P. carmen were on strike in Missoula, so Lonely imagined most of the town's cops would be hanging around the shops. It should be easy tonight, slipping into the city unobserved. At least, Lonely hoped it would.

Lonely drove silently down through Front Street and parked the car in a garage beside the Bucket of Blood. He sat down at a table in the back room. He'd invited Bud Bailey in from the bar. The kid looked kind of sappy to Lonely. Either the drinks had been going to Bailey's head or Bud was slaphappy from the punch in the head Joe Vuckovich'd give him in the yards.

"What's eatin' you?" Lonely asked. "You look weepy, no foolin', you look weepy, for sure."

"My thinker's been actin' up," Bud answered. "I got pains in the head."

"I got something'll fix that," Lonely suggested.

Bud Bailey was willing to try anything once. Even a shot in the arm. He didn't see how it could hurt him. Any case, his head had been going around in circles. Ever since that yard bull had beat him up, he got dizzy spells and felt faint. That was the reason he couldn't run in the track meets no more. Why he'd quit school, as a matter of fact. No use trying to study when you got aches in the head!

If this stuff Lonely was giving him did any good.

"You need more, there's plenty where this came from," Lonely said.

Chapter 32
Stiff Gets Burned

†††

Put up or shut up! Wilson tells critics. Throws gauntlet before Peace Treaty opponents.... Gus Peters of Camas Hot Springs, familiarly known to most people as "The Hobo Kid," has returned home after an absence of four years.... After drinking a quantity of moonshine, James Richards died in agony outside a lonely cabin in the hills near Yellowstone last Thursday.

Doctor became more friendly, it seemed to Pauly, as the fall came on apace. Mother must have put in a good word for him. Mother must have realized that a boy's life was unhappy at best. Doctor had invited Pauly to come up to the Lolo ranch to watch a duck hunt.

Long before daybreak, Pauly was out of bed. He was taking the bitch bird dog along to see whether she was any good with ducks. The ride up to Lolo took no time at all. Before the sun had come over the Sapphire Mountains, Doctor braked the car in front of the big grey house in which his brother had died, and they all walked down through the meadow and over to the swamp.

Wading out into the cold water of the slough, George Baggs and Doctor hid themselves from view behind some cat-tails, and waited for the ducks to show. They wore rubber boots that encased their legs and thighs, but Pauly, who was not so fortunately clothed, poled a scow over to a little knoll of high ground, which cropped out of the water lilies, and sat down.

In a whisper, George Baggs was discussing politics. This fellow should be elected! Mr. Baggs advised. Among the younger generation of public men in Montana, this fellow was the best! according to Mr. Baggs. During the war, this chap had prosecuted and convicted more than a dozen seditionists, among whom were Smith and Dunne of the *Butte Daily Bulletin*, the Red sheet that had caused all the trouble. Lawbreakers of all kinds had gone down before this fellow George Baggs was rooting for. Among other things, he'd cleaned out Wood Street, known from the earliest territorial days as one of the worst vice districts in all of the West.

Mr. Baggs wanted this fellow elected.

Some mallard and teal flew in a bevy over the slough.

Doctor raised his Winchester Repeating Pump Action Twelve Gauge shotgun, firing twice.

Bang! went Mr. Baggs' single action.

Four birds fluttered slowly through the morning mist and the water, in little junkets of anticipation, rose to receive them whose wounded wings would tangle the lilies of the swamp. The fish paused in their slippery slither, popping their eyes, with their fins confounded.

Cringing beneath the tents of her ears, the bird dog whimpered with fright.

Rowing the scow across the yellow September water, Doctor transported Pauly, George, and the ducks to the meadow's shore. The bird dog could look out for himself. Doctor congratulated himself upon his fine shooting. There'd be plenty of ducks for dinner this week!

Augie Storm hated Stiff Sullivan.

The mick's cousin was in the pen for sedition. And now that Stiff's uncle was back in Butte, and Stiff was bragging about it, there was no putting up with the son-of-a-bitch. But Augie wasn't fighting Sullivan—not yet, he wasn't! Augie thought bitterly of the bright red, raspberry cheeks of Norval Storm—the brother who would have put Stiff Sullivan in his place!

Augie, punting the pigskin down the field, cut his cleats into the frosty ground.

There wasn't anything good Augie had to say about Sullivan. Consequently, the Pastor's son was pleased when Sarah put the mick on the sick list. Sullivan would be playing no football this season. The coach wouldn't have it. Stiff was too valuable a quarterback, a triple threat, and the coach was taking no chances of burning him out. Gleefully, Augie thought of that little chippy, Sarah, who had caused all the trouble.

Some day he'd have to give Sarah a present.

Something nice!

After football practice, Augie shadowboxed around in the bathroom while getting ready to take a shave. *Benjamin Franklin's brain—like his razor blade—was a thing of exquisite balance. By stropping his mind on other men's brains, he always kept Fresh-Edged!* Augie sliced the soft peach-like fuzz on his face and wiped the lather out of his ears.

"Ma!" he yelled. "Where's that Idaho football jersey I been wearin' lately?"

Mrs. Storm scurried up the stairs as fast as she could.

Now that Norval was laid away in the family album, and memoried on the fly-leaf of the Holy Bible, the Pastor's wife ran to fulfil Augie's every whim.

"Yes, Augie! I'm coming," Mrs. Storm answered, as she flew up the stairs.

Pauly decided to take his life in his hands and ask Doctor to invite the Darlings for a trip up the Bitterroot. "We could ask the Roberts, too!" he suggested. "That way, there'd be two cars." Fortunately, mother put in a good word. Pauly was afraid of Doctor, with his long cigar like a pea-shooter in his mouth, and the smell of the hospital on his clothes. Pauly would never get to know Betty if things went on the way they had been! He was afraid to approach her all by himself.

So it was a good thing Doctor decided to help.

Driving up to Medicine Hot Springs, which was on the far side of Darby, Hutch, Betty, and Mr. Darling rode in Mrs. Roberts' car. Doctor drove Pauly, Crystal, and William Tell in the Cadillac. Up past the Lolo ranch, beyond Florence, Victor, Hamilton, and Darby, they sped. They followed in reverse order the route of Lewis and Clark. To the east, Pauly could see the deer-like flanks of the Sapphire Mountains. To the west, there were the high teeth of the Bitterroot Mountains, where forest fires were burning.

Darby was a small settlement of log cabins and frame buildings with false fronts. To the stores of Darby came prospectors from the hills. They tossed their poke on speakeasy bars and drank their liquor straight. Or so Pauly had heard.

As the two cars continued southward over the rocky road that led through the heavily forested mountains to Medicine Hot Springs, it began to grow dark.

Doctor pulled his car to a stop behind that of Mrs. Roberts' and everybody piled out. Ahead was the ramshackle, weatherbeaten hotel. To the right was the plunge. The steam from the hot-water mineral springs of the hills rose through cracks in the swimming-pool roof and merged into the general atmosphere of the dark.

Lights blinked vaguely through the misted windows that invited entrance out of the night....

Hutch Roberts bounced manfully up and down on the tip of the springboard. He pounded his chest and got ready to dive.

Pauly slipped into the pool like a question while Betty cut into the water as cleanly as a white fish, and as silent.

Pauly fought the waves away from his nose as his ears rang like saxophones sobbing the blues.

A Pretty Girl Is Like A Melody!

But how to catch her eye?

Stiff Sullivan walked disconsolately into Kelly's Empress Cigar Rooms and perched himself on a stool to watch some guys shooting a game of pool. That's what came from Sarah's chippying around!

Stiff Sullivan was burned.

Chapter 33
God Figures the War

:::

A great deal has been said about the change the war made in the soldiers, that they were more serious, more religiously inclined. But of all the men represented on that service flag not more than half a dozen have returned to this church after their military service was over.... The men complained about prison stockades and general conditions surrounding the American occupancy in Siberia. There were on board sixteen bodies of American troops killed in battle with the Bolsheviki.

Augie Storm had taken Stiff Sullivan's place as quarterback on the Missoula High School football team, which was playing the Helena eleven in a fine mist of early October snow. Tubby Ross, six axe-handles across the butt, was at center. Jake Sterling, tall and lean with a cadaverous look of determination, stood on ten-terhooks at right end.

14-19-21-2.

The famous double-back signal of the Missoula team!

The pigskin lifted from Tubby's chin, flew straight through Tubby's legs, and slammed into Augie's outstretched hands. Doubling back fast behind where the halfbacks had shifted to right end, Augie pivoted and faded ten feet into the rear.

The ball went sailing through a fine mist of snow, high into the afternoon air. Jake picked it out of the sky.

First down and ten to go!

On the bleachers, which were strange to him at a time like this, Stiff Sullivan cleared his throat, spit, and blew his nose. It was damn rough being benched this way! No chance of the team's beating Helena with Sullivan out of the play. Stiff turned around to see who was poking a shoe into Stiff Sullivan's behind. He discovered it was the little punk, Harold, who'd caused Freckles Ferguson, the boyhumping music teacher, to get canned.

Tubby Ross waded through a mass of arms and legs. He was like a locomotive crashing a tangle of trees, the branches and trunks exploding with that sharp lumberjack sound.

Third down and four to go!

Stiff Sullivan pivoted on his seat and slapped Harold into the aisle.

"You want more, just let me know!" Stiff Sullivan said.

Harold ducked under the bleachers and ran for dear life. He didn't like football, anyway. It was such a *brutal* game.

Stiff Sullivan was sore! No drinking. No running down to the Snowshed on Railroad Street or hanging around at the Bucket of Blood. At least, for some time to come. He wished to Jesus he'd never seen Sarah. He should have known better than to pick up with a chippy whose face had been caved in by a horse! Take Penny, for instance. Now, there was a girl! Safe and sanitary.

Augie punted out of danger.

The game was nearing the end of the second half.

The Reverend August Storm, wrapped warmly in a white Hudson Bay blanket, four beaver, sat proudly in a box reserved to himself alone. He was delighted with his son's generalship on the football field that fine October afternoon. But the war had been a trial to the Pastor. He thought of his friend, the minister, from Anaconda. Visiting in Missoula, he'd made a splendid sermon about the war. He admitted that swearing was prevalent among soldiers, but was happy to relate that, aside from his bedroll having been taken when he was a chaplain over in France, he'd seen no stealing to speak of. It was the vile language he wished to complain of. Nothing more!

The Helena halfback, Sweeney, broke away and cut out into a stretch of open-field running. The Pastor sprang out of his chair and gripped the railing in front of him. But Augie lifted his feet from the ground behind him and dived like a swan to clip the legs of the Helena halfback as clean as a bird clinches a worm with its beak.

Pastor sat down.

Pauly peered out of the corner of his eye to see if Betty was watching him. Over the heads of the crowd, Pauly could see the sturdy shoulders of Stiff Sullivan. Dr. Craddock's stepson hoped that Stiff would be able to go a few games with the Lucky Streaks. He ought to be better by that time, and Pauly had arranged for some basketball frays with Arlee, Darby, and Thompson Falls.

Pastor was proud of his son!

The Reverend August Storm shifted in his chair, and considered the sermon he'd deliver the following morning. He'd tell his congregation the story his friend, the minister, from Stevensville had told him.

Jake Sterling pole-vaulted into the sky, intercepting a short pass on its interrupted flight to Archambault, Helena left end, and struck out as fast as he could, completing one leg of his voyage. He hit the ground's cold slush face downward and came up spitting teeth through a set grin of ferocity.

First down and ten to go!

The Reverend August Storm looked back up the field to see what Augie'd been doing. Well, you couldn't expect your son to be a hero all the time, Pastor considered. As his son said: No use playing the grandstand or the coach would throw him off of the field.

By paying so much attention to Betty, out of the corner of his eye, Pauly had missed some of the play. At this moment, the banker's daughter, with the snow like a prayer on the soft hood of her hair, turned her head and looked straight through him.

Pauly felt weak!

His blood burned in a swift retreat, leaving his face white and his lips faint.

The Reverend Storm hoped Augie would win!

For it was getting late. But God moved in a leisurely sort of way His Wonders to perform. *On the other hand, they do not have the sanitary conveniences in France that we have over here. In fact, they are a great people. Otherwise, how could they have built their cathedrals? the minister from Stevensville asked.* The timekeeper gripped the pistol as if it were a chain that would flush the people out of the bleachers. The game had lasted too long, as it was, in weather so cold.

Augie stiff-armed McGinley, Helena fullback, and started out over a broken field. The Pastor's heart caught in his throat, he bit his lips to keep himself together, and he leaped from his seat. Like a hare beaten out of cover and with thunder in his ears, Augie raced in the slim, sweet color of the wind.... But he didn't get far—Sweeney, the Helena halfback, laced his fingers around one driving ankle, and Augie hit the slush.

The pistol cracked like a blacksnake whip.

The game was over!

Score: 0 to 0.

Stiff Sullivan looked sourly at the *M.H.S.* on Mount Jumbo, which was spotted with patches of snow, and he turned on his heel and walked home.

Just after midnight, the high-school juniors painted their numerals conspicuously on the store window of the Greek's candy shop. An hour later, however, the senior clan assembled at this point and proceeded to transform the '21 into a '20, thereby, everyone would agree, establishing a great victory over their rivals!

Conscious of the fact that Betty Darling was right behind him, Pauly kept his face front. Self-consciously Dr. Craddock's stepson marched resolutely through the slush of October snow, careful to avoid spattering his new rust-colored suit with mud.

Russet was a good color for autumn!

Pauly hoped that Betty was properly impressed with his good taste. But he'd certainly failed on that trip to Medicine Hot Springs! Not once had he spoken to the banker's daughter. The words just wouldn't come out. What made it more difficult, girls were bothering him more and more. And there was nothing he could do about it. He couldn't follow in Augie's footsteps. He couldn't pick up with a chippy like Sarah, the way Stiff Sullivan had. Crystal had said to Pauly: *If you take a drink you're a drunkard!*

If you kiss a girl, you'll get sick.

But horribly! Malformed, and rotting away like a whisper!

The constant fears that Pauly faced made a nightmare of his days and nights. His terror that Doctor might beat him again, his dread that Augie or Stiff Sullivan might call him a sissy and kick him around, the trembling that tore at his teeth whenever Betty Darling came walking down the street! Out of whiskey, breasts of women, and beer, he constructed nightmares.

If God should strike him.

He'd stolen a .22 pistol out of the hardware store!

Pauly told himself that he didn't believe in God. So how could God strike him? Even mother was kind of tentative in her references to the Lord. Yet, there was no use taking chances!

Arriving at the house, Pauly could smell the ecstasy of broiled elk steak floating out of the kitchen window. Doctor had killed a big bull whose six-pronged antlers had a spread of five and a half feet.

Elk meat was wild!

Wild as Calamity Jane come walking around the mountain, her biceps like Big Berthas, she was so strong.

Betty Darling had walked by Pauly, without a word. As the melancholy years that pass like brant[1] into the sunset!

Pauly was sad.

---

1   A small goose with a mainly black head and neck.

Chapter 34
The Kill

░░

The man who was lynched at Centralia Tuesday has been identified as Ernest Everetts.... Prosecuting Attorney Allen announced that D. Lamb, sixteen years old, who was arrested as an I.W.W., confessed to belonging to the radical organization.... That the thugs of the lumber trust were hiding behind the uniform and the name of the American Legion in Centralia, no one can doubt who is familiar with the conditions on the coast.... Sweden declares the fall of Petrograd certain within short time. Red Cross preparing to step in for relief work as soon as possible.

It was Armistice Day in the year 1919.

The worst blizzard in years had descended upon Missoula. Heavy snow drove on the vicious velocity of high winds down through Hellgate Canyon and the thin memory of Lover Lemire and Betty Darling there. The railways fought the storm with every locomotive and fireman at their command. *Delayed further to the east, N. P. train No. 3 arrived two hours late, while train No. 1, due at 12:25 a.m. reported three and one-half hours late at Logan.*

Gassed and wounded, awarded the Croix de Guerre, the ghosts of Missoula soldiers paraded down Higgins Avenue through the blinding snow. The blare of hidden trumpets reverberated even unto the heavily laden limbs of larch, spruce, and alder upon the mountains. The thin whine of undecorous clarinets cut through the canyons and the drumbeat of the clouds caught their columns unawares, who had fought with such devotion, over and under the hallowed soil of France, whose bruised and bitten cheekbones were death-bare and vacant.

The wind rattled their skeletons like drumsticks!

Mr. George Baggs, official of the Anaconda Copper Mining Company at Bonner, was reading the newspaper with considerable difficulty, but with considerable pride:

President Wilson today set Thursday, November 27, as Thanksgiving Day, in a proclamation which says the country looked forward "with significance to the dawn of an era where the sacrifices of the nations will find recompense in a world at peace."

Mr. Baggs stayed inside the house on Armistice Day.

The streets outside were cold.

The day following the blizzard, Stiff Sullivan returned from a visit with Uncle Mike. Hell was popping in Butte. Out on bail, Bill Dunne was working day and night on the *Butte Daily Bulletin*, and with the workers, trying to meet hysteria calmly, trying to keep his eye on the facts. *Nevertheless, anarchy threatens the bloody annihilation of private property throughout the world! Religion, the opium of the people, man without God or master, described as beautiful ideal, stolen Soviet document held.*

Astounding revelations!

While Russia on the brink of madness....

Excitement radiated from Pig Alley. Here the news kids gathered to pick up their papers. Stiff Sullivan walked north from Front Street. He continued along Higgins Avenue until he reached the alley that led behind the newspaper plant. Billy Toole was waiting to get his bundle of the latest edition; and Augie, Lover, Pauly, Tubby, and Jake Sterling were horsing around. The Pastor's son strolled into the newspaper building and returned with a copy just off the press. *Ex-soldiers marching down the streets of Centralia shot by Wobblies. Entirely without warning, the I.W.W. laid down a barrage!*

Augie Storm felt the hot anger electric in his veins.

He'd make somebody pay for this! Augie would, whose brother had been killed on the fields of France. The Pastor's son was loyal to the Legion and proud of Norval's memory in the war. It was Stiff Sullivan's fault! Stiff Sullivan, who'd never renounced his Red uncle in Butte; who never apologized for his cousin in prison; who'd taken money to beat up scabs that were helping the country to arm. It was people like Stiff Sullivan who had killed the ex-soldiers in Centralia! Stiff Sullivan should pay for this.

If Augie were only strong enough, wary with his eyes, fast with his fists, bitter of heart enough.... *At this moment, one of the bullets struck the legionnaire in the neck. "They got me this time!" he yelled, as he grappled with the ground. More I.W.W. fired as the ex-soldiers advanced over No Man's Land, contesting every inch of the terrible terrain. George Stevens, another member of the crowd, kicked the guy's teeth in. According to this report, they took the Wobbly just outside the city limits, disfiguring his groin, which several of the legionnaires split up for souvenirs.*

Augie bit his tongue so hard that it bled!

If he could only bash Stiff Sullivan's brains out and smash them like a pink watermelon all over the street! But the mick was too mean for the Pastor's son to take on at this time. Any guy Sullivan tangled with got mangled like in a machine! *So what can we say of these men? Murderers of a type so revolting, pure horror is no name for it! Consideredly, I say that this massacre should mark the end of the Wobblies in this land. If there exists so much as a remnant of sympathy for them, henceforth a lunatic asylum is the proper place for such sympathizers.* Augie went the whole hog on that. He'd like to see Sullivan in the bug house, out of his life!

Billy picked up his bundle of papers, folding the sheet he'd been reading for headlines under his arm.

"Wuxtry! Wuxtry!"

"Read all about it!"

Posses hunting I.W.W. fire upon each other in the dark. "Read all about it!" Billy scurried down Pig Alley, skidded around the corner onto Higgins Avenue, and headed up the street.

"Wuxtry!"

Billy's voice grew faint in the distance.

Other kids mounted on their bicycles or trudged off through the snow. Bud Bailey, however, moved in a fog. He was practically out on his feet! Ever since he'd started using the stuff Lonely had given him, his eyes bright and vague by turns, Bud Bailey had walked around in a daze. His tongue felt foolish in his mouth and his lips were dry. "Looks like the Sammees are still fighting the war!" Bud Bailey cracked, his laughter spidery in the thin air.

Stiff Sullivan didn't say anything. What went on in Centralia was none of his affair.

Inadvertently, in turning to leave, Stiff jostled Augie, who lost his balance and fell on the ground.

"Fer Chrissake, why don't yuh watch where your goin'?" the Pastor's son swore in exasperation.

"Shut your face or I'll bust your trap wide open!" Stiff Sullivan said.

Laughing, Bud Bailey turned to leave. He'd have to drop by the Snowshed to pick up some snow from Lonely.

"What's so funny?" Augie snarled, brushing off his shoulder. Bud tittered.

Augie, in two swift strides, swung Bailey around, and let him have it. A dark, bruised stain spread over the side of Bud's face. The Pastor's son whipped a handkerchief out of his hip pocket and wrapped it tightly around the knuckles of his right hand.

Bud, as if in a daze, lifted his fingers to the bruise on his cheek. "I didn't say nothin', did I?" he asked.

Augie eyed Bud Bailey, calmly. Pressing his advantage, he feinted with his left, cut over and down with his right on Bailey's nose. Collapsing flat on the pavement, with his arms outstretched, Bud bled brutally in the surprise of his broken face

Climbing groggily to his feet, he tasted strangely the blood that was flooding his under lip. It seemed as if he were coming out from beneath the coal dock. It was dark and Joe Vuckovich was beating his brains out.

Sturdily, Bud Bailey leaned against the flying formation of Augie's fists. The ribs recoiled into the belly, and it felt as though they were sticking out of his back.

Like a jack-in-the-box, but each time more slowly, as if in some deep delirium, and the snow fading into darkness all around, Bud Bailey came up for air. Instinctively, he forwarded his fists to the front, his arms flapping up and down like the wings of a monkey.

Augie lifted a right uppercut from the ground that split Bud's jaw and splintered it like toothpicks.

Stiff Sullivan spit carefully in the general direction of a telephone pole, and blew his nose with his fingers. Unconscious, Bud Bailey bled quietly in the alley.

The blizzard that had drifted the streets of Missoula had stopped the street cars, but some sections were swept clean and blue as larkspur, bright and metallic as the iron railings of the Higgins Avenue bridge. In some places, the drifts were ten feet high! But over and under, to the full stentorian symphony of the storm, the ghosts of dead soldiers marched double-quick. Nor unkind word nor thoughtless gesture. Armistice Day had passed without delay, except for that disquieting mist of death, which floated through the alleys and by-ways of Missoula. As the storm let up, the ghosts of soldiers who had marched away to war so merrily with the scent of casual kisses on their lips—Vanished!

"You cheap pimp!" Stiff Sullivan said quietly.

Walking over to the prostrate and battered body that was Bud Bailey, death-like on the snow, Sullivan lifted the kid in his arms and strode westward toward St. Patrick's Hospital.

Bud Bailey would need some help.

"To the citizens of Missoula County, Mont.:

"Whereas, it has been rumored that some of the citizens of this community are preparing to take steps to prevent Mr. W. Dunne from speaking at the Union Hall on Sunday night, and

"Whereas, Mr. Dunne has been invited by the Missoula County Central Trades and Labor Council, A. F. of L., to speak on behalf of labor problems, therefore be it

"Resolved, that no such action be tolerated and every member of organized labor have pledged him their support through the central body; and be it

"Further resolved, that we ask the support of all law-abiding citizens to cooperate with us in this action."

(signed) "Missoula County Trades and Labor Council."

Aghast at what he had seen, Pauly walked home as the moon cut over the mountains. Through Hellgate Canyon, an N.P. train sped over the wind-swept track, whistling twice in the sadness of the mountains.

It twisted around the bend and disappeared.

Chapter 35
Redskins Bite the Dust

‡‡

Wheeler, W. Dunne, and Ford in their proselyting visits to Missoula have not failed in turn to publicly pay their respects to The Missoulian. *We are rather proud of their dislike for us. Otherwise, we would feel neglect of a duty to the people. Of the three, we have more respect for Dunne. Dunne is rough and self-conscious, but comes from the bottom and has had hard swimming against the currents of life. He fights in the open and we never heard that he was a grafter.... Claiming he fired three shots in the air to frighten three boys he found looking for coal in a fuel yard for which he is nightwatchman, M. F. Gill is in County jail held responsible for the death of Henry Patrick Green.*

Shop early! But sixteen days until Christmas! Better get that gift for Uncle Henry right now! Pauly bought a present for Mother and charged it to Doctor; and purchased a gift for Doctor and charged it to Mother.

Doctor and Mother were quite pleased!

The afternoon the Lucky Streaks left for Arlee, the sparkle of frost was bright on the ground.

Stiff, Pauly, Jake, Tubby, and Billy comprised the outfit that would play basketball with the Arlee Indians that evening. With Augie out of the running because of his broken knuckles—and Lover no good, anyway—the Lucky Streaks had been stumped for a substitute, until Stiff Sullivan thought of Abraham Lincoln McGinty, colored.

Because of the cold weather, Pauly was glad that he'd lifted so many jerseys from the various football teams that had visited Missoula! In one intercollegiate conspiracy, to keep him from freezing to death while beating his way on the N.P. train to Arlee, were the football jerseys of Gonzaga, Washington, Idaho, Utah, and Montana Aggies. And Pauly had ordered a turtle-neck orange sweater with two red service stripes on the left sleeve to denote the number of seasons he'd played with the Lucky Streaks. The front of the sweater would bear the initials *L. S.*, also in red. If the Missoula High School basketball team wouldn't give Pauly a sweater, he'd give one to himself! Stiff Sullivan kept warm with Whitman, Oregon, Wyoming, and a few high school sweaters.

Talk about Siberia! The weather was cold! Pauly's rabbits were dying fast, bleeding their life out through their ears.

Pauly thought the train would never reach Ravalli. His toes felt like rocks of ice in his shoes. Like the fellow was saying—*Free, that's Siberia! There is no country in the world with so much freedom as there is in Siberia. On the other hand, it must be admitted that the Russians are most hospitable people. Personally, they are likeable. Though they have little, they will give you everything they have.* The gale sweeping down from the cramped canyons of the cold was as free and easy as Pauly ever wanted to see it.

The people that liked Siberia could stay there! was the way Pauly saw it.

Tubby Ross did nothing but complain all the way to Arlee. The sweaters from Bozeman, Dillon, Butte, Billings, and North

Dakota couldn't possibly manage to keep him properly clothed. Tubby was so fat the jerseys jumped up around his neck like a goiter. If he'd thought to bring some weights along to hold them somewhere within hailing distance of his belly button—for safety pins just wouldn't do! As it was, Billy Toole's ears were aching from Tubby's complaints by the time the Lucky Streaks reached Arlee.

The Missoula kids jumped off the tender as the train slowed to the station, and they trudged off through the drifts of snow while Abraham Lincoln's teeth chattered. Stiff Sullivan led the way to a pool hall he knew about.

It was an hour or so before the game would begin. Sullivan lifted a cue from the rack on the wall and chalked its tip with vigor. Abraham Lincoln and Tubby were hugging the stove.

"How about a game?" Stiff asked Pauly.

Pauly felt flattered that Sullivan should treat him so well. Picking up a cue that was leaning against the table, he tested it by rolling in on the floor. It was straight and perfect. Pauly broke.

The two ball slopped into the left side-pocket.

Pauly shot twice and that was the end of his game.

Methodically, with rolled-up sleeves, Stiff Sullivan ran the rest of the balls right off the table.

He never scratched once!

"How about you, Billy?" Stiff Sullivan asked. "You want to play a game?"

After a small dinner in the local beanery, Stiff and the kids cut over to the barn in which the basketball game was to be played. Already, the sidelines were jammed with spectators. In one corner, a wood stove burned noisily, its belly a red glow of contentment. After the walk from the restaurant, the barn felt good to the Missoula kids, who sauntered into one of the back rooms to change into their basketball togs. Outside, the wind was rising to tug at the ice-clad crags and glaciers of the Mission Mountains.

Abraham Lincoln looked funny as hell, with his teeth chattering. Instead of warming up on the floor, Abraham Lincoln wanted to hug the stove, but Stiff Sullivan was against it.

"That shine get close to the stove, he'd be no good for the rest of the evening," Sullivan explained.

The referee held the ball at the center circle.

After Jake Sterling and Montgomery Ward Two Bellies had shaken hands, the referee blew his whistle, tossed the ball in the air between the two contending centers, and the game was on! Shouts and cheers rose rapturously to the roof, for the ball had been tipped by the Arlee center toward Tubby Ross and James Two Medicine Tail.

Tubby moved like a mountain under James Two Medicine Tail. The Indian's feet flew into the air and his flat hands slapped the floor.

Stiff Sullivan had the ball and was dribbling fast. Pivoting around Rides Pretty, he bounced it to Pauly.

Pauly, feinting at Oscar Other Medicine, dropped the ball to one side, caught it, and ducked it under one arm to Jake Sterling, who was coming rapidly down the center of the court. It was a good game. But Montgomery Ward Two Bellies was taller than any Salish Indian had a right to be. Reaching up one hand, he tipped the ball away from the Lucky Streak basket as soon as it hit the backboard.

Stiff Sullivan was sore!

Calling time out, he replaced Jake Sterling with Abraham Lincoln McGinty.

Abraham was high ebony!

He out-touched Montgomery Ward by a hand.

Billy Toole cut around fast, pivoting on one heel, and shot the ball to Pauly in a corner, who relayed it to Sullivan, who passed it to Abraham Lincoln, who was coming like a cannon ball down the middle of the floor. Score!

This shine was good!

Stiff Sullivan blew his nose through his fingers and wiped them on his pants. Foul! Tubby had moved under James Two Medicine Tail just once too often, for the referee was on.

Ben Long Ears recovered the ball as it banked from the board and bounced a long one to Rides Pretty, who was skirting the other end of the court.

Back and forth, so fast that the play seemed dizzier than the eye, but Pauly moved without consciousness, without fear. Ducking under Ben Long Ear's arm, he reached out a hand and cut the basketball short, bounced it to Stiff, and got clear, Stiff shot it back to him. Pauly tossed a basket from the center of the floor. The ball rose like a shapely swallow in flight, paused for one perilous moment in mid-air, and swished through the net.

The Indians on the sidelines started to howl.

It was the middle of the second period. Score: 10 to 9, Indians' favor.

The Arlee coach stopped the play just long enough to replace Oscar Other Medicine with Bull-Dog-Falls-Down-Too-Often.

And the game went on! The excitement and the perfect rapture of the play was stinging in Pauly's ears. Perhaps, because Augie wasn't there, or because Stiff Sullivan had spoken to him so nicely before that game of rotation—whatever the reason, Pauly's hands and feet were working together! Shot another basket from the side of the floor.

Out of bounds!

Bull-Dog-Falls-Down-Too-Often passed the basketball to Rides Pretty, who cantered behind center and swung it to James Two Medicine Tail, who lassoed it with his arms. Pausing in a scientific crouch, with his legs at the proper stance, he let the ball rise from his chest in an upward, free and easy motion. Montgomery Ward Two Bellies followed through nicely.

Score: 19 to 20 in favor of the Arlee Indians.

There were only a few moments left of the play. The referee took his time about tossing the ball up between centers. He was stalling for time. And the Indians on the sidelines were yelling fit to be tied!

The ball sky-rocketed into the air. Abraham Lincoln slammed a fast one towards Stiff Sullivan, who pivoted and dribbled cagily to one side, and bounced it to Billy Toole, who'd sneaked up from behind guard and under his own basket.

Pauly, in the meanwhile, had circled through center and was returning down the middle of the floor as fast as his legs would carry him! Billy shot from beneath the basket. Teetering crazily upon the rim of the iron rung, the ball slipped the wrong way. In spite of Rides Pretty blocking, Pauly leaped high, lifting the ball with one hand back to the board.

As it banked and swished through the net, the whistle beat the game to a period.

21 to 20.

And five more redskins bit the dust.

Pauly had won!

As the Lucky Streaks walked down to the railroad station, Stiff Sullivan glanced somewhat quizzically at Pauly Craig.

"Who Played Poker With Pocohontas?" Stiff Sullivan said.

Chapter 36
Dr. Craddock Passes Away

Government combs country for radicals. Most extensive roundup
ever attempted puts 3,896 behind bars. Federal Agents from coast to
coast are turned loose to hunt down those advocating overthrow of
American institutions.... All good Americans in Missoula should feel
like climbing to the top of Mount Sentinel and shouting thanks to the
heavens for the great round-up of the red revolutionists. Thousands
of these aliens were taken in every corner of the country and will be
deported as rapidly as possible.... Messages of New Year have opti-
mistic ring despite great unrest.

The day that Pauly started wearing his *L.S.* sweater around the
house, Doctor came down with pneumonia. Dr. Craddock had
been on a case at St. Ignatius. After attending to his patient, he'd
stopped in to see the Fathers at the mission, before starting the
long drive over the snow-covered road to Missoula.

In the Coriacan Defile, Dr. Craddock had had car trouble.
Climbing from under the wheel, he'd gone out in front and raised

the engine hood. It looked all right to Doctor. The only trouble was the engine wouldn't run. Doctor fooled with the ignition, monkeyed with the gas feed, and tried to crank the car. But the Cadillac wouldn't go. Fixing a man was one thing, fixing a car another. Doctor walked back to Evaro and got a man to come back with him and fix the car.

When Doctor returned to the house on Kootenai Street, Crystal put him to bed.

Doctor was sick!

Doctor lay flat on his back in a private room at St. Patrick's Hospital. Although it was almost three o'clock in the morning, Crystal and Pauly were standing on either side of his bed.

Dr. Craddock closed his eyes. Across the canvas of his eyelids passed the ragged soldiers he had seen as a boy. In the War Between the States. Westward from Missouri, he'd hopped a ride on a covered wagon, his rifle resting in the cautious crack of his arm. The years of trout-fishing and deer-hunting had been good! The Big Horn buckled in his stride as the rifle shot rang out in thin air. His antlers knuckled into the wind. Struck center, he slipped and fell, from crag to mountain slope, for fifteen hundred feet!

As the sky grew grey to the east, Doctor lifted his eyelids. "Bunch some pillows under my head," he asked.

Doctor closed his eyes again, but even this slight operation wearied him more than he had expected.

He wondered if Gil would be riding the pampas? These few short months he'd been married to Crystal! If only William were at his bedside! Doctor would never know what William Tell would grow up to be like.

As Doctor opened his eyes for the last time, the sun was rising over Hellgate Canyon. He lifted his right forearm from the bed, the hand hanging limply. It fell.

Pauly was stunned!

For Doctor was dead.

Bill Dunne was writing an editorial: *A union organizer walks into Missoula and is arrested because the A.C.M..... A friend comes to visit this organizer and he's arrested, too.... While at a recent farewell dinner party which was held at the Silver Bow Club in honor of Jack Rochambeau, a high official of the Montana Power Company, who is going to New York on a more important job.... Frank Little, jerked out of bed and carried down stairs in his nightshirt. In self-defense, shot from the windows of union headquarters in Centralia.*

And now another workingclass leader has been lynched: Wesley Everest!

Men who are proud of what they do work in broad daylight, Bill Dunne wrote.

But these men:

Frank Little and Wesley Everest

Are martyrs that the workers won't forget!

Bill Dunne got up from his typewriter and slammed on his hat. Descending the front steps of the church, he turned left at the sidewalk and continued down the hill.

Beside a garbage can in the alley, Bill Dunne paused to strike a match. After lighting his cigarette, he shoved his hat to the back of his head and knocked three times on the rear door of The Bar of Justice.

Mr. Gambetti opened the peep hole, looked out.

"Why, come right in, Mr. Dunne," Gambetti said. "Come right in!" And he opened up.

Standing at the bar, Bill Dunne drank three straight slugs of bootleg whiskey fast, and scowled. It was getting so's the West was no place for the workers! Maybe, after his appeal was decided, he'd go east....

It wasn't that Pauly was unfeeling! But that he was the victim of conflicting emotions. His mother was upstairs in her room, crying with those dry sobs that would tear the lungs right out of her body.

Numbly, Pauly sat down in the living room to think things out. In the parlor, Doctor's body was laid out in a seven-foot coffin, the grey face of him still in the twilight, his eyes closed. But Doctor in death looked very little like Honey Pie Buchard! *Walking over to the Cadillac, Pauly climbed under the steering wheel, stepped on the starter, and turned the car around—narrowly missing a steep embankment that fell away to the meadow below.*

As Pauly pulled the car to a stop, killing the engine. Doctor came tearing out of the farmhouse, his face white with concern.

But Doctor had his own sons, Arthur, who would be coming from California to cry on his father's grave, thinking that he should have written to him more often, remembering all those small but so important things Doctor had done for him! But as for Gil—Gil was working in Venezuela!

Gil would come back to Montana, perhaps, many years after his father had been buried. He'd walk down the streets of Missoula and turn into some bar he'd patronized before the War.

Hello! Jimmy, Gil would say. And one thing would lead to another. After about the third shot of rye, Doctor's oldest son would treat the bartender to a drink. Your mother know you're off the wagon? the bartender would crack. And from there, Gil would start talking about the time he'd been a bootlegger over at St. Regis.

Who'd you say your old man was? the bartender would ask.

Dr. Craddock. He used to have a ranch up at Lolo, Gil would explain.

Why, of course! the bartender would exclaim. I knew your old man well! He brought me into the world, did Dr. Craddock. Yessir! A fine old gentleman, I always used to say. Though, mind you, he was a stern one, was Doctor. Remember like it was yesterday. And Doctor says to me: Jimmy, he says, Jimmy! Just like that.

Jimmy! he says. You been drinkin' too much. Now, cut it out! Doctor would say.

Yes! Gil would muse, as he fingered his drink on the bar before him. Yes! Doctor was like that.

But Pauly didn't know what to feel. Should he be excited? Or scared, with death like this in the house. Or should he be glad that he'd get no more beatings, now that Doctor was gone? But of one thing Pauly was certain: Life would be less sure than it had been to this moment. What would happen to the house? And to the few rabbits that hadn't died off?

Crystal might not want to stay in the house, now that Doctor was laid out in the parlor!

Walking upstairs quietly, so as not to disturb his mother, Pauly slipped into his room and picked up the orange sweater with the red letters, *L.S.*, faced boldly upon it.

Drawing the sweater over his head, he tiptoed down the stairs and out the front door.

While Doctor lay like a nail in his coffin....

When Augie saw Pauly coming down the street, he nearly split his guts! Pauly sure looked funny with his sweater loud as a forest fire.

Chapter 37
Girls Leave Home

The efforts of some of the "intellectual" periodicals, such as The Nation *and* The Dial, *to create sympathy for the deported alien radicals are wholly misdirected and can result only in adding to further unrest.... "'What are the sirens shriekin' for?' said Percy Parlor-Red./ 'To speed the guest, to speed the guest,' the Loyal Native said./ 'For they're done with Bolshe Viki, an' his serpent breed must go./ The People, they are thinkin'—but thinkin' very slow!/ Ho! America must arm herself to fight an unclean foe!/ And be shippin' Bolsheviki every mornin'!'"*

Mr. Darling, the banker, had been worrying about the Reds so much that he'd gotten into a little difficulty. Naturally, he'd heard rumors. His son was up to no good! That much was certain. It was even buzzed about that some of the high-school kids were smoking marijuana.

Mr. Darling thought bitterly of his son! The banker knew that he was making Polson his headquarters, that he was running booze through the Flathead Valley, and that he would come to a bad end. *Attorney Vandeveer, however, at the close of Allen's statements, asked the prosecutor whether the state took the position that there was no attack on the I.W.W. hall before the shooting?*

And Betty wasn't looking any too well! the banker worried. *"In other words," said Vandeveer, "it is equivalent to a statement that there was no attack on the hall and the doors were not smashed in before there was any shooting?"*

"That's about it," the state's attorney said.

On account of the Reds, and Lonely, and Betty, it looked as if the banker would lose his bank....

Penny was going down the line.

As she packed her few belongings, her bright pajamas, her slippers and instruments, she wondered what the cribs would be like in Billings. *Oh, the days that used to be and how oft I've wished them back, as my thoughts go idly wandering o'er the well-remembered track!* Penny had worn out her usefulness in Missoula, it seemed.

Penny stuffed her bedroom wearing apparel into the suitcase and climbed into the only street dress she had to her name.

Poor Little Butterfly Is A Fly Gal Now!

Turning for one last look at the crib which had been her home, she walked slowly down the stairs. It was hardly like the one that mother used to make! Yet, she had lived there for a considerable period of time.

Reaching the sidewalk, Penny handed her suitcase to the driver. The sunlight almost blinded her—she'd not seen it for so long! The street looked strange in the glare of noon.

"All right, Tony," she said. "Where do we go from here?"

"Cowpunchers' round-up," Tony laughed. "Them guys is strong fer the broads."

As Tony gunned the car through Hellgate Canyon, Penny tried to remember some of the men she'd known in Missoula. If there had been but one face she could have isolated from the others, somehow, it would not have seemed so bad!

Penny sighed, for the good days were gone forever!

Tony sped through Milltown. Up the Blackfoot, Penny could see the erect gun of the refuse burner, poking at the sky. It was all she knew of Missoula!

But the country was pretty, she'd heard.

As Betty Darling walked down Higgins Avenue towards Front Street, and the Bucket of Blood, she saw Mrs. Storm drive by with Mrs. Craddock in the Pastor's car.

Betty entered the Bucket of Blood through the alley entrance. Walking over to Red Eye, the bartender, she asked him whether he'd seen Lonely lately.

"I hear he's been over in the Tobacco River country," Red Eye said, "but he oughta be here later this afternoon."

Sis carried a glass of whiskey over to the table in the corner of the room. She'd have to see Lonely.

But soon!

The bartender hadn't paid his dues since Prohibition, but he was worried about the Centralia business. *On the counter-march, shortly before the command to halt, he heard three shots and fired, apparently in self-defense. It did not knock him down, however, although he fell on his face as soon as his right foot hit the pavement. The bullets passed between him and the flag he was carrying, I think.*

Lonely opened the back door and walked into the saloon. Immediately upon entering, he caught sight of Sis sipping her liquor like it hurt her lips to drink.

Sensing Sis was in trouble, Lonely flipped the butt of his cigarette into the gobboon, walked over to the table, and sat down beside her.

"Spit it out!" Lonely said. "You're in trouble!"

Betty started to cry. If only Lonely would take her back with him to his house on Flathead Lake's blue shore. She wept as if her heart would break!

"All right! All right!" Lonely said. "Forget it!"

It was getting so's you couldn't trust nobody, it looked like. Helluva banker that couldn't even hold onto his own bank! And this was the guy who was gonna make his son cut out the drink. A screwball that had let his own daughter go wrong from loneliness in a big and empty house!

Lonely was through with his old man for good.

"Come on, Sis," Lonely said. "You and me's got a date with a guy I know in Polson."

Anissimow, Wolin, Serafimovitch, and O'Hara were in the Blackjack Dugout, in Butte, drinking. Since a falling beam had bashed in his old man's skull, Wolin was starting in at the mines tomorrow.

Wolin was stiff!

Chapter 38
The Showdown

██

The jury in the trial of ten alleged I.W.W. for the murder of Warren O. Grimm, Centralia Armistice Day Parade victim, brought in a verdict tonight, finding seven of the defendants guilty of murder in the second degree.... Our high-school lads held a mock convention the other night and through a coalition of Democrats and Socialists nominated Upton Sinclair for President. This will be great news to Lenin, who will probably cable W. Dunne to drop everything to start a Bolshevist kindergarten in Missoula.

In a nightmare, Pauly led his regiment into the trenches west of Fort Missoula. During the course of the winter, the battlefield had become somewhat cluttered up by storms. The first thing to do, of course, was to dig them deeper! Stiff, Lover, Jake, and the others went across No Man's Land to the Boche trenches. From where Pauly was standing, you could see their cautious eyes peeking over the sandbags. Augie snarled in a manner peculiar to modern warfare. Wrenching the .22 four-barrel revolver out of Pauly's hand, the Pastor's son whipped a handkerchief out of his hip-pocket and wrapped it tightly about the butt of the gun. Billy on one side and Bud Bailey on the other. Some of the Butte kids distributed themselves along the end of the trench. Anissimow, Serafimovitch, and Wolin. Spread Eagle Red Eyes and some of the Arlee Indians, this being a strictly patriotic affair, were over on the other side.

I didn't say nothin', did I? Bud Bailey quavered, as sixteen platoons of Colonials, including Dead Eye Dick and Charging Antelope Blue Thunder, came galloping over No Man's Land with Big Berthas in their fists.

Pauly turned over in bed, as he felt the full flavor of Betty's sweet mouth on his lips. This was the life for a soldier! The girls kissing the Sammees goodbye.

But it was completely wrong that Augie should be fighting on the same side as Pauly. The Pastor's son would have to stop laughing at him! Pauly had made up his mind.

Lay down the barrage! Augie commanded.

On all sides, you could hear the crack of bee-bee guns. Pauly shot high in the air, so that none of the Boche would be hurt, while the Butte kids on either side of No Man's Land heaved cobs and comported themselves generally as the Reds were expected to comport themselves. In night flying, however, each wing of the ship was lighted with a small electric bulb, which sprouted radiance like tulips all the length of the plane. The rudder was lit up, too, so that the machine could be seen from all angles. After reaching an altitude of about two thousand feet, sideslipped, Immelmanning,[1] and stalled—while the ship's lights chased themselves through the darkness!

Pauly, peering out through the periscope of his caution, saw Lover's face white as a ghost in death.

Fire! the Pastor's son commanded.

---

1 Performing an Immelmann turn, an aerobatic combat maneuver.

No, not that! Pauly screamed. Not that, please! he pleaded. For Augie had trained the pistol dead center on Lover's brain.

They should equip themselves with mud guards, he suggested. Then, gas masks and the usual armor should follow. You are instructed, said the court, that any person or persons has or have the right to defend himself, themselves, or their property from actual or threatened violence, and to that end to arm themselves, but the right does not go to the extent of stationing armed men in outside places for the purpose of shooting the persons, red or apparent, from whom force or violence is expected.

Pauly stood stock still in agony. As Augie pressed the trigger and fired, Pauly watched the bullet fly like a hornet, stinging Lover's eye.

Through the magic marvel of his clairvoyance, Pauly saw Lover's left eyeball, twisting like a snake in terrible pain, recoil and then pop out like an agate, to hang quizzical and cold at the end of a memory tied to Lover's brain.

Quietly, blood dripped out of the empty socket.

Spring had come out of the ground early. Already, up around Salmon and Seeley Lakes in the Blackfoot country, the high-priced automobiles of millionaires' sons were ushering in the excitement of summer. *When the warrant was handed to him charging him with the murder of McElfresh, fifteen years to life imprisonment, Elmer Davis laughed out loud, then began an I.W.W. song to the tune of* John Brown's Body, *the others joining in....*

Pauly picked up a baseball bat and walked over to Pastor Storm's residence. Hiding the weapon behind his back, he walked up to the front door and knocked.

The Pastor's wife answered. "Why, come in, Pauly, come in," she said. "We were just sitting down to dinner."

"No thanks," Pauly said grimly. "I come to see Augie about a matter."

"Nothin', ma, nothin' at all!" the Pastor's son answered.

"Well, Pauly's outside and he's got some club or stick behind his back," Mrs. Storm said.

"Nuts!" Augie laughed. The Pastor put down his knife and fork and looked stern. "There'll be no fighting!" Pastor observed.

Mrs. Storm returned to the front porch where Pauly was waiting. "Whatever it is, Pauly," Pastor's wife said, "Augie apologizes. He's really sorry."

Wordlessly, with his heart's pressure in sudden nervous collapse, Pauly turned and walked down the steps to the street.

As he started the journey home, out of the corner of his eye, he noticed the Gold Star in Pastor's window.

While out in front of the house on Kootenai Street, William Tell Craddock lifted a basketball, which completely blotted him out from nose to navel, and toddled across the lawn.

Author's Postscript
In Two Parts

1. A Historic Point

"Hellgate and Missoula.

"In the Indian days the mountain tribes had a road through here which led across the Continental Divide to the buffalo. The Blackfeet, from the plains, used to consider it very sporting to slip into this country on horse-stealing expeditions and to ambush the Nez Perce and Flathead Indians in this narrow part of the canyon. Funeral arrangements were more or less sketchy in those days even amongst friends, so naturally enemies got very little consideration. In time the place became so cluttered up with skulls and bones that it was gruesome enough to make an Indian exclaim, *'I-sul!,'* expressing surprise and horror. The French trappers elaborated and called it *La Porte D'Enfer* or Gate of Hell.

"From these expressions were derived the present-day names Missoula and Hellgate. If the latter name depresses you, it may be encouraging to know that Paradise is just seventy-nine miles northwest of here."—A Historic Marker, 1.5 miles east of Missoula on U. S. 10, erected by the Montana State Highway Commission.

2. Author's Acknowledgement

Of thanks due:

Dr. H. L. Nossen, without whom this book would have been impossible;

That warm-hearted, hard-boiled Western newspaperman, Mr. French Ferguson, editor of *The Daily Missoulian*;

Deane Jones and Billy Dugal, for stories told out of season;

Robert Park Mills; and,

Most of all,

Vivienne C. Koch, for helpful criticism.

Norman Macleod
Missoula, Montana
August 25, 1940.

Afterword

Running into the Past:
Norman Macleod and The Bitter Roots
by Gabriella Graceffo

"Toward the blue-lipped western hollow of the sky, with the thin severity of birds flying over the ridgeway home where the years were buried like fossils in cool stone, I was returning to the mindless bridlepaths of my melancholy youth." So begins Norman Macleod's journey home to Missoula, Montana in the summer of 1940, described in his unpublished autobiography. Bundled into an old Chevrolet with his younger brother, Robert, the thirty-five-year-old author drove across the country with a single purpose: to write *The Bitter Roots*. He worked in a rented cabin nestled in the shadow of Mount Jumbo, retracing memories etched into the footpaths of a hometown which never quite felt like home. On off days, he drove along the routes Lewis and Clark had taken through the Bitterroot Mountains and gambled his way through the valley with his brother, once hitting a horse on the way back, though he was adamant both the Chevy and the horse went their separate ways without much damage. His day job directing the New York City Poetry Center and years helming magazines as

a formidable literary figure seemed lifetimes away as he redis-
covered the sun-dappled Western landscape with entertaining
company at his side.

But Macleod spent the summer haunted by the past. Despair
and yearning seep through this section of his autobiography,
common emotions throughout the materials on his life and work
archived at the Beinecke Library that shape this article. He was
separated from his second wife, Vivienne Koch, and under con-
tract to write a second novel more likely to sell than his first, *You
Get What You Ask For*. He found solace in looking back, desperate
to understand the man he had become by returning to where all
his troubles began.

As America inched closer to World War II, Macleod retreated
into his cabin in the Rattlesnake Valley and created a lightly-fic-
tionalized version of his life in Missoula during and after World
War I, intertwining the past and present. The author had always
felt connected to Westerns—perhaps a form of wistfulness as he
admitted to never living up to the mountain machismo of those
around him, a sore point all his life. After one of the book's orig-
inal publishers, Hilton Smith, was accused of being a Japanese
undercover agent and shot dead in Texas by the FBI, *The Bitter
Roots* seemed steeped in bloody potential. And the book *is* bloody,
featuring police brutality, traumatized soldiers, labor violence,
and an unrelentingly bleak political landscape. But we see it
through the bewildered eyes of a shy boy, Pauly, just as Macleod
experienced the world in his youth.

This book offers key insights into the author's mind and
unique perspective on the time period. Macleod's papers at the
Beinecke Library exist because of his remarkable influence shap-
ing the literary community in Manhattan and his contributions
as poet, editor, and teacher. Even old grocery lists are housed
among the dozens of archival boxes. But his time in Missoula
isn't featured in the catalogue description or materials apart from

Alice Wicklund Macleod Mills, around 1923

the contents of his autobiography. This new edition of *The Bitter Roots* allows us to fill that absence, especially as it is so intimately connected to his life.

Norman Macleod moved to Missoula early in his childhood when his mother, Alice Wicklund Macleod, became an instructor at the University of Montana, one of the first women to hold the position. He came of age looking down on the grassy lawn beneath his mother's office in Main Hall, where he saw a glimpse of Barbara Sterling, the banker's daughter, in a scene reproduced in *The Bitter Roots*. Despite his tongue-tied nature, he was deeply enamored by language from an early age and got his first job selling newspapers for the *Daily Missoulian*. Fellow newsies, including Wild Bill Kelly, gave him "hotfoot" by chasing him all over town "until my white bones rattled in my shoes like dice," but he was determined to make a place for himself at the press. We see this connection right away in the headlines opening each chapter in *The Bitter Roots*. Macleod could explore the world's wonders and horrors through the newspaper from the comfort of his hayloft, hiding out from bullies and writing poetry about the beauty of the wheat fields and watersheds around him. Writing was and always would be an escape, a way to run away from his life.

Like Pauly's mother in the novel, Alice married a doctor, William Park Mills, in 1917. They moved into a house on Stephens Avenue, and Macleod woke to squawks and coos of peacocks next door, an unwelcome change to the tender affections of his dog, Wolf, who Dr. Mills banished from the house. His stepfather mostly ignored him unless Macleod memorized the human skeleton and recited the list of bones to him. Macleod wasn't interested in biology, though his friend Shandy[1] had him steal illustrated medical textbooks so they could look at female anatomy. It only made Macleod more terrified of girls. His mother was distant, soon pregnant and preoccupied. Isolated from his family and surrounded by teenagers who he "identified with the wild violence of the frontier," Macleod was desperate to force himself into a masculine mold that he never fit into. One bully called him a "mildly Eastern tenderfoot with no possibilities of Western growth." He was determined to prove them wrong.

Macleod spent most of his time converting the old barn behind the house into a basketball court, founding the Sataspian

---

1   Shandy was a nickname of Paul Maclean, brother to Norman Maclean, the author of *A River Runs Through It*. In *The Bitter Roots*, Augie Storm is the fictional counterpart of Paul Maclean.

team—renamed the *Lucky Streaks* in the novel—to become the athlete he always wanted to be. This is described in Macleod's poem, "We Played the Flatheads At Arlee" (see Appendix). Once he had a team assembled, they bummed their way across Montana for games via the Northern Pacific or electrified Milwaukee railroad, riding on the freezing tender or between the whistling blinds. Sneaking around vicious railroad guards and nearly losing an arm to the grinding shock absorbers, Macleod began to see the gritty underbelly of the West as a young teenager. He jumped off the train covered in coalsmoke and ran with the other boys to their basketball games, sometimes in towns glittering with new money, sometimes in ones falling apart, avoiding road agents and local police who were both ready to spill blood at a moment's notice.

Politics that Macleod had only read about became much more tangible on these trips: visiting his "red hot socialist" uncle who hosted radical political dinners and had regular brawls with another uncle, a Ku Klux Klan member; witnessing the neglected buildings and impoverished people on the southside of Missoula; and watching a boy drown in the Clark Fork River without comment or ceremony, an episode recounted in an opening chapter in *The Bitter Roots*. Macleod could not ignore the tumultuous and brutal place he lived in.

In the novel, this violence is highlighted in the scenes set in Butte. The mining town was established in 1864 and boomed with the discovery of rich copper deposits, raking in huge sums and becoming one of the wealthiest cities in the West. However, as the ore dwindled and greedy companies exploited workers, Butte became a site of intense political activity with labor unions on strike and Army troops brought in to suppress this upheaval. Augie Storm, the pastor's son, and Stiff Sullivan, the high school quarterback, meet with political activist Bill Dunne, learning about the reality of censorship and worker abuse before Dunne is dragged away and arrested. The boys had come for a fun night

Norman Macleod, around 1920

looking at girls in a bar, only to find themselves knee-deep in political intrigue. While Augie and Stiff Sullivan both embody the masculinity Pauly yearns for, they are forced to grow up fast and reckon with the complexities of what it means to be a man in the West. Macleod's focus on politics adds nuance to a simple case of failed gender expectations. From there, the novel further explores party-influenced violence with the beating of Bud Bailey, a poor Missoula teenager, and the real-life barbaric lynching of Frank Little, a union organizer. The conflict between Wobblies—members of the International Workers of the World—and the establishment parallels the end of Pauly's boyhood and his subsequent politicized entrance into manhood.

But what of Pauly, Macleod's alter ego? For most of the book, he is consumed by his personal goals—chasing after Betty Darling (the fictional counterpart of Barbara Sterling), trying out for (and not making) athletic teams, and slowly garnering the approval of fellow boys. This parallels Macleod's own experiences as an early teenager: the inclusion of scenes and reflections from other characters paint aspects of the social landscape beyond Macleod's own experiences. By the end of 1918, war had ended in Europe but a new one was festering in Montana between unions and corporations, with the boys caught in the crossfire. Stiff Sullivan, affected by Bill Dunne's arrest, retreats from the patriotism expressed by Missoulians upon the return of American troops from France and becomes more and more aligned with the Wobblies; Lonely Darling does not receive a hero's welcome because he has been judged "not man enough" due to his suffering from shell shock; and Augie Storm is fired with nationalist anger when he hears that Wobblies have shot former soldiers in the street as a political message. By this point, Pauly has pushed himself into a more mature role, smoking cubeb cigarettes and introducing gambling to the *Lucky Streaks*. But he isn't on the same playing field as the other boys; he doesn't see himself as manly enough to stand up to his stepfather when he whips him, let alone pursue political gambits.

While not having the hero be particularly heroic or aware of the harsh reality around him perhaps appears an odd choice for a Western at first, this literary choice serves a critical role: to embody a feeling of being left behind when not living up to the rugged, politicized characteristics of Western masculinity. Pauly expresses a different form of masculinity, one that is tender and bookish and innocently clueless, but beaten down by the other men around him. He is still deeply impacted by politics but does not directly engage with them. Unlike Pauly, who tries to take matters into his own hands at the end of the novel, Macleod ran away, into writing and out of Missoula.

Beginning at the age of twelve, Macleod wrote and published poetry, which he described as "reflective verse," on his memories of train-hopping, trying to process his experiences with the protective distance of language. He could write his observations but not take a stand in the way the boys and men around him wanted him to. To build up a more athletic physique during high school, he began working at a lumber mill in Bonner. There, he met Corneil O'Hara. Unlike Shandy, who had been Macleod's former hero and masculine ideal (along with all the negative characterizations we see presented in Augie), O'Hara was a quasi-dandy, a lover of literature, and offered a path away from machismo. He introduced Macleod to Arthur Schnitzler's plays, the erotic memoirs of Casanova, and gossipy humor in the magazine *Smart Set*. O'Hara validated Macleod's literary interests while still working in the context of manual labor, sharing their poetry with each other while brushing sawdust off their clothes. Unfortunately, Macleod was injured on the job and forced to convalesce at St. Patrick's hospital back in Missoula. As he brooded each day in his hospital bed, French Ferguson, the columnist at the *Daily Missoulian* who had published his poetry, visited and reassured him that he *might* be a good poet one day.

After graduating from high school, Macleod left Missoula and went to the University of Iowa. There, he found himself enamored with the work of E. E. Cummings, F. Scott Fitzgerald, and Theodore Dreiser (whose novels were restricted in the library, until he schmoozed a librarian for special permission). From these, he moved on to literary magazines like *Palms*, *Poetry: A Magazine of Verse*, and *The Measure*, as well as the socialist magazines *The Masses* and its successor, *The Liberator* (also restricted, also schmoozed for). Although he was finding a home in literature, he couldn't find one among his peers, who were either intensely dedicated to their studies or gallivanted through "freelance sex, sports, fishing, and hunting"—neither lifestyle a good fit for him. This tension sent him fleeing once more, hitchhiking his way into misadventures. During a semester at the University of Arizona, he met a young woman, Catherine Stuart, and traveled with her to visit her family in Alabama. After he declared his love for Catherine one evening, she then announced to her parents they were getting married, sealing the deal at church the next day as the preacher's "snot-nosed kids" watched from above, mooning the couple as they said "I do." Despite the unexpected marriage, Macleod dove headfirst into trying to be a husband. But when he felt inadequate, he ran once more, this time back to Montana to serve as a park ranger in Glacier National Park in the late 1920s, and then fleeing once again to become a caretaker at the University of New Mexico in Albuquerque, where he enrolled in literature classes part-time. Catherine always followed him a few months after each departure, desperate to catch up.

In New Mexico, Macleod fell in love with the literature of the Southwest, particularly Washington Matthews' translations of Navajo chants and *Laughing Horse* literary magazine. He was so impressed with *Laughing Horse* that he used it as a model to begin his own magazine, *jackass*, in 1928 while also publishing his own work in other periodicals. He eventually became a contributing writer for *New Masses*, where he continued to write about his boyhood experiences, but this time clearly siding with the labor unions. The reason for this, he emphasizes in his autobiography, was because he had recognized the tremendous power of the Anaconda Copper Mining Company—how it and other corporations controlled newspapers, schools, and colleges in Montana, dictating all aspects of life and how people perceived the world. During a stint as custodian of the Petrified Forest National Park, he wrote constantly, railing against social injustices, but his personal life was as spectral as the trees around him: haunted by Catherine's need for him to be a good husband and father to their newborn daughter, he was consumed with shame and watched himself becoming a shadow of his former self, only feeling present when writing. Those years are a blur, hardly dated in the autobiography, until he finally completed his degree in 1930.

After starting two more journals, *Palo Alto* and *Morada* (which Ezra Pound proclaimed to be a stellar regional magazine dedicated to the complexities of experimental Southwest literature), becoming the American editor of *Front*, and publishing his own work widely, his network expanded, including a turbulent relationship with Pound and later a father-son dynamic with William Carlos Williams. Mike Gold, the editor of *New Masses*, invited him to be assistant editor of the magazine, and Macleod left Catherine and their young daughter behind to live in New York City. When Gold fell ill, he took over as editor and this cemented his place in the politicized literary world. In 1931, he wrote features on the effects of the Great Depression, then gnawing its way through the city, including one on a hunger march at City Hall that turned violent, with police breaking up the crowd as Macleod hid in the doorway of a cigar store and watched an innocent man be brutally beaten. Langston Hughes, a close friend, organized a trip with Macleod to see the Hoover Dam so they could write on the injustices occurring to Black men there by construction companies, the first of many similar articles he produced for *New Masses* as a writer dedicated to civil rights. But despite Macleod's "revolutionary red typewriter," he quickly lost the "fervor of radical devotion and passion," an emotional predicament that threatened his ability to properly run the magazine. He ran once more, this time to Russia, to learn to be a better Communist.

He became the writer the English column of Moscow's *Daily News* in late 1932 or early 1933. His Montana life and family became a distant memory as he immersed himself in trying to live in a communist country. But he saw Russian people starving and he himself became skeletal, subsisting on squab and vodka. Now fully disillusioned with politics, seeing the reality of poorly executed ideology, he bolted back to America, only to be met with divorce papers from Catherine and an acute sense of emptiness at not living up to personal or political goals. Writing was his only solace. He published volumes of poetry and tried his hand at teaching the University of New Mexico and then a boys' school, only to realize he didn't live up to the ideal of the erudite male professor, and retreated once more to New York City.

There, he married Vivienne Koch, a literary critic he had known for years, and felt he could make a home with her, to finally be the "right kind" of husband. Fellow writers called him a "proletarian poet," but he never fully meshed with the leftist movement, chafing against any strict template he was meant to live in. His marriage with Koch was increasingly strained as he moved across the country again and again, searching for projects he saw himself in, growing progressively more depressed. By the summer of 1938, he was consumed with memories of Montana, of sharing "flapjacks and sourdough biscuits with grizzled prospectors in the mountains" and the "bald skulls of rock above the snowline and the supporting silence of the foothills below." He had a sense of impending doom as WWII loomed and after settling his affairs, fled the present and dove into the past by retreating to Missoula.

Macleod's childhood in Missoula had been full of a sense of not living up to expectations, but it was a familiar ache that perhaps felt strangely comforting in the face of new conflict. "The divided world now is somewhat different from the one I knew during my anxious high school years in Missoula," he acknowledges. He then quotes William Carlos Williams, from a letter the author wrote to Macleod earlier that year: "Life is burning its bridges so fast behind me I've scarcely the time in which to turn around and look but keep going at a faster and faster pace the less able I become to go fast at all." Montana was where Macleod first felt constrained by the masculinity he couldn't live up to, but he had since developed the skills to unpack that by writing and reexperiencing memories through Pauly.

However, as tensions rise and the characters buckle under the weight of the political climate, the novel suddenly ends, deflating the conflict between Augie and Pauly. Some readers may feel this is a major flaw in the book, an unsatisfactory conclusion. In real life, Shandy had tormented Macleod psychologically. Macleod carried a burning hatred for him for years. When Macleod arrived back in Missoula, he looked into what had happened to his old friends and discovered that Shandy had been found in a Chicago alley in 1938 with a bullet hole in his head and no gun nearby. Norman Maclean included his brother's death in *A River Runs Through It*, reconsidering his sense of grief and guilt. Both Norman Maclean and Norman Macleod used semi-autobiographical fiction to process the events of their lives, Missoula serving as the beating heart of both novels.

Macleod confesses in his autobiography that he "felt responsible for the murder...that I was in a true psychological sense the murderer" through a kind of subconscious "voodoo." He felt guilty for surviving when Shandy and so many other Missoula boys hadn't. So, he couldn't bring himself to write Augie's murder at the hands of Pauly. Doing so would express a traditional hero's journey and finally let him—through Pauly—achieve that coveted Western machismo. But it would also solidify Macleod's sense of guilt regarding Shandy's murder, to allow the hatred he felt to be validated and victorious on the page when he was doing everything he could to let it go. So, instead, the novel concludes with Pauly's kind heart protected from the violence that would corrupt it, easing some of the guilt from Macleod's own conscience.

The Bitter Roots is a novel deeply informed by Norman Macleod's struggles with masculinity, which itself is bound up with politics, then and now. The novel was created by Macleod running from expectations he felt he couldn't live up to in his life, but it was also a deeply meaningful exercise in rooting himself in his past to understand who he was and the larger issues that shaped him. He felt he needed "something besides the bitter past," so he infused the book with investigations of the psychological condition regarding gender and oppression. He wanted to accurately portray Pauly as the awkward boy desperate to fit into a world not designed for him. Language was a safe haven for Macleod as a child; it was no different at thirty-five. It was something he could run *to* instead of *from*, where he could speak the truth of his way of moving through life that didn't fit into the neat boxes of rugged individualism, toxic masculinity, or political ideology. *The Bitter Roots* offered Macleod a way of moving forward by looking back.

Macleod went on to publish more collections of poetry and continued teaching, including a position at the University of Maryland and later Briarcliff College, where he gained confidence in himself as a literary scholar and editor. After moving to Pembroke State University, he started *Pembroke Magazine*, which featured poetry by students and faculty as well as leading poets like W. S. Graham, Simon Ortiz, and William Carlos Williams. He continued to advocate for poetry in communities throughout his life, from New York to San Francisco and eventually across Europe and even in Iraq at the University of Baghdad. In 1973, he was awarded the Horace Gregory Award from the New School of Social Research for his extensive contributions as a teacher and his literary achievements. No longer the shy boy uncertain of his place in the world, he had finally found a home, one not tied to place but to the people around him.

In August 1940, with the first draft of *The Bitter Roots* complete, he and his brother Robert tucked themselves once more into the gray Chevy and drove by night back to New York City, the moon lighting the road. According to his autobiography, Macleod never returned to Missoula. He had no need to: he had done what he set out to do, giving himself grace for simply having a tender heart, finally ready to live his life instead of running from it.

Appendix
Four Poems by Norman Macleod

Like Chief Joseph the Nez Perce
The unpublished afterword to The Bitter Roots

Since I can no longer remember
the poems of my youth (nor even

the five fingers which brought
them to birth) I recognize that

I am issue of a lean length of
men whose serial inheritance is

taxed by time, deep distortion
or anger until the man I now am

is less memory than shadow: so
like Chief Joseph the Nez Perce,

I see the receding saw of rock
roaring in a cataract of sunset,

breathe the bitterroot valleys
and touch with despair a tender-

ness that is not anywhere, and
tasting the larkspur of retreat,

hear the black drums reminding
tomorrow the son I then will be

will renounce not only the men
who were his anchor in the past

but also his race, name, those
poems he will never know: there-

fore he will die as I will die,
grey as the ultimatum motorized

transport move upon, atomizing
our tablet in this world's mind.

We Played the Flatheads At Arlee

From miles around the Indians came to see us
Play basketball against the Flatheads at Arlee.
The stakes were high and the floor narrow—
The Indians wore their black hair parted,
Drawn back sharp as the split edge of a tomahawk
From both sides of the copper forehead.
  The game was angry—
Never until the dead end were we
Sure of winning.
  But if they lost,
We knew it had not always been their habit
To be losing.
  Never had basketball on a Jesuit court
Been a game of their own choosing.

Before the Smog Buried Missoula

The kinnikinnick
Or shooting stars—
The flowers were
Purple and yellow
Close to the ground—
Remind me of days
When I was young

Smoking cubebs
In tunnels beneath
A woodpile stacked
In the cellar beside
A furnace I stoked—
Reminds me of
The cow I milked
And the Cadillac

My stepfather drove
To Flathead Lake
Or the Bitterroots
To the farm at LoLo
Where ducks were shot,
The trout caught
And cherries picked—

I climbed the canyon
To Medicine Springs
Or hunted jackrabbits
Through winter snow
Unless a blizzard
Howled and bent

The tamaracks
Until the Chinook
Melted the ice
In promise of spring
With wild pink roses
And huckleberries—

Before the smog
Buried Missoula
And orchards died

The Bitterroots

In the Bitterroots were sapphire mires
And ticks were a menace to the cattle.

I followed the myths of mica and gold
And shared flapjacks with the grizzled

Prospectors. The cabins were of spruce
And pines were a forest along horizon.

The bald bench of the black mountains
Was above the snowline and ptarmigans

Were a thin white silence in the hills.
The beavers gnawed the edge of winter

Where jackrabbits zigzagged along the
Creek bottoms. My mackinaw camouflaged

A stag shirt and my breath was a frost
Sparkling like the skies on a blue day.

I hunted beneath the ridges for sheep
And the trails led from one cabin to

Another: there were no women for me
To look upon. The mountain men were

Starved from a wariness of body hunger
Until their skulls encased a hardness

No possible cold could ever penetrate
—I warmed my hands at many fires.

Norman Macleod was born in Salem, Oregon, in 1906 and lived in Missoula, Montana, from 1913 to 1924. He earned degrees from the University of New Mexico and Columbia University. He taught at institutions including San Francisco State College, the University of Baghdad in Iraq, and Pembroke State University. He died in 1985.

Joanna Pocock is an Irish-Canadian writer currently living in London. Her first book, *Surrender*, won the Fitzcarraldo Editions Essay Prize in 2018 and was published in 2019. Her hybrid memoir-roadtrip, *Greyhound*, is coming in spring 2025. Her writing has appeared in *The Nation*, *The Spectator*, and elsewhere. She teaches at the University of the Arts, London.

Gabriella Graceffo is Managing Editor of *Poetry Northwest* and a graduate student at the University of Montana pursuing a PhD in Interdisciplinary Studies, building on her MFA in Poetry and MA in Literature there. Her work has been published or is forthcoming in *Poets & Writers*, *Pleiades*, *Gulf Coast*, *Hippocampus*, and others.

The Bitter Roots
By Norman Macleod

First published in this edition by Boiler House Press and the
University of Montana Press, 2024
Boiler House Press is part of the UEA Publishing Project
The Bitter Roots copyright © Norman Macleod, 1941
Introduction copyright © Joanna Pocock, 2024
Afterword copyright © Gabriella Graceffo, 2024

Proofreading by Sarah Wilson

Photograph opposite title page: Norman and Catherine Macleod,
Glacier National Park, late 1920s.
Photographs of Norman Macleod and Alice Wicklund Macleod
courtesy of Norman G. Macleod.
Photographs at the start of sections 1-3 by permission of Archives
& Special Collections, Mansfield Library, University of Montana.

Cover Design and Typesetting by Louise Aspinall
Typeset in Arnhem Pro

ISBN: 978-1-915812-38-4

9 781915 81238